DYLAN HARSON

In this spellbinding saga of the American West, Dylan Harson captures the glory and adventure of the brave men and women who dared to venture into the untamed land. Full of breathtaking action, realistic characters, and grand historical drama, *Kansas Blue* will sweep readers to a long-ago time they will never forget.

After her husband returns from the Civil War suffering from injuries to both body and spirit, Danni Coopersand can only hope that a move from their Illinois home to the Kansas Territory will help him recover. But when she joins a wagon train heading across bloody Indian lands, Danni soon faces a relentless struggle against storms, floods, and brutal attacks from ex-Rebel soldiers turned outlaws. And worse yet, Danni's loyalty to her invalid husband is tested by her growing attraction for the cavalry officer leading the settlers to their homesteads....

KANSAS BLUE

DYLAN HARSON

LEISURE BOOKS NEW YORK CITY

For John

A LEISURE BOOK®

January 1996

Published by special arrangement with Donald I. Fine, Inc.

Dorchester Publishing Co., Inc.
276 Fifth Avenue
New York, NY 10001

For further information, contact: Donald I. Fine, Inc., 19 West 21st Street, New York, NY 10010

Printed in the United States of America.

KANSAS BLUE

Chapter One

Fort Leavenworth, Kansas, May 1867

Austin Bourke entered the gates of Fort Leavenworth, spoke with the guards, and made his way across the grounds to the barracks, where he slipped in to find a grinning Will Drake lying on a bunk and using a piece of charcoal to sketch a nude female on the wall beside him. When Will sensed Austin's presence, he turned with a start. His eyes rounded in surprise at sight of his former commander, and he lifted his long legs to sit up on the edge of the bunk.

"Bourke. Who let you in here?"

"Captain Bloom," Austin responded. "He sent word he wants to see me. I thought I'd see you first."

"I haven't forgotten the twenty dollars I owe you," Will said quickly. "How'd you know where to find me?"

The corner of Austin's mouth curved. "I saw the rest of the company at morning drill. What's the ailment today?"

"Gout," Will said seriously.

Austin lifted a brow and Will reached inside the shirt of the blue cavalry uniform he wore. "I've got a doctor's certificate to prove it."

"Your brother-in-law the doctor?"

Will's face split in a grin. "He's the one. The post is presently without a doctor."

"What does the captain want with me?" Austin asked, and Will's grin widened. "General Hancock changed his mind about that honorable discharge they gave you. He wants the papers back."

The complete lack of expression on Austin Bourke's face soon dampened Will's enthusiasm for the joke. He sobered as he gazed at the dust-covered clothes Austin wore. "I hear the captain has a favor to ask."

"A favor?"

"Yeah. How's the coach business?"

Austin lifted one gloved hand to rub some of the sweat and grime from his face. "Not good, with the railroad on its way. Folks are putting off trips until it's done."

"That's a shame. Did I hear you're part-owner?"

"I am. I'll see you again, Will." Austin turned his back on the smiling malingerer and headed for the captain's quarters. As he entered, an aide rose from his desk and knocked on the captain's door. A moment later Austin was shown inside. The gray-haired captain stood and paused, as if waiting for a salute. Austin removed his hat and glove and smoothed the thick brown hair from his forehead. He replaced his hat and stood waiting.

"Mr. Bourke," said Captain Bloom finally, and he stepped away from his desk to hold out his hand. Austin took it and shook it firmly. He saw none of the old animosity in Bloom's eyes. He saw nothing but intent.

"They tell me you're in the coach business now."

"You heard correctly."

The captain nodded. "I'm sure it's not as lucrative as in years past, now that the railroads are coming. Where are they now? Outside Ellsworth?"

"That's right."

"You were a fine officer, Bourke. You should have stayed in

the cavalry. Conflict has damaged many a good man, trampled his spirit. I never thought it would happen to you."

Austin met his look. "You sent word you wanted to see me. What about?"

"I have a dozen people camped outside the fort who want to go west across Kansas. Stragglers. They have few wagons and little money. With the majority of my men away on off-post details, I can spare no one from the fort, with the exception of Corporal Drake, whom I believe to be a friend of yours. The stragglers have pooled funds and will pay you two hundred dollars if you accept the job. The government will provide you with a horse to ride. You know the route, Mr. Bourke. The Smoky Hill Road from Leavenworth to Fort Wallace. Will you accept the job?"

Austin stood silent.

The captain lifted his chin. "Mr. Bourke, I rode in one of your coaches from Atchison last month. Your horses are tired, and your tack needs replacing. I'm doing you a favor. Once the railroad arrives, your coach line will be obsolete."

"Any women?" asked Austin.

"Four or five."

"You're not doing them any favor. There was slaughter on the Smoky Hill Road last month. Our stage stations are repeatedly attacked and burned. At White Rock Creek the Sutzer family and the Wards were—"

"General Hancock is on top of the situation," the captain interrupted. "He's mounting defenses against the aggressors now."

"Would that be Custer?"

"It would. I believe he's stationed in the mud at Fort Hays. Will you take on the job or not? If not, I have other names on my list to consider."

"Then do so. Goodbye, Captain Bloom." Austin turned on his heel and left the captain staring at his back as he retreated from the room. He crossed the grounds once more, and in the barracks he walked over to Will Drake's bunk and nudged the dozing corporal. Will's eyes opened immediately.

"Well?" he said when he saw Austin. "What did the old man have in mind?"

"A trip west with a dozen stragglers. Wagons. Women."

Will made a face. "Are you going?"

"No, but you are. Nice to see you again, Will. Drop in and see me when you're up Atchison way. Bring the twenty."

"Wait a minute." Will shot up off the bunk. "Did Captain Bloom tell you I was going?"

"Yep," said Austin.

"You bastard. You'd leave me to make a trip like that by myself?"

"Bloom said he had a list of men to choose from."

"He was lying and you know it. No one knows that road like you. You've been driving it for two damned years now."

"You've made it before," Austin replied.

"As a teamster for the quartermaster, hauling freight and supplies just like I did all through the war. I never had any women with me."

"The women won't be the problem, Will. The Cheyenne and the Sioux will be your problem. The cavalry's chasing them all over the western half of the state."

"Scattered renegades, I heard."

"If you call families renegades. An entire village slipped out from under Hancock's nose last month. These Indians are desperate, driven by fear."

"Is that why you turned Bloom down?" Will asked. "You're afraid of being attacked?"

"It's reason enough," said Austin. "Be seeing you."

He left the barracks and the open-mouthed Will Drake and made his way to the sutler's store just outside the fort. The post's sutler had been his reason for coming to Fort Leavenworth. Staples were available in Atchison, but the store provided for the soldiers at Fort Leavenworth had many items not available in the tiny trading post beside the stagecoach station Austin managed with his partner, who was also his cousin. Like the bolt of blue silk cloth coveted by his cousin's wife. She had seen something similar draped over the wife of a fort officer and could not sleep until she herself owned a blue silk dress.

Austin didn't mind the trip. It was good to get away from his cousin's wife. She had made the last few months miserable for everyone at the station. When she lived in New York, everything had gone well. There were no problems between Austin and his cousin, and business had been good. Since her arrival in late February, however, relations between the two men had been strained. The woman routinely threw herself at Austin, and pouted and claimed to be insulted when he ignored her. She flirted outrageously in front of her husband, daring him to grow angry and accuse Austin of encouraging her behavior. It mattered little that Austin had no interest in the woman. Neither of them believed him.

As a result, he found himself ready to move on. To what, he didn't know. He could handle most any job that came his way, but having been part-owner in his own business, he knew he would find it difficult to take orders from anyone again. Austin thought it best to move off on his own and have only himself to consider when it came to making decisions.

Inside the sutler's store was a bounty of treasures and a melange of pleasing, enticing odors. There were scented soaps and spices; canned meats and fruits; whiskey and beer and tobacco; books, clothes, hats, and boots. Austin looked at the wealth of goods the store offered and had to wonder if perhaps he should have remained a lieutenant in the cavalry. He wouldn't mind reading a dime novel now and then, or having a new pair of boots. Most of the money made in the coach business was spent on upkeep, leaving little room for purchases of a personal nature.

He picked up a neatly folded shirt from a table and eyed it. When he looked up again he saw the store sutler shaking his head and frowning while speaking to a female customer. Austin put down the shirt and moved to look at the covers of the dime novels on the counter. The exaggerations by the artists always amused him.

"Can't go," a voice said, and Austin turned to see a tall, thin, black-haired man addressing him. He opened his mouth to speak, but the man swerved away from him and stepped into a table of carefully folded trousers.

"Can't go. Just can't. Can't do it." The black head first began to nod and then to bob. "Oh, no. No. No."

As he watched, Austin suddenly realized he had seen the man before. Not the man, necessarily, but the symptoms. The vacuous gaze. The dazed expression.

"Can't go!" the man said louder, almost a shout, and the sutler stopped talking to the woman and looked over.

"We can't go, I tell you! We can't! C-c-c-can't!"

The man began to shake. His arms began to twitch and his eyes began to roll. Austin looked for something to put into his mouth. He found a leather quirt and reached forward to shove it between the man's lips as he collapsed onto the floor. Austin went down with him and held on to his arms and legs as they jerked spasmodically. A female voice was shouting something above him, but he couldn't hear the words; all his concentration was on the man beneath him.

Finally the jolting movements began to subside. The heaving chest relaxed, and the whites of the man's eyes rolled slowly back in his head. When the limbs beneath his hands went limp, Austin released the man and stood up to step away. He bent down and retrieved the leather quirt and handed it to the woman behind him.

The sutler looked angrily at the quirt. "I'll ask you to pay for that, ma'am. What in the devil is wrong with this man? Will someone please tell me what just happened?"

The woman, a fair-faced blonde, was staring at Austin. "You knew what to do. You knew how to help him."

Austin nodded. "I've seen men like him before."

"Men with fits?" she said with a frown. "Men who shout and curse and scream at nothing?"

"Yes, ma'am. He was in the war?"

She nodded and looked back to the man on the floor. "The Illinois infantry. My husband isn't alone, then? It's not something peculiar?"

"Not at all," Austin assured her. "Maybe your husband had a head wound that brought on the fits, I don't know. The war did different things to different men, none of it good. He's not alone."

"Thank you," the woman said, and she turned clear gray eyes on Austin. "Thank you for helping him."

"It was no trouble, ma'am." He looked at the sutler then. "I'll pay for the quirt."

"It's a good thing," said the sutler, and he walked away from the man on the floor to stand behind his counter. "She had no money anyway. Came in here trying to peddle her wrap in exchange for cash."

The woman heard the sutler's words. She coldly turned her back on him to look after her unconscious husband. Austin looked outside the store and saw no wagon. "The two of them just passing through?"

"It looked that way for a while," said the sutler with a curled lip. "But now we'll probably be stuck with them. Them and the rest of that ragtag band wanting to go west. They've been camped outside the fort for three weeks now. There's even a group of Mormons among them. A man and two or three of his wives—I'm not sure how many he has, exactly. They want to go and join up with the rest of their kind in Utah."

The sutler paused then, as if remembering himself. He smiled hugely and said, "That quirt won't be all, will it? Do you have a list?"

"Yes," Austin said, and he took it from his pocket and handed it to the man. "I'll be back for everything."

He returned to the woman, who was trying to rouse her husband, and motioned for her to stand. "I'll get him out of the store if you'll tell me where to take him."

"I don't know where to take him," she said, flustered, and her frustration and distress were evident in the deep pink of her cheeks. She took a deep breath and said, "We're camped north of the fort, but that's too far. I'm certain no one will mind if we settle Jack outside the store until he comes around and can walk for himself."

Austin nodded and bent down to lift up her husband. Jack was a big man, but Austin was used to hefting trunks and travel cases and his muscles were well toned. Once he was off the floor, the man's wife got on the other side of her husband and she and Austin carried him outside the store. After they put him down and leaned him against the wall, Austin turned to the woman.

"You and your husband are members of the party camped outside the fort?"

"Yes."

"Why?" he asked.

"Why?" she repeated, confused.

"Why do you want to go west?"

She looked away from him and began to speak as if reciting from memory. "The Homestead Act. A hundred and sixty acres of land all ours to claim if we build on it within six months and farm it for five years. We'll only have to stay a year, though, since the time Jack spent in the army will be deducted from the five."

Austin cast a doubtful glance at her husband. "Just you and him?"

She refused to meet his eyes. "Me, Jack, and Kiowa, a mixed-blood Indian boy we brought along with us." As if in explanation, she offered, "Kansas has been a dream for us. We need . . . something permanent. Something no damned war can take away from us."

Austin blinked at the softly spoken profanity from her mouth. "You're certainly entitled to it, ma'am. What about the others? I hear the Mormons want to go farther west."

She glanced at him. "They plan to go on to Utah Territory. But they need help to get across Kansas first. We all do. We're waiting for the captain of the fort to find a guide for us. It's taken longer than expected."

"I imagine it has," Austin murmured.

The woman looked strangely at him. "May I ask why you're so curious about us? And how you know what you do?"

Austin took a deep breath and released it. She smelled good, he noted. Like a field flower of some kind. And her nose didn't wrinkle up at the smell coming from him.

"I'm the man the captain had in mind to guide you," he said finally.

Her eyes rounded slightly, but she waited, watching him.

"There's a lot you don't know," Austin said to her, and he

went on to tell her about the killings and the rough trails and the weather they were likely to encounter. As he talked she began to nod. For a moment he was reminded of her husband, but then she spoke.

"I know the dangers. I'm aware of the risks we're taking."

Austin wasn't so sure. He searched for a delicate way to phrase what he wanted to say, then he decided to be blunt.

"Do you know what happens to white women caught by raiding Indians?"

Her lids lowered. "I think so, yes."

"If they don't kill her immediately with a rock or a tomahawk, they sometimes haul her off and subject her to repeated rape. Then she becomes a slave."

"Yes . . . I've heard." She swallowed hard and forced herself to meet his gaze.

"You're aware, and you still want me to lead you west?" he asked.

"Yes," she said, nodding again. Then her lips parted in a brilliant smile. Her gray eyes shone. "I can see now why the captain wanted us to wait for you. I've known you less than half an hour and already I know I'd follow you anywhere. When do we leave?"

Austin was disconcerted. He stared at her a long moment. Then he said, "In three days."

CHAPTER TWO

LOUISE DANIELLE Coopersand hurried to revive her still-unconscious husband after the stranger had turned and walked back inside the sutler's store. Her chest was bursting with excitement and anticipation and she couldn't wait to get back to the others with the news. The man with the intense eyes and grime-covered face was wonderful. She didn't know his name—hadn't thought to ask it—but she knew just by looking that he was going to have special meaning in her life, probably in all of their lives. The words out of her mouth had surprised her as much as him, but instinctively she knew they were true. She would follow him anywhere.

"Jack," she said anxiously. "Jack, please wake up now. We have to get back to the others. I have the most wonderful news to share with them."

Jack Coopersand's lids fluttered. He groaned low in his throat. When his eyes opened and focused on his wife, he looked worriedly at her. "Are they coming?"

"No," his wife told him. "No one is coming. We'll be going in a few days. The man who helped you, the one in the sutler's store, he's going to be our guide."

"He is?" her husband said and looked up at her in surprise.

She nodded.

"Oh," said Jack. "That's good, Danni. We need a man in front of us. God, yes, a man who's . . . I'm no good anymore, Danni. I can't go."

"Yes, you can," Danni told him. "And you will. We'll all go together, me, you, and Kiowa. Now, let's hurry and tell the others."

Danni led her husband back to the tiny camp outside the fort, where five wagons were arranged in a circle and three women were doing wash in tubs near the cook site in the center. Danni took Jack to their wagon and instructed him to lie down inside while she spread the news. She looked for Kiowa and saw him sitting beside their tethered horses near the walls of the fort. She gestured for him to come, and the lanky seventeen-year-old unfolded himself and gave a last loving pat to the horse nearest him before striding over. His dark eyes were alight with curiosity as he approached, and when he came close to her, Danni gripped his hand between hers and smiled happily. "We have a guide, Kiowa. I met him today. He said we leave in three days."

Kiowa blinked and turned his head to look past her at the women doing wash. In the bright morning sunlight the scar on his throat was a vivid pink. The scar went from ear to ear, the route the blade of his would-be murderer had traveled the day before Danni found him.

"We leave in three days?" he echoed, his voice low and unnaturally hoarse as a result of his injury.

"Yes," Danni said happily, and she turned away from him to approach the women doing the wash. Eve Blaine pushed her long black hair from her face and smiled at her, as always, while Kora Blaine and the fair-skinned Ingrid Corle ignored her and went on with their work.

"I have news, ladies," Danni announced, and she beamed at them as one by one their heads lifted. When she had their full attention, Danni said, "I met our guide today in the sutler's store. He said we're to leave in three days."

Eve Blaine smiled and looked away. Kora Blaine heaved a long sigh and said a quick prayer. Ingrid Corle muttered something in Swedish under her breath. Then she looked at Danni with wide blue eyes and asked, "Who is he?"

Danni blinked. "I don't know. I forgot to ask."

"You forgot to ask his name?" said Kora. "Well, what does he look like? Is he a decent sort?"

"Decent enough," said Danni. "He's medium height with a good build and was dressed as though he'd been on the trail awhile. He helped us in the store when Jack had one of his fits. He knew just what to do for him."

"He was alone?" the freckled, auburn-haired Kora asked. "There was no one with him?"

"No one that I saw."

"How do you know he's our guide?"

Danni smiled. "He told me." She kept her mouth closed about the other things he had told her, about the people killed and the rough trail they were certain to encounter. No sense in frightening the other women.

"Surely there will be others," Kora commented. "I understood we were to have a military escort."

Danni shook her head and walked away from the women. To the waiting Kiowa she said, "Mrs. Blaine doesn't seem to understand that the soldiers of this fort have enough to do without acting as personal escort to our group. The captain has been incredibly generous to us."

Kiowa nodded as he walked along with her. "Your news upset her. She's frightened of the journey."

"With good reason," Danni said. Then she smiled at him. "I'm thrilled at the news myself. We're that much closer to having our own claim, Kiowa."

"Yes," he said, and he looked over his shoulder again at the women tending the wash. Danni watched him and wondered if he was looking for Susannah, the fourteen-year-old daughter of Kora and Ormond Blaine. Susannah was a pretty girl, with auburn hair like her mother's and dark brown eyes like her father's. Since camping outside the fort, Danni had often found Kiowa staring with brooding eyes into the camp of the Mormons. Yet when Susannah spoke to him, invariably when her mother and father were out of earshot, Kiowa would pretend not to hear her. Danni had thought to tease him about it once, but good sense and respect for the young man kept her quiet. It wasn't so long ago that she was seventeen and painfully shy around the opposite gender. At twenty-five she felt like an old woman.

Once back at her wagon, she directed the boy to help her shift her husband in the wagon's bed. Jack slept like the dead, and he slept often, as if he preferred his tortured dreams over reality. When they had made him comfortable she took the lace shawl from her shoulders and placed it carefully in her trunk. The shawl had been given to her by her grandmother. In a way she was glad the man at the store had refused to buy it. She would have missed it. It was such a beautiful, delicate thing, and it made her feel like a lady when she wore it. They needed the money, certainly, but the shawl was all she had left of her family.

Louise Danielle Ogden had been born in Independence, Missouri, in 1842, to a family waiting to follow the Oregon Trail west. Sick and bleeding, Danni's mother had begged the rest of the family to go on. She and her baby girl would be fine until Papa could come back for them. Danni's mother never recovered, and the ailing woman died enroute to the home of Danni's grandmother in Mattoon, Illinois, where mother and child were to wait until her husband's return.

When Danni's father received word of his wife's death, he decided his newest daughter could live with her grandmother in Mattoon. He wouldn't travel two thousand miles to pick up a child he had never seen, even if it did belong to him. Danni was raised by her grandmother and never learned the circumstances of her birth and abandonment until accidentally stumbling on the missive written by her father in a bundle of old letters. Hurt beyond words at the falsehoods told to her by her grandmother, Danni married the first man who asked, a young farmer named Jack Coopersand, and vowed to create for herself the family she had never had.

Shortly after Danni's marriage, her grandmother died of a

stroke, leaving Danni bereft and lonelier than she had ever imagined possible. Danni had her first miscarriage that year, and another the year after. A year after that, the call to arms was heard, and Danni lost her husband to the war. She had nothing but a farm and a mortgage, both of which she would lose. When her man returned from battle a helpless and needy stranger, Louise Danielle Coopersand was convinced that any God in any Heaven had forsaken her at birth. Whatever she gained in this life was going to be by her own hand and certainly not by divine providence.

At one time she had thought of going to Oregon to find the rest of her family—father, siblings, uncles, aunts—but pride would never allow her to thrust herself and her two wounded males upon them. The Homestead Act, passed in '62, was the star she chose to follow. She didn't need the family who didn't want her. She didn't need anyone except a guide to get her safely across Kansas.

"I'll know it when I see it," she had told Kiowa of the claim they would stake. "People say most of the best places are already taken, but there are always one or two left that no one has bothered with. I want good water within at least half a mile, and a stand of trees, if it can be had. If not, then sod will do us just fine. I'm not asking for much. Not much at all."

Her funds were few. She had just enough to get them started. The government gave her a small stipend to help with Jack, but it wasn't enough to live on. Kiowa didn't eat much, bless him, and he hunted most of what he ate, providing Danni and Jack with food as well. Danni was glad she had taken the boy in, for he helped her in ways that Jack no longer could, and he would be a good farmhand once they were settled on their claim.

There had been talk among the other women about Kiowa, Danni knew. She had heard speculation about her own relationship with the boy, most of it from Kora Blaine. All of them had asked questions about Kiowa: Where had he come from? Who were his people? Not even Danni knew these particulars, since Kiowa had never spoken of them to her. She had asked him, of course, but he told her he preferred not to speak of it.

So politely spoken was his request that she was compelled tc honor his wishes.

Danni had questions of her own about her traveling companions, mostly about the pretty, black-haired Eve Blaine, who seemed never to say much. Eve was Ormond Blaine's second wife, though she had no children by the man. Mr. Blaine's three children, Susannah, Joseph, and John, were all by Kora Blaine.

The Corles made up the rest of the group traveling west. They were Quint, Ingrid, and Arthur Corle. Quint and Ingrid were man and wife, and Arthur was Quint's father. They, too, were looking for land to claim somewhere in Kansas. Quint claimed he wouldn't know what land he wanted until he had seen all of it, and that was his reason for the trip. Danni had met the Corles back in Illinois and had traveled with them to Kansas, having the same goal in mind. They were quiet people, rarely initiating a conversation and keeping largely to themselves.

Danni liked it that way. Good neighbors were important to her, but neighbors who minded their own business were even more important. She thought it would be nice if she and the Corles could settle on adjacent claims.

Noises from the bed of the wagon brought her attention back to her husband, and Danni turned to check on him. He was awake and he smiled when he saw her, in one of his rare lucid moments.

Danni smiled back. "Hello."

"Hello. Any news today?"

"Yes, there is. Do you remember the man we met at the store today? The one who helped us?"

"Yes," Jack said, his brow furrowing. "Yes, I do. Did you say he was going to be our guide?"

"That's right," Danni said, pleased. "Isn't that wonderful? We're finally going."

Jack sat up and reached forward to put his arms around his wife. "That is wonderful. I'm so sorry, Danni. God, I'm truly . . . I know it must be hard for you. I wish it could be different. I wish . . ."

His eyes filled, and Danni lifted her arms around his neck and held him against her bosom as his shoulders shook. Her husband cried often, long shuddering sobs that made Danni ache for him.

She wished she knew how to help him. She wished she knew the terrible horrors he had beheld, so she could better understand his illness. His regiment had fought in several battles, bloody ones, if the papers were to be believed. Jack had seen two of his boyhood friends blown to bits before him; he had watched half a regiment fall under the merciless cannonfire of the Confederate artillery. And yes, Jack had sustained many an injury himself, not a few of them to the head. But the most serious injury had been inflicted on the mind of the poor, gentle farm boy from Illinois. In her heart, Danni knew the Jack Coopersand she had married would never be back.

Still, if there was anything she could do for him, she would. Anything to relieve his daily misery.

Perhaps she would question the stranger who was to guide them west in three days. He had seemed familiar with men like Jack. He might be just the man to ask about the debilitating effects of those horrible years of war.

Chapter Three

Austin passed by the group of wagons on his way into the fort, and several of the people gathered outside looked expectantly at him, and then at the blonde he had met in the store, as if to ask, *Is that him?* The woman nodded and smiled brightly at Austin. Austin tipped his hat to her, thought what a brave little fool she was, and went inside the fort's gates. He had told her most of what happened to white women caught by the Cheyenne. He had used ugly language to make the point. And still she said she would follow him anywhere. Her immediate trust in him was unnerving.

But here he was, about to enter the captain's quarters for the third time in four days. The captain's aide rose and knocked on the door, poked his head inside a moment, then ducked out again and gestured for Austin to go in.

Austin hated the smug smile on Captain Bloom's face, the knowing look in his eyes.

"Is everything under control? Have you inspected the wagons and their teams?"

"No. I came here for my money."

The captain lifted a brow and dropped a hand to open his desk drawer. "You'll receive half now. The rest will come when you reach Fort Wallace."

"Fine."

"I'm sure there'll be no problems," said the captain.

Austin glanced out the window. "The only problem I can see at the moment is the Mormon family. They should be taking the Oregon Trail west. After Fort Wallace they'll be traveling some of the roughest country on the map to get to Utah."

Captain Bloom shrugged. "That's hardly your concern, Mr. Bourke. Mr. Blaine tells me he has been asked by the church to make this southward journey and explore a different route. Naturally, it will be difficult, but the trek through Kansas seems to concern him more than the perils he'll face in the Rockies. Here you are . . ."

The captain handed him an envelope with money inside. "Your horse is tethered outside the barracks, under the care of Corporal Drake, who as you know has orders to accompany you. Have a safe journey, Mr. Bourke."

Austin put the envelope inside his shirt and wondered for the hundredth time that day what the hell he was doing. Then he left the captain's quarters and headed for the barracks. A fine chestnut gelding was tied out front and Austin stopped to look over the animal.

"He's mine," a voice called, and Austin glanced over his shoulder to see Will Drake leading a large black animal from the dark interior of the stable.

"This one's yours," said Will. "Meet the Butcher."

"The Butcher?"

"Yep. Sliced up two men with his hooves and chewed the hell out of at least three more. He's all yours."

Austin stared at the menacing red eyes of the large black horse.

Will sputtered and started laughing. "Naw, I'm just kidding. He's only kicked and chewed a little. Just gotta stay away from his mouth and feet is all." He held out the reins to Austin.

"You're a cavalry man, Bourke. You know how to handle a horse."

Austin looked at the black animal and thought of postponing the start of the trip until he could find another mount. But a good horse would cost him at least a hundred dollars, and that would be a major setback at the moment.

He strode forward and took the reins from Will. He murmured low to the horse and allowed the flaring nostrils to take in his scent. Then he swung up into the saddle and braced himself for trouble. Butcher yawned and passed wind.

Will burst out laughing again and Austin gave him a dark look. "Are you ready?"

"Yeah," Will managed. "Let me run back into the barracks and get my pack. I'll meet you outside for wagon inspection."

Austin nodded and reined Butcher toward the gates of the fort. Outside he found a dozen people standing in a group. The blonde he had talked to earlier in the week smiled and stepped away from her companions. Austin opened his mouth to tell her not to come near his horse's snout, but Butcher allowed the woman to place her hand on his bridle and stroke his velvety nose. "My name is Danni Coopersand," she said. "I forgot to ask your name the day we met. Everyone's gathered here so we can introduce ourselves."

Austin climbed out of the saddle and stood beside his horse. "My name is Austin Bourke. I'll get all of your names in a minute. Any questions you want to ask, ask them now before we get started. Corporal Drake and I will briefly inspect your teams and wagons before we leave."

"Corporal Drake?" a red-haired woman echoed. "Isn't anyone else coming?"

"No, ma'am. Just Corporal Drake and myself."

"Have you done this before?" Danni Coopersand asked. "I mean, you've traveled the trail before, obviously, but have you traveled with wagons?"

"Before today I was part-owner in a coach business," Austin told them. "We made this run and others on a regular basis with myself, my partner, and a few other men doing the driving. As for wagons, I've made a few trips with them, mostly supply wagons, like Corporal Drake. You should all be fine if you listen closely, follow my instructions, and do exactly as I say."

"What if we're attacked?" an older man standing beside a young couple asked. "Wagons aren't the same as coaches. Coaches can sometimes outrun trouble."

"Are all of you armed?" Austin replied. "Rifles, pistols?"

Everyone nodded.

"If you know how to use them, and you do as you're told, we should be able to ward off any attack."

Someone in the group snorted, but Austin couldn't make out who it was. He ignored it and stepped forward to hold out his hand to Danni Coopersand's husband. "Mr. Coopersand, it's good to see you feeling better."

Jack Coopersand's shake was limp. "I'm glad to meet you, Mr. Bourke. I didn't get a chance to thank you for your help. They were coming for me again, and I didn't have time. I had to get away."

Austin glanced at the man's wife, whose smile had faltered. "I understand," he said. "Perhaps you should go and rest again before we begin. You won't get any decent rest on the trail."

"That's a good idea," Jack said. "I am tired. So tired I'll never get to sleep, but I might as well try."

He wandered away, back to his wagon, and Austin and the others watched him go. There was pity in most of their glances, Austin noted, and derision in others. He reached for the hand of Danni Coopersand and gave it a firm shake. "Pleased to meet you, Mrs. Coopersand." He dropped her hand then and moved on through the small group, shaking hands and feeling like a politician. By the time he finished, Will Drake had come through the gates and was staring at him. Austin walked over and asked what he was looking at.

"What was that all about?" Will asked.

"They had questions. Do you?"

"Yeah," Will said, and he gave a low whistle through his teeth. "Tell me that little redhead ain't married."

Austin shook his head. "All of them are married, Will."

"Even the redhead? That one."

Will pointed and Austin looked. "She's fourteen."

"So? My mama was fifteen when she had me."

"And she died two years later. Are you ready to inspect the wagons and their teams?"

Will shrugged and slid down off his horse. "Let's get to it."

Will Drake wasn't exactly shiftless, but he wasn't ambitious, either. Will had served under Austin at Fort Leavenworth, where Austin was transferred after the war. If there was ever any work requiring physical effort to be done, Will Drake could tell you just the man to do it. As a lieutenant, Austin hadn't shown any favoritism, but he couldn't help liking the prankster. Will was usually optimistic, quick with a joke, and he had been good for the morale of the fort. Austin hoped he would be the same for the journey west.

Together they moved from wagon to wagon, looking for weaknesses and overloading. Will stopped at the Mormon's two wagons and began to marvel over their four teams of mules. "These had to cost a pretty penny. Good stock. You must be a man of means, Mr. Blaine."

Ormond Blaine's smile was proud. "The wagons were a hundred apiece and the mules were ninety dollars a head. The Church considers this a very serious effort, Corporal Drake, worthy of the finest animals and equipment money can buy. The cattle were paid for by the Church as well."

Will looked at Austin, then at the small herd behind the wagons. "Indians'll love 'em."

Austin shoved him away from the Mormon's new wagons, and they moved on to the Corles. Arthur Corle owned one wagon and its contents, and the young married couple owned the other wagon. Both conveyances were in good shape, with two yoke of oxen apiece and two milk cows to make the long haul. Will and Austin talked with Arthur Corle only briefly before moving on to the wagon belonging to the Coopersands.

One glance told Austin that an old grain wagon had been hastily fitted with a seat and some iron bows to hold a cover. There was no jockey box for tools, nowhere to hang a grease bucket. The bed was split underneath, the tongue was cracked, and the iron tires looked wobbly. Austin looked inside the wagon and spied an odd jumble of belongings. Danni saw his look of dismay and her face colored. "It was all I could afford. We don't have much money."

"Are those your horses tied in back?" Austin asked.

"Yes," she said. "But I couldn't sell them. Kiowa needs a horse to hunt, and I need . . . well, my husband always said I should never be without a horse. Never. No matter what else I had to sell, I should always keep a horse. So I did. I paid for the wagon, the oxen and the milk cow with the money I got from selling everything else."

"You have plenty of supplies?" Austin asked, with a worried look at the interior of the wagon.

"I think so," she told him, and she began to count on her slim fingers. "A hundred twenty-five pounds of flour per head, fifty pounds of salted ham, thirty pounds of sugar, three pounds of salt, a bushel of dried fruit, beans, rice, and a list of other items that Mr. Corle helped me with. Whatever else we need, Kiowa can get. He's a very good hunter. He'll be useful to us on the journey."

Austin looked at the silent, dark-eyed Kiowa and nodded.

"What's wrong with the fellow in the wagon bed?" Will asked as they walked away from the wagon.

Austin looked straight ahead. "War nerves. Trauma."

Will appeared uncomfortable. "That's a shame. What about the Indian?"

"They call him Kiowa," said Austin. "He's half-white."

"What happened to him? Where'd he get that scar on his throat?"

"Ask him," Austin said, and he walked over to his horse. As he reached for the reins he nearly had a finger removed by the black brute as the horse lunged forward, teeth bared. Austin snatched the reins and jerked his hand back in time to save himself. Will began to laugh as he swung himself up into his saddle.

"What'd I tell you? Butcher's a mean one. The captain wanted you to have him special."

Austin gritted his teeth and climbed into the saddle. He gave an extra hard yank on the reins in punishment and wheeled the horse around smartly to the front of the small wagon train. He stopped in front of Danni Coopersand's wagon and said, "I want to make sure I understand something. You want to go west across the state, and though you're looking to homestead somewhere in Kansas, you want to go all the way to Fort Wallace. Is that right?"

Her gray eyes turned serious. "All the good land in the eastern half has already been claimed, what with all the preemptions and land sharks around. A body has to travel west to find unclaimed land. I suppose if we find the perfect spot before we get to Fort Wallace, we'll just drop out and let the rest of you go on. Mr. Corle says he has to see all of it before he makes a decision. At the moment, I'm of the same mind. Does that answer your question, Mr. Bourke?"

He nodded and tipped his hat to her. Her smile returned and he was tempted to tell her not to do that, not to smile at him like that and remind him just how much she and the others were counting on him to get them where they wanted to go. But it was late to be having such thoughts, and they had some trail to cover before daylight ran out.

He was tired of smiling women. The scene with his cousin and his wife had been an ugly one, with both accusing Austin of abandoning a failing business. When Austin told them how much money he would make, and what he intended to do with the cash, they were not impressed. They remained icily skeptical, until Austin became angry and said to hell with both of them. They could have the goddamned coach business, his share included. He had gone and packed his things and that was the end of it.

It was a great relief to be away from his cousin's conniving wife, but he hadn't counted on throwing away his share of the business. Now he wasn't entirely certain that it had been the right thing to do. Money was money, and Austin liked it as well as the next man. Better than some, he guessed, which was why he had always been interested in operating his own business.

He'd have plenty of time to think about that now. The days

on the trail were going to be long ones, and the nights even longer, since Austin had his problems getting to sleep. He wouldn't call himself an insomniac, but he couldn't say he wasn't.

Such were the fortunes of war.

He thanked God every day he hadn't gone that final step beyond and become like Jack Coopersand. He had been close many times. Too close. Perhaps it had been his recognition of impending insanity that kept it at bay. He didn't know. But he did think about it often.

He wondered why men like his cousin had been allowed to shine the boots of generals and shovel up the excrement left by their horses rather than fight in the muddy fields and bloody trenches with other troops. Was it his cousin's gentle breeding and Harvard education that kept him away from the gore?

Perhaps it was that particular bitterness, Austin acknowledged, and not the trouble with his cousin's wife that had eaten away at their relationship. Perhaps her arrival and subsequent behavior had merely been the excuse Austin used to get away.

He suspected it was, but he wasn't going to think too seriously about it. He had other things to concern himself with now. Like what he was going to do after he got these people to Fort Wallace. If he got them there.

He rode his big black horse to the sutler's and picked up his belongings, then he returned to the wagons and signaled that he was ready to begin. Will lifted his hand in an instinctive salute before giving a shrill whistle and a shout that said to move out. An ox bellowed as someone in the train cracked a whip. Wheels creaked and wood groaned as the wagons began to move.

Austin moved out in front and rode slowly down the dusty road, giving everyone a chance to get into position. After a moment he turned in the saddle and looked back at the small train. All he could see was the wagon directly behind him, and the excitement on Danni Coopersand's bright, shining face in stark contrast with the dark, somber features of the half-Indian youth beside her.

Austin ignored the woman's engaging smile and turned to face the road. For the first time since his discharge he was responsible for other people again. He wondered why he hadn't thought about that before he agreed to take the job.

Chapter Four

After only a week on the trail, Austin discovered the naked, mutilated body of a man not more than five miles away from Fort Riley. Dread tightened his stomach as he dismounted his horse and walked over to view the corpse. The sun was high in the cloudless sky; the flies were numerous. Austin took his kerchief from his neck and put it over his nose to filter out the stench. He didn't want the wagons a mile behind him to see this sight.

The man's eyes had been gouged out, his nose, ears, and chin sliced off. His head had been split open, the brain removed. His hands and feet were gone, and his intestines littered the ground around him. His skin had been stripped away in places, and great chunks of muscle removed. He had also been castrated.

It took Austin only a moment to decide to cover the man rather than move him. He turned to look for some brush when a sound behind him made him whirl, revolver drawn from his holster. Kiowa was in the middle of the trail, watching him from the back of his sleek bay mare. His dark eyes flickered over the revolver in Austin's hand before lighting on the corpse in the tall grass.

Austin held up a palm, but the youth was already off his horse. He walked over to stand beside Austin and the dead man. His face registered no emotion as he glanced over the mottled remains.

Austin shoved his kerchief in his pocket and returned his revolver to its holster. "Help me find enough brush to cover him. I don't want the others to see this."

Kiowa nodded briefly and walked away. Moments later he returned with his arms full of leafy branches. "It was a cavalry man," he said to Austin.

"What makes you say so?"

"There's a boot," he said, and pointed to where a cavalry boot lay beneath tangled limbs.

Austin looked. He nodded. "What else?"

Kiowa glanced questioningly at him.

"What else do you see?" Austin asked.

The youth looked hesitantly at the corpse.

"You've obviously done some tracking, Kiowa. I've seen this before, and from your lack of reaction, I'd say you've been exposed to something like it yourself. Tell me what you see here."

"I see a dead man mutilated by two Indians and maybe three white men."

"Not the Cheyenne?"

"No, it looks like the Sioux. I could be wrong."

"What makes you think white men were here?"

"Besides the shod horses?"

"The whites may have come later," Austin suggested.

Kiowa shook his head as if to say it wasn't likely.

Austin eyed the tracks again. He had suspected renegade whites when the raids on his stagecoaches appeared too sophisticated in orchestration for the usual mob of angry Cheyenne to have planned.

"Was it a white who tried to kill you?" Austin asked, and he looked at the scar on the boy's throat.

"Yes," Kiowa answered, and he bent to lay his armful of brush over the body.

Nothing more was forthcoming, so Austin placed his own camouflage and stood back. The oxen and mules would shy away from the smell, but no human eyes would pick out the dead man in the tall grass beside the trail. He felt Kiowa look at him as he walked back to his horse. "When we reach Fort Riley I'll inform the commander," he said over his shoulder. "Don't speak of it to anyone else."

"No," said Kiowa in his unnaturally hoarse voice.

Austin climbed on Butcher and waited for the youth to mount before kicking the black horse forward. Together they rode back to the wagons, and as the train passed the hidden corpse, both Austin and Kiowa were there to keep the nervous oxen and mules in place on the trail. Later that day, as they made camp outside Fort Riley, Austin pulled Will Drake aside and told him about the body. The corporal's face paled as Austin relayed his suspicions.

Finally, Will shook his head. "I can't believe a white man would be capable of something like that."

Austin Bourke knew better. In the last seven of his thirty-three years he had seen unspeakable atrocities committed in the name of God and country, all of them perpetrated by coldly sadistic white men. They were more than capable—they were experts.

"I believe Kiowa knows what he's talking about," Austin told Will. Then he excused himself to speak to the commander of the fort.

His welcome was cool, so Austin passed on the news of the body and its whereabouts and left the commander's quarters as quickly as possible. The man had looked at Austin's papers and eyed him as if he were a murderer and mutilator of men rather than a guide in the employment of the U.S. government. Austin hadn't expected anything less after reporting the condition of the body. The bearer of such news bore no small amount of guilt when it came to the reporting of facts. He was glad when he passed through the gates of the fort undisturbed.

Outside, Will Drake approached and asked what the commander had to say.

"He said to be on our way shortly after reveille in the morning."

"Kill the messenger," Will muttered. "Did you tell him what the breed said about the white men?"

"No."

"Maybe you should have."

Austin looked at him. "I thought you didn't believe him."

"I don't say I didn't believe him. I just don't *want* to believe him, is all."

Austin commiserated with a nod and walked over to Butcher to remove his bedroll. His mind kept flashing images of the dead soldier, the way it flashed images of every dead and dying man he had seen lying in the slime and muck at Salisbury, North Carolina. He gritted his teeth and willed it to stop. He willed himself to think of something—anything—else.

"Mr. Bourke," a nearby voice called, and he turned to see Danni Coopersand approach. He sighed in relief as she came and handed him a cup of coffee.

"We're ready to eat now," she said. "Would you care to come and sit with us?"

"I would," he said, and he hoped he didn't sound as eager as he felt. Anything to get away from the thoughts he was thinking. He followed her back to the cooksite and thanked her as she prepared a plate for him. Beans, dried beef, and bread were the fare, with hot coffee to drink. Jack Coopersand sat like a stone with his plate before him. His eyes didn't blink, and nothing but his chest moved. Austin glanced at Kiowa and Danni to gauge their reactions, but they appeared not to notice. It was normal, then.

After Danni had served everyone else she prepared a plate for herself and sat down across from Austin. He looked at her, told her the food was good, and thanked her again for asking him to join them.

"I noticed you've been eating by yourself," said Danni. "You're welcome to eat with us whenever you like." She put down her plate then. "May I ask you some questions?"

Austin looked at her before nodding.

"You said you'd seen men like Jack before," she began. "Where?"

"Everywhere, ma'am."

"You were in the Union army?"

"I served under Philip Sheridan and Wesley Merritt as a lieutenant in the United States Cavalry."

She blinked. "A lieutenant? Under Sheridan? Why aren't you still?"

"Still a lieutenant, or still under Sheridan?" Austin asked.

"Both."

Austin stopped eating. "Sheridan's on the Mexican border, and I'm about as fond of that location as I am of him. As for no longer being a lieutenant, that was my choice. Many men were demoted after the war was over; I wasn't one of them, but it was time to leave the cavalry."

"Did you see many battles?"

"More than I wanted."

"So you know some of what Jack has seen. You know why he is the way he is."

"I can guess. You said he was in the Illinois infantry. Who was his commander?"

"A man named Prentice. Benjamin, I believe. Jack was at Shiloh when General Johnston surprised Grant. My husband was a part of what they called the Hornet's Nest, the men who held back the enemy for six hours until the Confederacy brought in their cannons."

Austin stared at Jack Coopersand. Few men he knew had mentioned the battle of Pittsburgh Landing without using the word *bloodbath.*

Danni was staring at him, her eyes unblinking. "You know about Shiloh."

"Yes, ma'am. We all did."

"You've seen the same horrors," she said softly. "I can see the memory of it in your eyes. Which only leads me to ask why? Why him, and not you? Why didn't it affect you the way it's affected Jack?"

Austin forced himself to look at her. "What makes you think it hasn't?"

"Because you . . . you're sane."

Austin gave a bitter smile and felt the stirrings of irritation mar his pleasure in his dinner. "Some would argue. I took this job when there's a real and serious danger of everyone here being slaughtered and left out on the prairie to die. That's not sane. You want to go out and homestead on land the Cheyenne have been roaming and raiding for two years now. Is that sane?"

"It's desperation," said Danni. She looked at his hard features and clasped her hands together. "I don't want to pry or make you angry. I want to know if there's anything I can do to help Jack. You seem so good and patient with him I thought you might tell me something I could do for him."

Austin glanced at the silent Kiowa, who was cleaning up his plate with a piece of bread.

"I don't know what to tell you," he said tersely. "I don't know what would make a difference, or even if anything can. I'm sorry, Mrs. Coopersand. I can't help you."

She gazed at him before picking up her plate again. "You're an honest man, Mr. Bourke. Thank you. I'm sorry to have ruined your dinner with my conversation. I hope you'll forgive me."

Her gray eyes were on him, waiting, and Austin said, "There's nothing to forgive, Mrs. Coopersand. I'm sorry if I seemed brusque."

Their eyes met for a moment, then both of them slowly started eating again. Kiowa finished off his plate and took it and washed it before returning with a deck of cards in his hand. Austin watched him attempt to shuffle and the corner of his mouth curved as he remembered his own first attempts at shuffling a deck. Kiowa saw the smile and narrowed his eyes. He handed the deck to Austin.

"Show me."

Austin wiped his hands on his trousers and shuffled the deck twice. Then he handed the cards back to Kiowa.

Kiowa picked up the deck and tried again. Cards flew everywhere. Danni Coopersand laughed and helped the youth retrieve them. She looked different when she laughed, Austin noted. Younger. Sweeter. Like the girl she must have been at one time. His irritation with her dissolved as he watched her careful treatment of Kiowa. She was good to him. Better than most might be to a strange, wounded half-Indian youth. She treated him with affection but also with respect, and she didn't attempt to mother him. Rather, she treated him as she would a dear friend, laughing and gently teasing until at last she coaxed a smile from his somber face.

She was just as good to her husband, he realized, and suddenly he felt guilty for his earlier sharpness with her. How could he explain it to her? How could he tell her that what she yearned to understand was beyond simple understanding? Austin had been there, and he still didn't understand. He carried the struggle with him day after day, night after night, and wondered how other men, like Sheridan, went on to fight other battles and kill other men. Was there no satisfying their taste for blood? Had the war merely awakened their thirst?

The Indians did what they did for a reason. They mutilated corpses to prevent the spirit happy access to the afterlife, believing the corporeal form would somehow transmute into the hereafter. The white man mutilated for no other reason than savagery. And it was witness of that savagery, Austin wagered, that had sent the gentle Jack Coopersand into the depths and pain of insanity.

As if sensing Austin's thoughts, Jack Coopersand shook himself and lifted his head. He looked directly at Austin.

"Enjoying your supper, Mr. Bourke?" he asked. "Danni's a fine cook. Her grandmother taught her well."

His wife glanced up and pointed to her husband's plate. "You should eat now, Jack. Please."

"Yes. I'll eat. I see you're playing cards again, Kiowa. Kiowa learns awfully quick. Have you figured out poker yet? I'll sit in for a hand if you'll have me."

"Jack . . ."

"I'm eating, Danni. I am, see?" He lifted a forkful and placed it in his mouth before looking at Austin again. "Sometimes I forget to eat. I've always been bad about it. My father and his brothers used to call me 'string bean' when I was a boy. Tall and skinny." He paused then and sniffed himself. He looked around. "Is there anywhere around here a man who smells like a skunk can bathe, Mr. Bourke?"

"You can wash in the bucket later," said his wife.

Jack looked cross. "I asked Mr. Bourke."

"Not to my knowledge," Austin said. "A dip in the river might be risky at this time and place."

"I see," said Jack. He rose and brought his plate over to sit next to Austin. "I need to converse with you, sir. We should do it privately."

Austin felt Danni Coopersand look at them. He glanced at her and saw that her expression was worried.

"If you like," Austin said, and he rose. "We'll go check on the horses." He left the camp and Jack Coopersand sauntered along after him. When they were out of earshot, Austin turned. "You had something you wanted to say?"

"Yes," Jack said, and his face twisted with sudden intensity, as if he were willing himself to stay focused. "You can see the man I've become, Mr. Bourke. My mind is never constant. Much of the time I don't know who I am, and when I do know who I am, I cower from the world like a . . . a frightened, pathetic animal. I can't help it, and I can't seem to stop it."

Austin said nothing. He only stood and listened.

"I haven't been a husband to Danni in a long, long time. She hasn't had a man to look after her or see to her needs. When she found Kiowa and took him in, I thought he might find his way to her bed, but they're more like brother and sister than . . . well, like lovers." He stopped and wiped his nose as tears dropped out of his eyes.

Austin swallowed hard and wondered why he was the one hearing this. He concentrated on the nearby horses and saw a few hogs loose from the fort pens come snuffling around.

"Danni likes you, I know," said Jack. "She's got a light in her eyes when she looks at you. It's a look I've never seen before. I—"

"Mr. Coopersand," Austin interrupted, "your wife scares the hell out of me. She thinks I'm some messiah with a mission, come to lead her to the promised land. That's the light you see in her eyes. She's had it since the day I met her, and God help me if I fail her and these other people, because I'd hate to see the reverse of that woman's smile. Now I'm aware of your predicament, but I'm not the man to talk to about this."

Jack's hands covered his eyes and he began to weep. He sat down hard in the grass and his shoulders heaved as if some terrible burden weighted his lungs. "I hate this, oh, Lord, you don't know how much," he sobbed. "But I have to try and do right by her. I've got to put things right somehow. I'm not a man anymore, Mr. Bourke. I'm not anything."

"Mr. Coopersand, please . . ." Austin bent down to lift him, but when he touched the man's shoulder, Jack suddenly sprang up from the ground. His eyes were wild as he stared at the hogs a few yards away. Austin spoke to him, but Jack didn't hear. His gaze dropped to the revolver at Austin's waist, and a high, hysterical note came from his throat as he swung wildly at Austin.

"They're eating the dead!" he screamed. "They're eating them! Shoot, damn you!"

"Jack!" a voice shouted, and Austin saw a horrified Danni Coopersand running toward them, followed by Kiowa. Jack didn't respond to her call. He swung once more at Austin and then turned and began to run away from the camp. Austin went after him, and within fifteen yards he grabbed the wild-eyed Jack around the waist and slung him hard to the ground. Jack turned and fought as if against death itself, kicking and pummeling and scratching, but Kiowa and Danni arrived to help pin him down. In moments his limbs were jerking and his eyes rolling. Kiowa thrust a stick between his teeth and the three of them held on until finally he lost consciousness.

Danni was first to let go. She sat back on her heels and wiped at the streaks of dirt on her face. Her breathing was quick and shallow. "What did he mean?" she asked when she could speak. "What did he mean when he said they were eating the dead?"

After his own breathing slowed, Austin said, "The hogs, I think."

Danni appeared confused. "The hogs? From the fort?"

Austin got up and drew a deep breath. "At Shiloh it was said hogs wandered the fields eating the unclaimed dead after the fighting was over."

Danni's face lost its color. "What else did he say?"

Austin looked down at Jack. "Nothing."

She paused a long moment, waiting. Then she said, "I'm sorry my husband assaulted you, Mr. Bourke. Kiowa, let's get him back to the wagon."

Austin offered to help, and Danni Coopersand politely accepted, though she refused to look at him.

She walked in front of them back to the wagons, her gait uncertain. When Jack was inside the wagon and comfortable, she thanked Austin again. "I'll do my best to see that we're no more trouble to you, Mr. Bourke."

Austin opened his mouth to speak, but he closed it again. She was embarrassed, ashamed, and sick at heart for her husband, and nothing he could say would change that. He only wished Jack hadn't told him so much.

Chapter Five

Eve Blaine watched the struggle with Jack Coopersand from the back of her wagon. Everyone in camp had watched and no one uttered a word. No one but Kora, who said there were hospitals for men like Jack Coopersand, and why his wife didn't give up and put him away she would never know. The government money Danni Coopersand received for him was one reason, Kora surmised. God only knew what other reasons there could be.

Ormond Blaine told Kora to be quiet then, and she turned prissily away to help Eve finish washing up the dishes from supper. Ormond also ordered the children to stop staring and to make themselves busy with their lessons. Susannah, Kora's daughter, sat in the back of the wagon and plucked in boredom at a fiddle. The boys lay on their stomachs under the weak light of a lantern and looked at their schoolbooks.

When the dishes were done and put away, Eve tossed out the water and poured a fresh bowl with which to bathe herself. She took the bowl into the back of her wagon and drew a blanket across the opening behind her. After a moment the blanket was pulled aside and Ormond joined her in the wagon. His white face creased into a smile as he saw her fingers move to rebutton her blouse.

"No, don't. I'll watch you bathe, if you don't mind, Eve. I have that right, don't I?"

"Of course," she murmured, and she undid her blouse again and removed it. She sponged inside her loose-fitting chemise until he reached forward and pulled it down over her shoulders. Eve looked uncomfortably at the blanket hanging between them and the outside.

"Don't worry," said Ormond. "I've instructed the others not to bother us. Come now, Eve. Don't keep me waiting. It's been a while for us."

Eve sighed inwardly and lifted her skirts. Ormond came to her, and when he had positioned her exactly the way he wanted her, he let down his trousers and mounted her.

"Slattern," he said as he forced himself inside her.

Eve concentrated on the canvas over her head.

"Whore," he whispered fiercely. "Come to God."

"I come," she said tonelessly, "with love and thankfulness in my heart."

"Yes," he cried low in her ear. The entire exchange was repeated again, and moments later it was over. Soon he was fastening his trousers and leaving the wagon, the entire time spent with her no more than twelve minutes. Eve sank her sponge deep in the water and cleansed herself thoroughly after his departure. She found the pasty-skinned man repugnant.

But he was just one man, and he didn't touch her often. She was better off with him than where she had been before, and eventually she intended to leave him and his family and make her way west to California. He didn't know that, of course. Neither did Kora, for all her claimed omniscience. The two of them believed Eve would be happy to remain forever a part of their little family as maid, cook, whore, and watcher of children. And yes, Eve was grateful to have been rescued when she was. But she saw more than was intended for her to see, and what she saw guaranteed that she would leave these people the moment she was able.

None of it made sense to her in the beginning. Why Kora Blaine would allow her husband to seek out a second wife. As Eve understood it, only a few Mormons actually engaged in polygamy. Most did not. Most wives wouldn't allow it. And with a woman of Kora Blaine's temperament, the consent to add an additional woman to her household, particularly a woman such as Eve, was most puzzling. Kora knew Eve had sold her body to men for money. She knew everything about Eve, and still she encouraged her husband to offer himself. Not until Eve had become familiar with the family did she understand. Not until she had lived with them, watched their movements day in and day out, did she realize why she had been introduced into the family.

Eve was there so Ormond would keep his hands off his daughter, Susannah. A whore had been brought in to sate his lust so his little girl might be spared his unclean attentions. Eve knew it, and the moment Kora saw that she knew it, Kora's treatment of Eve worsened. The two women barely spoke to each other to begin with; now they addressed each other only when necessary.

The trouble was, Kora's plan had failed. Even with the addition of Eve to his stable, Ormond Blaine still found time to fondle his teenage daughter. Eve imagined he found time to do other things as well. The idea sickened her, but young Susannah seemed to accept it as normal. She doted on her father, and he on her. The two of them laughed and talked and tickled and played all manner of games while Kora looked coldly on. Susannah, knowing fully well that her mother viewed her as an adversary for her father's affections, took full advantage of her position and often smiled like a cherub while incurring her mother's wrath.

Eve saw all of this in six months of living with the Blaine family. Six months of being called names and co-existing with the hateful, red-haired Kora. She was grateful at being rescued from penury, yes, and for being taken care of at the hospital in

St. Louis with its wonderful medicines. But her dignity was suffering, perhaps more than it had ever suffered before.

She finished her bath and put on a nightdress, but her eyes and her mind were not ready for sleep. She thought of Jack Coopersand and pitied his wife, who was such a strong-willed woman. She had to be, Eve guessed, and Eve admired her for it. She thought of Austin Bourke and the carefully hidden wounds he carried with him. Then there was Will Drake, the soldier; Eve had slept with dozens like him, all of them hungry for and willing to give as much as a month's pay for something as simple as a woman's touch.

Eve had kept her head above water during the war, and she had kept her ailing father alive . . . for a time. He had been sick before the war, in the grip of consumption, and then he contracted cholera. Eve had no more furniture or dresses to sell for medicine, and begging was no longer effective. After being mistaken for a whore and roughly taken by a drunken officer one evening, Eve made her decision.

Illness and disease came to her eventually, and she found herself in the hospital, the place where Cora Blaine, the ministering Mormon, found her.

Eve wasn't sorry for any of it. She had done what was necessary to keep her father alive for as long as she possibly could. She felt she owed him that much.

He died, of course. And, of course, his death had devastated her. Even now her throat thickened to think of him.

Restless and perspiring, she rose from the bed of the wagon and pulled the blanket aside to step out into the coolness of the night. She had walked no more than ten yards when she saw movement to her left. She turned her head and saw Kiowa, the dark-haired youth, watching her from where he sat on the ground beside the Coopersands' wagon. His bedroll was beneath him.

"You couldn't sleep either?" she inquired, and he gave a small, almost imperceptible shake of his head, all the while steadily watching her with his dark eyes.

Eve approached and gestured for him to shake out his bedroll, so she might sit down beside him and share his company. He rose instead, and made to walk away.

"Kiowa," she called, and he stopped and turned to look at her. "Won't you sit and talk?" she asked.

After a moment he returned and shook out his bedroll.

Eve sat down and beckoned him to join her. He sat down beside her, and she noticed his flesh had goosepimples.

"Are you cold?" she asked him.

"No."

She looked at his goosepimples again. "I am. A little. But it's a pleasant evening. My head was just too full of things to sleep."

He nodded.

"Would you mind if I talked?" she asked, looking at him. "Just for a time. I feel the need to talk about my father. It makes me feel close to him."

Kiowa's assent was in his eyes. Eve smiled and looked at the evening sky. "My father loved nights like this one. He loved an unimpeded view of the moon and stars. He was a professor in St. Louis. He taught literature to young boys like you. He gave them Shakespeare and Homer, and sonnets of love to carry home in their angry young heads. He sang every morning and prayed every night and I used to love to hear the sound of his voice. Wherever I was I would stop and listen. It was magical.

"His students loved him nearly as much as I did. He was the kindest, most gentle man I have ever known. When war came he did all he could for his boys, even giving away his books so that love of literature could be carried even into battle.

"He kept Byron," she continued. "He did love Lord Byron's works, controversial though they were. I was raised on Byron, you might say. I heard Byron in my cradle, as my father used it to soothe me. My mother died soon after I was born. I have a picture of her in my trunk. I look like her. She had the same black hair and green eyes, my father said. She loved poetry and literature and my father, so they were quite happy together . . . until I came along and ended their happiness."

She grew silent and thoughtful. Then she turned to look at Kiowa. "You do speak English, don't you?"

He chuckled.

Eve smiled. "Do you? Have I been telling my sad story to someone who doesn't understand a word I'm saying?"

Kiowa leaned his head back. Soon he began to recite in his hoarse voice:

She walks in Beauty, like the night
Of cloudless climes and starry skies;
And all that's best of dark and bright
Meet in her aspect and her eyes;
Thus mellowed to that tender light
Which Heaven to gaudy day denies.

He turned to look at Eve, who stared at him. "You're quite a mystery, aren't you? How is it that you know Byron?"

"My mother," said Kiowa.

"Your mother was white?"

"Yes."

"Your father was—"

"One of five Cheyenne warriors."

Eve blinked. "Cheyenne? Where were you born?"

"Oregon. My mother traveled west with her family when she was sixteen. She was captured and then left to die. She survived and was later reunited with her people."

"I've heard stories of such things," said Eve, her voice hushed.

"She died last winter."

"I'm sorry."

They were comfortably silent, then Eve turned to face him. "If the warriors were Cheyenne, why are you called Kiowa? Surely it wasn't your mother's idea?"

"No," he said. "It was the man she married, after she returned to the east. She met him in Virginia, and he said I resembled a Kiowa he once saw. He never called me anything else, and my stepbrothers soon followed his example."

"What is your given name?"

Kiowa didn't answer. He only looked at the starry night sky. Eve leaned toward him, hoping the conversation would continue. "Is your stepfather still alive?"

"Yes," he said.

"Where are your brothers now?"

"I don't know."

The flat note in his voice was a warning, but Eve ignored it. "This man your mother married, was he good to you?"

Kiowa abruptly stood. "You should try to sleep now. Good night, Mrs. Blaine." Just as abruptly he walked away from her, and Eve was left sitting on the blanket by herself. She looked around in the darkness and finally made out the sleeping form of Will Drake. The alert Mr. Bourke would be on watch. Over by her own wagons snored Ormond Blaine; beside him were his two sons.

Eve got up with a long sigh and walked quietly back to her wagon. As she settled herself on the lumpy mattress in the back she thought of Kiowa's hoarse recitation of the lines from one of Byron's poems. She decided she had never heard the words more beautifully spoken.

Chapter Six

Kiowa padded silently around the perimeter of the camp to check on his mare. He had stolen the bay and another horse eight months ago, from a trader in Illinois who cheated Danni on several items she was selling to raise cash. Danni disapproved greatly of the theft, but rather than see Kiowa hang for the offense, they left Illinois all the more quickly. The bay was a fine animal, worth every penny Danni was owed by the miserly old trader. The man had no idea who had taken his animals, but Danni wanted to be safely away. And though she angrily scolded him, Kiowa followed her. He had no choice; Danni Coopersand was the kindest person he had ever known.

He could still remember the first time he saw her, his head spinning from loss of blood, his mind uncertain. He had believed her to be a spirit of some kind, come down from the sky to take him away. He saw the pretty face and the clear eyes, framed by a halo of blonde hair, and he had wondered when he was going to start floating. When he realized how worried her expression was, he knew he was mistaken. She was no spirit from the sky.

But she proved to be an angel all the same, nursing and tending his wound and keeping him fed and free of infection until he began to regain his strength. And all of this while she looked after her husband and made plans to leave the farm she had lost to the bank. When she asked Kiowa how he had come to have his throat slit, he knew he would not burden her further with his problems. He resolved to aid her as she had aided him, and that included keeping his troublesome business to himself.

It helped, of course, that Danni had decided to travel in the direction Kiowa himself felt bound to go. His brothers had come to Kansas after slitting his throat and leaving him to die, and they were probably among the men who now rode with the Sioux, attacking stagecoaches and murdering innocent citizens. The loss of the war and the destruction of their home in the Shenandoah Valley had left his Confederate brothers miserable with hatred and bitterness toward the Union Army. Cavalrymen were their favorite targets, since it was the cavalryman Sheridan who had led his soldiers in the burning and pillaging of the valley.

Kiowa had heard Austin Bourke say he served under Sheridan in the war. He could only shake his head at the fate that would surely befall Bourke if Kiowa's brothers knew the same fact. Bourke would be hunted down and left in the same shape as the cavalryman found outside Fort Riley. His brothers had traveled all the way to Illinois, dragging Kiowa with them, in search of one unlucky man they held directly responsible for the destruction of their home and the homes of their surrounding neighbors. Kiowa had been forced to watch the live mutilation of this man and two of his former cohorts in the war. His brothers fled Illinois the same night, but not before slitting Kiowa's throat and leaving a knife in the hand of a dead soldier, to make it look as if Kiowa had been the murderer.

Bleeding profusely, Kiowa managed to drag himself away from the carnage and into the nearby woods. He continued to drag himself, heedless of direction, until he reached a stream. It was here he collapsed, and it was at the stream that Danni later found him. He wanted her to be an angel. Better to die than to live with the hatred that soured his belly. Better to leave the earth entirely than to spend the rest of his days hunting down the men he had called brothers . . . to kill them.

Kiowa volunteered, but for the Union Army, who rejected him because of his mixed blood. When his stepfather found out, he was enraged. Kiowa's mother felt differently. She was much enamored of Abraham Lincoln, and called him a rare, truly honorable man. Her feelings and Kiowa's attempt to join the Union sparked many a confrontation between his mother and her husband, and when Kiowa dared to intervene he was lashed with a strap and sent out to the slaves' shack. Kiowa spent many an hour with the slaves, reading to them from his mother's books and listening to their sad songs.

He often told his mother he wished she had stayed in Oregon, or at least gone north when she decided to come back east, rather than south. She would laugh and tell him many was the occasion when she wished the same. She didn't know how cold her husband could be until after marrying him and seeing him with his slaves. She didn't realize the sons he introduced her to would have so little regard for their new stepmother. She hardly knew her own daughter, for as soon as the baby girl was weaned from the breast she was given to housekeepers and governesses to raise, leaving her with little to say about her daughter's upbringing.

Kiowa was different. He was left alone to do as he pleased, receiving none of the education or attention accorded his stepbrothers or his baby sister. When he crossed the path of his stepfather in the big house, the man would stare him down and threaten to reach for the horse whip he carried out of doors. Kiowa avoided him and went to his mother when he was in no danger of being discovered with her. She was his teacher and she alone was his friend.

To know he had been kidnapped by his brothers had probably been the death of her. Kiowa wrote his mother when he regained his strength and told her what happened. His young sister wrote him back and told him their mother had died shortly after receiving his letter. Pneumonia had been the reported cause of her demise, but Kiowa tortured himself in spite of the facts, because his sister added that her father had flown into a rage and called Kiowa a liar and said should he ever attempt to return to the family he would be shot on sight.

His mother had known the truth, Kiowa told himself. She knew he would never lie about being kidnapped. Nor would he lie about murder.

In the long months spent recuperating and waiting to make the trip west with the Coopersands, Kiowa read everything available to him about Kansas and beyond, and he spent many a long hour in the shack of a trapper who lived near Danni's farm. The trapper's name was Bill Ottleway, and he taught Kiowa everything he knew about Indian and animal sign, giving Kiowa a taste of his own heritage and enabling him to *feel* like an Indian for the first time in his life. Bill taught Kiowa the lessons of silence and stillness, and the power gained over oneself and others simply by learning patience.

Under Bill Ottleway's tutelage, Kiowa became an able hunter, trapper, and reader of sign. Bill said he would make the army a fine scout if he was so inclined. Kiowa told him it was something to consider, but he knew he would not leave Danni alone on the prairie with no one but her husband to aid her in homesteading. His conscience would not allow it.

The nostrils of his bay mare flared and the animal snorted as Kiowa held its muzzle. He turned and saw Austin Bourke approach. Austin came and gave the neck of his black horse a swift pat, to which the animal responded by craning its head and trying to take a bite out of his ear. Austin ducked and Kiowa felt laughter bubble in his throat.

"Sonofabitch," Austin muttered. His lips curved when he saw Kiowa's smile. "How would you like to ride him?"

Kiowa shook his head and chuckled.

"Had any sleep tonight?" Austin asked, and Kiowa moved his head again. "No."

"Got your cards?"

"Yes." Kiowa dug in his pocket and produced the deck. "Poker?"

"Still learning?" asked Austin.

"I know the game. I just can't shuffle."

"All right, we'll play. But not for money. I don't need to be swindled by a perfect poker face."

Kiowa smiled again. He liked Austin Bourke.

They went and sat near the smoldering fire still burning at the cook site. Austin put another branch on the fire to rekindle the flame and then held out his hand for the deck.

"I'll deal," said Kiowa.

"You don't trust me?" Austin asked.

"Would you trust a man who never sleeps?"

"I'm sitting with one."

They looked at each other, then both slowly smiled.

"Deal," said Austin.

Kiowa shuffled the cards the best he could and then dealt out the hands. As he placed the rest of the deck beside him he heard a noise that made him look up.

Austin looked up at the same time and then glanced at Kiowa as the sound came again. It was a low, mournful whistle, carried and made eerie by the gentle night wind.

The horses and mules snuffled nervously and the oxen and cattle stamped their feet and jostled against one another. Finally Kiowa knew what it was.

"It's the dead man," he said.

Austin nodded. "A detail was sent out to get him after I left the commander. They're bringing him back to the fort now."

They paused together and listened as the whistle sounded again, tuneless for the most part, but making an attempt at linking the notes in a song.

Kiowa's eyes scoured the darkness and finally he saw the men emerge in the glow from the camp. Four soldiers on horses and a long, cloth-covered bundle slung over the saddle of a fifth horse.

The soldiers didn't look at Austin and Kiowa as they passed. Their faces were pointedly averted as they approached the gates of the fort, spoke to the guards, and were allowed inside.

Kiowa glanced at Austin and was tempted to tell what he suspected had happened to the man. He was tempted to confide his purpose, and to warn Austin of the danger he faced if his presence and past performance as a soldier came to be known to certain men now ranging over the prairie.

But he would not. Austin Bourke was aware of the dangers they faced as they traveled westward. He was aware of the threat from every quarter; it was in the nervous tension running through his hands and arms. It was in the alertness of his eyes and the way his head swiveled as if to trap every sound and isolate its cause. The man did not sleep for a reason, and though this westward trip had given him purpose, Kiowa believed this state of perpetual alertness was normal for Austin Bourke.

Bill Ottleway would have called him a "warrior of the senses," meaning that to Austin Bourke, living was in and of itself a war. A war that would never end.

When the gates of the fort closed behind the men, Kiowa returned to his cards. Eventually Austin did the same. The easy companionable feeling of a moment before was strained but not entirely gone. The two played with little more than grunts and snorts for several minutes, until Kiowa yawned. Austin saw and suggested Kiowa turn in. The fort had posted additional guards and lookouts after the news of the body, so there was little need to keep strict vigilance this close to the post.

Kiowa agreed and made his way back to his wagon and bedroll. He picked up the blanket to shake it out, and for an instant he detected the scent of Eve Blaine. His heart beat a little faster as he lay down on the blanket, but he willed himself to concentrate on other matters. Soon she would be gone, on her way to Utah, and he would remain in Kansas, with plenty of work to do for Danni Coopersand. After he helped Danni to settle and get started farming, he would leave for a while. He would come back, of course, but not before he had done what he promised himself he would do. He needed to find his brothers and kill them.

Chapter Seven

A HAND on her shoulder awakened Danni, and she came up with a start to see Kiowa kneeling before her in the bed of the wagon. "Time to rise," he said.

"Is Jack awake?" she asked, though the answer would make no difference.

"No."

She looked at Kiowa. "Did you sleep?"

"Yes. Bourke woke me."

Danni hauled herself off the beaten mattress in the bottom of the wagon bed. Jack still snored softly at the opposite end; his body twitched in his sleep.

"We'll have yesterday's biscuits and dried beef for breakfast," she told Kiowa, and he nodded and left the wagon as she searched about in the darkness for a dress to replace her nightgown. Her spirits were not as high as in mornings past, and she knew the reason was because of what had happened with Jack and Austin Bourke. A part of her had dared to hope Jack would get well in time. She had believed the presence of someone who knew his pain would help him. Last night had shattered those illusions. Seeing Jack swing at the man and hearing him scream about the hogs eating the dead had been like a glimpse into the future for Danni.

The faces of the people in the camp had deepened her dismay. Danni knew what they were thinking. She knew Kora Blaine believed Jack belonged in a hospital, and that the only reason Danni kept him was for the money the government sent, and because of the deduction in time his army service would grant them under a provision of the Homestead Act. Kora Blaine was right. But Danni wasn't ashamed of her decisions. No one could take better care of Jack than she could. And no one would. Not while Danni was still capable.

Determined to give her low spirits a lift, Danni lit a lantern and dressed, combed her hair, and put a bright blue ribbon around her ponytail to match the blue flowers in the yellow calico of her dress. When she came down from the wagon she saw Kiowa smile at her in approval. Danni smiled back and went hastily about the morning's preparation to move.

For the first time, she looked at Fort Riley and wondered about the fort itself. Austin Bourke had said Riley was built to consolidate other smaller forts. It seemed huge to Danni. It was said to have its own hospital, an extremely large dining hall for the men, and luxurious quarters for the officers. From the outside looking in, it appeared to be just another post to Danni, though larger than others she had seen. She had witnessed two women going in and out of the post the day before, and Danni had guessed them to be the fort's laundresses.

Most laundresses were married to enlisted men, but a few Danni had heard of were unmarried women who did more than launder clothes for the men of the fort.

"Good morning, Mrs. Coopersand."

She stopped what she was doing and turned. She forced a bright smile. "Good morning, Mr. Bourke. Have you had your breakfast?"

He seemed surprised to see her so cheerful. "Yes, I have, ma'am. Thank you for asking. How is Mr. Coopersand this morning?"

"Still sleeping. But we'll be ready to move when you are."

He tipped his hat to her and started away. Then he paused. "That's a very pretty ribbon you're wearing this morning, Mrs. Coopersand."

Danni blinked. "I . . . thank you, Mr. Bourke."

He nodded and walked on, leaving Danni to stare after him.

An hour later they were on the trail and moving west again. Fort Harker wasn't far, only a few days away, and simply being on the move again made Danni feel better. When they stopped for lunch, Ingrid Corle came and asked if she could ride with Danni in her wagon for a while. She was starved for the company of a woman. Danni laughed and told her she would be more than welcome, as Danni could do with some female companionship herself. She saw Quint Corle scowl in her direction when his wife told him of her plans, but Ingrid came anyway. As she climbed onto the seat beside her, Danni asked if anything was wrong.

"No, no, Quint's a suspicious sort."

"Suspicious of me?" Danni said in surprise.

"Of anyone," said Ingrid. "Aren't all men like that?"

"I haven't known enough to answer," Danni said. "Is his father the same?"

Ingrid nodded. "Quint and his father are two of a kind."

Danni smiled and changed the subject. "What do you think of Kansas? Is it what you expected?"

Ingrid's smile was sad. "Parts of it remind me of the home I left in Sweden. But only parts. So much is different here."

"Did you leave family back in Sweden?"

"No. All came here, before the war. My father and two brothers died for the Union. My mother is in New York."

"How did you meet your husband?"

"He was in New York with his father. They came to the city to find Quint's brother and convince him to go west with them. Quint and I met in the street one day. I worked for a seamstress and was carrying many fabrics when I tripped and fell. Quint came to help me."

"And your mother?"

"She works for the seamstress still."

"It must have been hard to leave her," said Danni, her fingers holding loosely to the reins. "What of Quint's brother? The one in New York?"

"He told them no. I said yes. Homesteading sounded exciting to me after the grime and soot of New York. And I was tired of the men in the city. Because I worked for a living, men treated me as if I were . . . a loose woman. Quint seemed an answer to my prayers."

Danni looked at the fair-skinned Ingrid and smiled in sympathy at her dejected tone. "And now?"

Ingrid lowered her face. "I'm pregnant."

Danni swiveled, ready to congratulate the woman, until she saw the dejected slant of her mouth.

"Ingrid?" she said cautiously.

"Quint doesn't want me to be pregnant," she said in a low voice. "He doesn't know. I haven't told him yet. He would be very angry with me if he knew."

Danni didn't understand. "He doesn't want you to be pregnant?"

"Not yet. He says he'll let me know when he's ready to have children. When we're settled, he says. When we have extra food and money."

"Surely he'll understand," said Danni.

"No." Ingrid shook her head. "He'll think I did it on purpose. When a woman becomes pregnant he believes it's because she willed it. He'll never believe I didn't want to be pregnant. He even rubs onion juice on himself as a preventative."

"I'm sorry," said Danni. "I don't know what to say."

"Say you'll help me end this pregnancy. You've been married a long time. You must know how."

Danni shook her head. "Both my pregnancies ended in miscarriage, Ingrid. I wouldn't know the first thing about ending a pregnancy."

Ingrid looked at her accusingly. "So you won't help me?"

"Ingrid, I swear to you, I don't know how. Please believe me. My grandmother never spoke to me of such things. Speak to your husband. Perhaps he won't be as angry as you think. Perhaps he'll understand."

Ingrid sat in stony silence for several moments. Her blue eyes were cold when she finally looked at Danni.

"I'll speak to him," she said. And then she got up and jumped off the seat of the moving wagon. Danni sucked in her breath and almost screamed, but Ingrid rolled once and sat up in the dust, her face disappointed.

Will Drake rode up to her and began to shout. "That was a crazy fool thing to do! You could've been killed!"

Ingrid merely looked at him and got up to walk to her husband's wagon. Drake rode up to Danni and asked her what was going on.

"Something I said," Danni told him. "I think I made her angry. I'm sorry, Mr. Drake."

"Not half as sorry as she would've been if she'd rolled under those wheels and been trampled."

Danni refused to believe that was what Ingrid Corle had hoped would happen.

"I'm sure she's fine."

"Lucky, is what she is," said Drake, and he rode off again.

Danni thought about Ingrid Corle for the rest of the day, and later, in that evening's camp, she heard shouting and crying in the Corles' wagon as she went about preparing supper. Kiowa looked at her, his dark eyes wondering, and Danni shrugged.

She didn't know why she felt so guilty.

When Austin Bourke rode by she asked him to join them for supper, but he declined. He needed to talk with Will Drake, he said.

Kiowa surprised Danni by smirking after Bourke was gone. "Drake's been hounding the girl."

"What girl?" Danni asked. "Susannah?"

"Yes. He eats near them, sleeps closer to her wagon every night, and spends much of the day riding beside the wagon she's in, making small talk."

"He does?" Danni was further surprised.

Kiowa nodded.

Danni grinned then. "Are you jealous?"

He lifted his gaze and stared at her. "No."

"Not even a little?"

"No."

"Oh. I thought you . . . well, I thought you were fond of Susannah. You always seem to be looking at . . . never mind, Kiowa. I'm sorry I opened my mouth."

As she glanced at him, she thought Kiowa looked positively heartsick for a moment. Then he got up and walked away, leaving Danni to kick herself mentally for her callous teasing. She would never mention it again, she promised herself.

After she cleaned up the supper dishes she walked tentatively over to the Corles' wagon and called Ingrid's name. There was a brief glimpse of Quint's angry face in the back, and then Ingrid was literally shoved out of the wagon. Her normally fair face was a bright red, with the distinct imprint of fingers across both of her cheeks.

Danni sucked in her breath. "Kiowa tells me there's a stream to the north of us. Would you like to take a walk and see if we can find it?"

Ingrid's blue eyes were made bluer by the tears that ran freely down her face. "Yes. Let's find it. If we're lucky the Cheyenne will find *us*. They're bound to be kinder to me than my own husband."

"I'm sorry," Danni said to her as they walked slowly away from the camp. "I'm so sorry, Ingrid. I wish I knew how to help you. Please believe me."

"I believe you," said Ingrid, and they walked in silence for several minutes, Danni feeling worse with each step. Suddenly Ingrid blurted, "The baby will die the moment it arrives. I can't let it be born. I have to do something now, don't you see?"

Danni stared. "Ingrid, what are you saying?"

"Quint said other cultures do it as a means to control the population."

"You mean he intends to kill the baby after it's born? Does his father agree with this?"

Ingrid nodded. "It was his father's idea. Both of them say it's too soon for children. They say they'll need me in the fields rather than in the house with a baby. I was brought along to be a field hand, not a wife."

Danni didn't know what to say. She'd never heard of anything so horrible.

A splashing sound directly in front of them made both women halt and stare at the brush ahead. Danni crept up and parted the branches. Ingrid came behind her, and soon both women relaxed. Eve Blaine had come to the stream before them. Dressed in nothing but her chemise, she was standing in the water and bathing herself.

Eve turned with a start and was ready to run when Danni and Ingrid pushed through the brush and approached her. When she saw them she laughed and clutched her chest. "You gave me a scare. I thought you were Indians."

Danni smiled at her. "We're all taking a big chance wandering this far away from camp."

Eve nodded in acknowledgement. "But it's been weeks since I had a proper bath."

"Who told you about the stream?" Danni asked.

"Kiowa mentioned it when he came by the wagon before supper."

Danni frowned and Eve said, "I asked him if he'd seen anything interesting while riding today. He told me about this stream and said it was good, clear water. It is. It tastes wonderful."

Ingrid needed no further invitation; she waded in upstream of Eve and cupped her hands to drink deeply of the water. Danni watched her and stepped closer to the stream. Eve pointed to a towel on the ground and Danni handed it to her. Eve took the towel and said, "Is Mrs. Corle well?"

Ingrid sat up and looked at Eve with red-rimmed eyes. "I'm not well at all, Mrs. Blaine. I'm pregnant."

Eve's brows met, and Danni glanced at Ingrid to see if she would go on. When she didn't, Danni said, "Mr. Corle doesn't want to have children . . . yet."

Eve looked at Ingrid. "Do you want to be pregnant?"

A short, bitter laugh was Ingrid's answer.

The black-haired Eve was thoughtful a moment. Then she said, "If you like, I can tell you how to be rid of the pregnancy. It doesn't involve much—a few plants to gather, is all. There will be some pain, of course, and you may feel ill for several days."

Ingrid's face became suddenly alert. "You have knowledge of these things? A keeper of the Mormon faith?"

Eve turned her head and went on toweling herself. "I wasn't born a Mormon."

Ingrid laughed, splashed the water, and came wading down the creek toward them.

In the next second Danni saw two Indians on horseback appear behind her. Seemingly out of nowhere they came, feathers and long black hair streaming behind them. The nearest Indian simply rode up, grabbed Ingrid by the hair, and dragged her off into the brush of the opposite bank. Danni stood in shock as she watched Ingrid's flailing arms and legs disappear into the dense growth. She heard Ingrid's scream long after she could no longer see her. Then her attention was jerked to the Indian bearing down on her and Eve. His hand reached for Danni's hair, but she ducked, swerved, and rolled to the right, avoiding his grasp and his horse. He circled and came back for another try, his hard brown face intent and his black eyes blazing. Danni screamed, ducked again, and saw Eve pick up a large stone and throw it at the Indian. It struck him in the head, causing a spurt of blood to hang suspended in the air for what seemed an eternity.

Then a shot rang out, and a neat red hole appeared in the lean brown chest of the Indian. The Indian gave a wild cry and raced away, leaning low over his horse. He crashed into the brush exactly where his companion had disappeared. Danni and Eve scrambled up the bank and headed for the brush and the safety of whoever was behind the gun. Kiowa called to them and they crashed through the branches and nearly barreled into him.

"Get on my horse and get back to camp!" he ordered, and the women didn't question him. Danni swung up and gave Eve a hand to pull up behind her. With only a glance back at Kiowa, they raced back to camp and told what had happened. An enraged Quint Corle and his father, Arthur, immediately took guns and left camp in the direction of the stream. Austin

Bourke and Will Drake conferred a moment, then both mounted their horses and took off, Austin shouting for everyone to get their guns and get inside the wagons until he returned.

Danni climbed inside her wagon and found a frantic Jack holding his gun and looking wildly around himself. "Danni, are they coming? What's happening? Where are the troops? God, he's flanking us again, isn't he? We need more men."

"We're fine, Jack," she told him, and she took the gun from his hands and patted his arm. "We're fine. Please don't worry. We're all right."

Her stomach in her throat, she turned away from him and aimed the gun out the back of the wagon. She could not help remembering her last glimpse of the fair Ingrid Corle.

Poor Ingrid.

Chapter Eight

AUSTIN RODE back to camp and saw frightened white faces waiting for some sign from him. He shook his head and dismounted. Arthur and Quint Corle sat near their wagons, their heads bent. Kiowa put a hand on Danni's shoulder. Will Drake rode in behind Bourke and got slowly off his horse. His face, too, reflected their luckless search. Ingrid Corle was nowhere to be found.

After walking to the center of camp, Austin gestured for everyone to come and listen to him. He looked directly at Danni and Eve when he said, "No one is to leave camp without my permission. No one. Were these Indians painted, Mrs. Coopersand?"

"No," she said. "They were not."

"No," said Eve in confirmation.

"Is that good or bad?" asked Arthur Corle.

"They paint up for a raid," said Will Drake. "And they paint up for a hunt. They don't need much excuse to paint themselves."

Quint Corle glared at Danni. "I'll say what's on my mind now. This wouldn't have happened if you had minded your own business, Danni Coopersand. I blame you for what's befallen Ingrid. She would never have gone off to that stream on her own. You coerced her into going with your female talk and your friendly ways. Shame be on you, woman."

"Shame?" Danni echoed, her cheeks red with anger. "You're the man who ought to be ashamed, talking of killing your own —" Abruptly she closed her mouth and turned her face away as she felt the stares of everyone in camp.

Austin looked away from her and turned to Kiowa. "You shot one of them. Was it a mortal wound?"

"Left upper chest," Kiowa responded.

"He's dead," said Will Drake.

"They haven't tried to steal the horses or livestock, so it appears they've only just stumbled onto us," Austin said. "We can look for trouble from here on out."

"What exactly does that mean, sir?" asked Ormond Blaine.

"It means we stay around Fort Harker longer than we anticipated, giving the Indians the idea that we've reached our destination."

"So they'll go on about their business," said Arthur Corle.

"Yes. With any luck."

"How long?" Kora Blaine inquired.

"I don't know, Mrs. Blaine. It depends on the post's commander. He may have a different idea."

"What if it doesn't work?" Ormond Blaine asked. "What if they don't fall for it and follow us west?"

"Then you can count on losing more people," Austin said bluntly. With that he turned and walked away from the camp. He led Butcher to where the other horses were picketed and removed his saddle and blanket.

From what he could tell, the Indians who grabbed Ingrid Corle had been two on their own, perhaps scouts. They had come upon the women and decided to make a quick raid. It might have been better if Kiowa hadn't killed one of them. They might have taken one woman and left it at that. Now there would be certain retribution.

As for Ingrid Corle, there was little hope she would be found alive, if at all. She was an attractive woman, so she might be kept alive for a time, though the abuse she could suffer at the hands of angry Indians might make death seem a blessing.

It was the same as with women used by invading Confederate forces. They were like pale, dazed ghosts, wandering aimlessly until someone spoke their name. He likened it to the experience of the thousands of men like Jack Coopersand, when the mind simply caved in on itself.

The others in camp were holding up all right. Danni Coopersand would torture herself with guilt for some time to come. Eve Blaine was handling the experience well. She was a tough one, Austin decided after hearing about the stone she threw at the Indian.

The person who surprised him was Quint Corle, Ingrid's husband. Quint appeared more angry than distressed at the loss of his wife, Arthur Corle even more so. They had both charged off to look for her, more out of duty, Austin thought, than genuine concern for the woman.

Will Drake had told Austin about Mrs. Corle jumping off the wagon being driven by Danni Coopersand that day. Austin decided to ask about the incident for himself and try to understand what had happened later. It was crucial for the people to travel as a friendly whole, with everyone interested in the welfare of everyone else, with as little antipathy and ill feeling as possible. If they failed that much, then all would be lost.

He waited until the rest of the camp was bedded down for the night before going to the Coopersands' wagon and asking in a low voice for Mrs. Coopersand to come and talk to him. She came, her eyes still haunted by earlier events, and looked questioningly at him. From beside the wagon, Kiowa sat up, his face watchful. Austin gestured for him to relax.

"What is it, Mr. Bourke?" asked Danni.

"Is Mr. Coopersand asleep?"

"Yes."

"I don't want to wake him. Come out for a moment."

Danni came out, her white feet bare beneath her nightgown.

She glanced down in embarrassment at herself. "I'm sorry, I don't have a dressing gown."

"Forgive the intrusion, Mrs. Coopersand. I'm curious to know why Mrs. Corle jumped from your wagon today. Mr. Drake said the two of you were arguing."

"No," said Danni with a look of guilt. "It wasn't an argument."

"Would you mind telling me what it was?"

She looked at him. "What difference could it make now?"

Austin said nothing, merely waited.

At length, Danni sighed. "Ingrid Corle was pregnant. She asked me how to end the pregnancy, because her husband didn't want children for some time. I told her I didn't know how to help her. She became upset and jumped off the wagon. Later I went to talk to her again, because I heard shouting from her wagon. We went to the stream together, and Eve Blaine had just told her she would help her when the Indians came."

Austin stared at her. After a moment he said, "What you said to Mr. Corle today, when he blamed you for the loss of his wife —you started to speak and then stopped. What were you going to say?"

"Nothing. He was hurt. I was angry."

Austin knew it was more than nothing. But he also knew he would get nothing further from her. He took off his hat and fingered the brim. "Thank you for telling me, Mrs. Coopersand. I'm responsible for you people, and I need to know your troubles, no matter how insignificant or private they might appear to be. If you learn to trust me, then perhaps we can avoid what happened to Mrs. Corle."

"I understand," said Danni. Then she relaxed. "Would you consider calling me Danni, Mr. Bourke? Mrs. Coopersand has always been Jack's mother."

He paused as if considering, then said, "I feel the same. Mr. Bourke was my father."

"Was? Your father has passed on?"

"Yes. He's buried beside my mother, back on the farm in Michigan."

"I'm sorry."

"Don't be. They lived well."

Danni smiled. "I'd like to call you Austin, but some of the others might get the wrong idea."

"What idea would they get if I called you Danni?"

She shrugged. "Everyone calls me Danni. My real name is Louise Danielle, but my grandmother shortened it to Danni."

"You don't look like a Louise," Austin told her.

They looked at each other, then both glanced away, suddenly uncomfortable with the turn the conversation had taken.

"Will you be on first watch tonight?" Danni asked.

"Yes," he said. "You should rest, if you can."

"I don't know if that's possible," said Danni. "I keep seeing Ingrid's face. It won't go away."

"You knew something like this might happen."

She looked at her feet. "I suppose I did, yes."

"Stay close to the camp from now on," Austin told her. "Don't go anywhere alone, and that includes nature's business. Go with the Blaines if you must, but don't go by yourself."

She was blushing in the darkness; Austin could tell by the way she turned her head.

"I'll say goodnight now, Mrs. Coopersand."

She nodded and turned to get back in her wagon. He offered a hand to help her, and she hesitated before accepting it. Her fingers were cool against his palm. He held on a moment longer than was necessary and said, "Try to get some sleep, Danni."

"I will . . . yes," she said. "Goodnight."

Austin turned and saw Kiowa watching him. He walked over and knelt down beside the boy. "Did you follow them to the stream today?"

"Yes," said Kiowa.

"To keep an eye on them?"

"Yes."

"You didn't want them to know you were there?"

Kiowa lifted a shoulder. "It didn't matter if they knew I was there. I was there."

"I'm glad." Austin lowered his voice. "We're likely to be stalked for a while; they'll want to get an idea of our size and strength. We may be attacked before we reach Fort Harker. If we are, we need to turn them away with everything we have. There are two Henry repeating rifles in my pack. I'll give one of them to you. Give your rifle to Danni. And give a rifle to Jack Coopersand when the time comes. We'll need him."

"He may shoot one of us," Kiowa warned.

"We'll have to take that chance."

Kiowa paused in silence. Finally he looked at Austin and said, "I've never shot anyone before."

"You did fine," Austin told him. "If you hadn't shot him he might have taken Danni, or Mrs. Blaine."

"Yes," Kiowa said, his look faraway.

"Get some sleep now. I'll wake you in a few hours and you can take the watch. Then it'll be Will's turn."

Kiowa nodded. Then he asked, "Do you trust him?"

"Will?" Austin stood up and shook his head. "I don't trust anyone, Kiowa. Not even myself. Get some sleep."

He walked away from the youth to the cook site in the center of the camp, where he poured himself a cup of cold black coffee. Cup in hand, he walked to the perimeter of the camp and began a slow circle. He didn't need the coffee; it was more reflex than thirst that made him drink it. His nerves were alive and on edge, humming with a familiar anticipation. War had awakened that awareness in him, and no other experience in life could match it. It was fear mingled with a peculiar dread-filled excitement that surfaced when the threat of losing one's life became very real.

Austin had to wonder sometimes if he wasn't addicted to the feeling, loathe it as he did. Volunteering to fight first the Confederates and now the Indians.

But he hadn't volunteered to fight the Indians. He had left the cavalry and taken on a job that involved only the threat of fighting hostile Indians. It wasn't the same.

Or was it? he asked himself. He could have taken any number of jobs, many of them having nothing to do with the possibility of warfare.

He shook his head to make himself stop thinking about it. Better simply to deal with the threat at hand than analyze it to death in his head and make himself crazy wondering about the possibilities. He was what he was, and if he was so addicted to the tight, hard ball of anxiety and fear in his gut, then he would have remained a soldier.

He finished the coffee in his cup and attuned himself to the darkness outside the camp. If they came tonight they would come for the horses and cattle. He posted himself near where the horses were picketed and sat still.

After an hour, Austin got up and stretched out his legs. As he stood, a high, agonized scream sounded from somewhere far in the distance. Austin froze and listened, his heart suddenly pounding in his chest. To the south, he thought, though it was hard to tell. Another scream sounded, this one worse than the first—hoarser, more desperate, like the cry of a wounded and frightened beast. The next scream was abruptly cut off.

Austin waited, his flesh raised in goosebumps, his entire body involved in the act of listening. But there was nothing further.

Ingrid Corle was probably dead.

Chapter Nine

Kiowa heard the screams, but he heard them in his dream, and they became the screams of the soldier being skinned alive by Kiowa's stepbrothers. The horror on the man's face, the terror in his frightened, heaving chest forced Kiowa to turn his face away in disgust. His head was snapped back from behind, his black hair held in the grip of his oldest stepbrother, whose grinning face was placed inches from his own. "You did this," he hissed at Kiowa. "You're a crazy goddamned savage, and you did this. That's why you're here, *little brother*."

The voice rasped on, and Kiowa listened, his mind rejecting all the words until he felt the kiss of steel below his left ear. The blade bit and bit deeper, and soon the front of Kiowa's shirt was soaked with bright red blood. He felt no pain. He felt nothing but his blood leaving his body from a place he could not see. The hands behind him released his head and his hair, and he was able to take a step forward. His vision darkened into a red-black cloud. Then he fell.

And awakened, his mouth open and gasping, his heart thudding. He looked wildly around himself and sat up.

"Kiowa?" a voice called, and he jerked his head around. Then he relaxed. It was only Danni, leaning out of the wagon and looking at him. Her voice was worried.

"Kiowa, are you all right?"

He waved an arm. "Yes."

"You were dreaming," she told him. "You were moaning in your sleep."

"I'm sorry I woke you," Kiowa said, and he got up and moved to stand beside her.

"You didn't wake me. I wasn't asleep."

In the dim light of the moon Kiowa saw her distress. "What is it?" he asked.

Danni shook her head and covered her mouth with her hands. "A few minutes ago I heard the most horrible screams. I think it was Ingrid."

Kiowa waited a moment, then said, "Maybe it was a bobcat."

"I know the difference," Danni said into her hands.

"If it was her, there's nothing we can do for her now."

"It was just her bad luck I led her to that stream—is that what you're saying?"

"Yes," said Kiowa.

Danni made as if to pull out her hair and Kiowa put his hands over hers and brought them to rest in front of her.

"We all knew the dangers when we started out. All of us. The same thing could happen to you at any time. Or one of the Blaine women. Settling on a claim won't make us any safer. It will make no difference to the Indians. That's why they hate us."

"Because we're taking their land," said Danni. "I know, I've heard it all before. But where are we supposed to go, Kiowa? Can't they live peacefully alongside us, and learn to farm as we do?"

"They live off the land as it is, Danni, not as it could be."

"They can learn differently, can't they?"

"Can you?" Kiowa asked.

"Yes," she said determinedly. "I'm learning something different every day. I'm learning to eat things I never dreamed I'd eat. I'm learning to pee in the tall grass and sometimes right in the dirt around my feet. I'm learning to drink water in sips and bathe with only a damp cloth. And I do it willingly, on the chance that our lives will somehow be better out here."

Kiowa's voice was quiet. "Indians don't know 'better,' Danni. They only know what is . . . and what is not. They are trying to make us what is not, so they can be at peace once more with what is."

"So I shouldn't blame them for killing Ingrid?"

"I can't tell you not to."

"But you don't?"

Kiowa shrugged. "If my land was being invaded, I might behave the same way."

"You wouldn't," Danni whispered. "I know you. You wouldn't."

Before Kiowa could respond, he heard Austin Bourke approach and call for him. Kiowa stepped away from the wagon and went to him.

His watch was quiet, with all the right animals making all the right nocturnal animal sounds. Bill Ottleway had taught him how to listen to nature, and part of Kiowa's mind stayed in tune with the crickets and the owls and the furtive movements of small animals in the brush, while another part of his mind dealt with what he had done that day.

Of course he had been watching Eve. He couldn't help himself. Just being close to her made him somehow unable to breathe properly, and his tongue became thick as a stump when he attempted to speak. He had told her about the stream, knowing she would go there. And he had followed, keeping himself hidden, delighting in being able to watch her without being seen himself.

When she took off her dress and stepped into the water, Kiowa nearly fell down. He had never imagined he would be able to view her thus, clad only in her thin chemise and allowing her thick black hair to flow free behind her.

Then Danni and Mrs. Corle arrived. And then the Cheyenne.

Kiowa made a fist of his hand as he remembered taking aim

with the rifle and shooting. The red hole in the man's chest had seemed unreal to him.

Later he went down and retrieved Eve's dress and shoes from the bank of the stream. Her thank you had been gracious and calm under the stern stare of Ormond Blaine.

Kiowa looked in the direction of the Blaines' wagons and saw movement out of the corner of his eye. He turned his head and stared, trying to screen the darkness. Then he saw it again. The girl, Susannah, was creeping through the camp, a blanket wrapped around her shoulders.

A full bladder, thought Kiowa, and he continued to watch until she was on the far edge of camp. Then he saw Will Drake roll out of his blanket and look carefully around himself before hurrying over to join Susannah. Kiowa was tempted to walk to the opposite edge of camp to ask what they were doing. But he knew what they were doing. And he knew neither Austin Bourke nor Ormond Blaine would be happy about it.

He still couldn't believe it was Susannah that Danni thought he wanted. Susannah was a spoiled, dull little fool.

The lovers weren't together long, and Kiowa was happy to go and awaken Will Drake for watch duty only a moment after the man settled down to sleep.

Will looked at Kiowa and yawned. "Where's Bourke?"

"He took the first watch. I had the second."

Will's eyes narrowed. "See anything?"

Kiowa glanced at the Blaines' wagon. "More than I wanted to see."

Will Drake sat up. "You didn't see anything, you hear? I mean it. You're good at keeping your mouth shut, so you just get better at it, and we'll all get along."

Kiowa opened his hands and walked away. Will Drake had nothing to fear from him.

The next morning breakfast was eaten in a hurry and the livestock were quickly bunched and made ready to move. Austin Bourke was snappish and Danni was pale and withdrawn and lacked appetite. Still, she smiled tiredly at Kiowa when he came for his coffee. "We've got ham this morning. Would you like some?"

Kiowa took a small bite and told her it was good. He looked at Jack Coopersand, who was staring intently at a forkful of ham, and then he asked Danni if she wanted him to drive the wagon that day. He would tie the bay behind the wagon along with her horse and allow her to sleep, if she could.

"Thank you, but I'll be fine," she said. She glanced in the direction of the Corles' wagon. "He's been glaring at me all morning. He must have heard the screams last night."

Kiowa doubted it. When he passed the Corles' wagons on his watch, the snoring from both conveyances had been deafening.

"Ignore him, Danni. Bourke is anxious to move out this morning. He wants to get as close to Fort Harker as possible."

"Perhaps we should go back to Fort Riley."

"I wouldn't," said Kiowa. "And Bourke won't. It's better to keep moving forward."

The words were barely out of Kiowa's mouth when an arrow grazed the side of his cheek, taking flesh with it. Another arrow came just as quickly, and then what seemed like two dozen more. Jack Coopersand gaped at the arrow protruding from his thigh and then stood up and screamed at the top of his lungs, alerting the whole camp to the flying missiles. Danni shrieked and grabbed her husband by the arm to shove him toward the wagon. An arrow caught her dress and pinned it between her legs, making her stumble and fall. Danni jerked the arrow out, ripping her dress, and scrambled into the wagon, dragging Jack with her.

Kiowa was struck in the right buttock as he reached for his rifle. He fell to the ground and crawled under the wagon, breaking off the arrow in his rump as he did. He howled in pain and then reached behind himself to jerk out the offending agent. He heard the crack of a rifle above him and knew Danni had begun to shoot. When an Indian shot back, he brought his rifle from beneath him and aimed into the stripling trees and thorny bushes where the arrows had come from. He fired and bit his tongue with the recoil.

"Kiowa!" a voice barked, and he jerked his head to see Austin Bourke slide under the wagon and thrust a rifle at him. It was a Henry. Kiowa snatched up the rifle and aimed at random into the brush to the south, sending fifteen shots into the dense growth. Austin Bourke sent out just as many shots, aiming with a little more care. Abruptly, the arrows and answering shots stopped.

Austin shouted for everyone to cease fire and save ammunition. He rolled out from beneath the wagon and Kiowa watched him move with skill and speed around the camp, stopping at each wagon. Kiowa couldn't see much from where he took cover, but he didn't hear any cries of anguish, and he assumed that meant everyone was all right. He made to slide out from under the wagon, but the pain in his backside stopped him and nearly made him black out. He gulped in deep breaths of air, willing himself to stay conscious, and soon the darkness receded.

He stayed where he was and concentrated on reloading the Henry with the ammunition he had been given. Austin was on his way back; Kiowa could hear him talking to Will Drake nearby. When Austin returned to Kiowa, he saw the blood on his face for the first time. "Are you injured?" he asked.

Kiowa felt his face grow warm. "It's nothing. What about the others?"

"One of the Blaine boys was stuck through the shoulder. Arthur Corle got an arrow through his side. What about Danni?"

"She's all right. Jack was hit in the thigh."

"Bad?"

"I don't know."

"All right. You stay here. I'm going up to check on them. Are you sure you're all right? Where are you wounded?"

Kiowa's mouth tightened and he pointed to his rear.

Austin frowned and leaned back to look. He came back up and said, "Stay put. I'll be back in a minute."

Kiowa silently thanked him for not laughing. Austin departed again and Kiowa's ears stopped ringing enough for him to hear the murmuring in camp and the rustling of the trees. He wondered when the Indians would return.

The wagon shifted above him, and he heard Austin speak to Danni as he climbed inside. There was a quiet exchange, followed by a sharp cry from Jack. A moment later the wagon shifted again as Austin climbed out. He knelt down beside where Kiowa lay and said, "Come on, let's get you inside."

Kiowa opened his mouth to protest, but the words refused to come out. He was tired and felt suddenly weak. His buttock hurt. His throat was parched.

Austin helped him inside the wagon and turned him over to Danni, who inquired after help. "Perhaps Mr. Blaine could spare Eve for a moment," she said.

"No," Kiowa said abruptly. "Not her."

Danni stared at him. "Kiowa, I—"

"Just you, Danni," he said in what he hoped was a firm voice. "You've fixed me before."

Danni sighed and Austin departed.

Kiowa exhaled in relief and allowed his eyes to close as he lay on his side on the lumpy mattress beside Jack.

"Jack?" he said.

"He's unconscious, Kiowa."

"Will he be all right?"

"He will be if I can get his bleeding stopped."

"The artery?"

"The arrow nicked it."

"Are you all right, Danni?"

"I'm fine." She paused then. "Do you think they'll come back? I never saw any of them."

"I didn't either."

"Was anyone else hurt?"

"Arthur Corle and one of the Blaine boys, both wounded."

"Mortally?"

"I don't know. I don't think so."

"All right. Rest now, Kiowa. I'll get to you in a moment."

Kiowa breathed in deeply and kept his eyes closed. Outside he could hear a child crying; the wounded boy, no doubt. He felt himself begin to drift, and he told himself he was already dreaming when he heard the voice of his youngest stepbrother outside the wagon. Luther said, "Everything's all right now, folks. We done run them Indians off, chased 'em for two miles. You can come out now, and don't be afraid. We're white men."

A choking sound came from Kiowa, and he sat up to grab for

Danni as she started out of the wagon. She cried out in surprise as he snatched her arm. "Kiowa, what—"

Kiowa put a finger to his mouth and violently shushed her. He pointed to the scar at his throat and then gestured outside the wagon, his eyes black, his stare meaningful.

Danni's eyes rounded.

Chapter Ten

Danni sat back against a chest bursting with her belongings. The smell of blood was heavy in the back of the small wagon. "The men outside tried to kill you?" she whispered.

Kiowa nodded. His eyes were black and hard, his expression fiercely intent.

"How do you know?" she asked. "You can tell just by hearing their voices?"

Kiowa's nostrils flared. "Yes."

"Then I should tell Mr. Bourke right away . . . shouldn't I?"

"Not now," Kiowa warned. "Not when they might see you and grow suspicious. Wait till he's alone and you can speak without anyone hearing." He paused to listen, and Danni heard a man with a southern accent politely ask for something to eat. Austin gave his consent.

Kiowa released a pent-up breath. "Danni, Bourke is in danger. If those men ask any questions about what he did in the war, you make sure he doesn't answer. His life depends on it."

Danni stared in confusion. "Kiowa, what—"

"Don't say my name," he said hoarsely. "If they find out I'm here they'll kill all of us. It may be what they're planning anyway."

Her mouth grew dry. "Why would they do that?" she asked in a cracked voice. "Why would they chase the Indians away just so they could kill us?"

"Maybe they didn't chase them away. Maybe they were together from the start and planned both the raid and our rescue." Kiowa closed his eyes, and Danni suddenly saw the torment in him. His hands were trembling. His shoulders were shaking. He was genuinely frightened.

She went to him and set about treating his still bleeding wound. After she had done all she could, she touched his arm and made to leave the wagon.

"Danni—"

She paused and turned to look at him. "Yes?"

"They're not what they seem."

Danni nodded and left the wagon. Outside she saw Eve and Kora Blaine preparing a hasty meal for their guests, three men wearing filthy, dusty clothes and tattered and worn hats. They sat on the ground around the cooksite, gnawing on bits of cornbread given to them by the women. As Danni entered the area, two of the men looked up at her. One smiled and knocked the crumbs from his beard.

"How d'you do, ma'am? My goodness, ain't you a pretty sight."

Her nod was timid. She looked at Austin and saw a small crease between his brows. The next moment he came over and placed an arm around her waist.

"This is my wife, Danni," he said.

The smiling man inclined his head and continued eating.

Several in the campsite stared at Danni and Bourke until Will Drake cleared his throat and said, "We certainly appreciate your help. A couple Indians carried off Mr. Corle's wife yesterday."

The man with the blue kerchief around his neck nodded. His

voice was smooth and somehow remote. "We found her a while ago. They stripped her."

Quint Corle came forward. "They took her clothes?"

The man grunted with mirthless laughter. "They took her *skin.*"

Quint's face turned pale. "What did you do with her?"

"Do?" the man replied. "We didn't touch her. Coyotes had already gotten to her. There's nothing to do for or with her."

Both Quint and Will Drake stepped forward angrily, but Austin held up a hand. "He's right. If you buried her she'd only be dug up again."

"Afraid so," said the man with the kerchief. He finished his cornbread and dusted off his hands. "My name is Robert McCandliss. This is my brother George and my brother Luther."

Austin's face was expressionless. "What are you doing in these parts, Mr. McCandliss?"

"Same as you, I expect. We're traveling the Smoky Hill Road, hopping from fort to fort. Was anyone wounded in the raid?"

"A few," said Austin.

"Serious?"

"Not at this point."

"Good. That's good. We arrived just in time."

Luther nodded. "Goddamned savages. Anymore we just shoot 'em on sight." He smiled at Eve then. "Is that grub ready yet, ma'am?"

"It's ready," said Eve. "Help yourself."

"That's very kind," said Robert McCandliss. "The rest of you have already had your breakfast, I suppose?"

Everyone nodded.

"Then you must be anxious to get moving." He turned to his brothers. "Let's allow these good people to be on their way and not hold them up any longer."

"I'm likin' the company, myself," said Luther, smiling around the crumbs in his beard.

Danni reached for Austin's waist and held on, her gaze even as she stared back at the young fool named Luther.

Robert McCandliss chuckled. "You might say we're starved for company right now. Tired of looking at each other's faces."

He sat up and lifted his hat to rake back his sandy hair. Danni heard the smile in his voice before she saw it on his face. "Would you be adverse to our riding along with you for a time, Mr. Bourke?"

"Eat your breakfast," Austin suggested. "We'll talk it over and let you know."

"Fair enough," said Robert. "Mind if I ask who's in charge here?"

"I am," said Austin.

"I assumed as much." Robert smiled briefly and leaned over to concentrate on his bacon.

Austin adjusted his hat and walked away from the campsite, still holding on to Danni's waist. As soon as they were out of earshot, she said, "These are the men who tried to kill Kiowa. He recognized their voices from the wagon. He's terrified."

Austin looked at her and took a moment to digest the information. "Do they know he's alive?"

"No. If they find out, he says we're all dead."

"Is he sure these are the same men? He was attacked in Illinois."

"He's sure. If you could see his face you would know."

Austin looked over his shoulder. "The others are behind us. We'll have to tell them what we know."

"What are we going to do? How do we get rid of them?"

"I don't know. Just play along as my wife and they should leave you alone. If anyone asks, Jack's my brother."

"What about Kiowa? How do I keep him hidden? And how do I keep the others from asking about him?"

"Tell them now. Ask them not to speak of Kiowa in the presence of the men, since they obviously hate all Indians."

Danni nodded and suddenly remembered what else Kiowa had said to her. "Austin," she began, and then she colored when she realized she had used his first name. He leveled hazel eyes on her and she rushed on. "Kiowa said not to discuss the war and your part in it with these men. He said your life could depend on it."

Austin frowned, and at that moment they were joined by the others. Danni was released as Austin stepped to the center of the impromptu gathering. He had expected to be assaulted with questions, but everyone was quiet and waited for him to speak.

He ran a hand over his cheek and said, "I believe these men are part of a raiding party that's been killing soldiers and settlers."

Kora Blaine's gasp was audible. Other mouths dropped, but still no one spoke.

"I'm sure they're not traveling alone," Austin continued. "There are probably two or three Sioux or Cheyenne hiding in the brush this minute. I think there are too many of us for them to handle without losing numbers of their own, so they've chosen the tactic of making friends. When they get what they want from us, they'll leave."

"What do they want?" asked Ormond Blaine.

"I don't know," said Austin. "Food. Maybe one of the women. That's why I claimed Mrs. Coopersand. Or they may intend to rob us. It's what they usually do to people they encounter on the trail."

"So what do we do?" asked Will Drake. "Hand over our food, valuables, and a female and hope they leave us alone?"

It was Susannah Blaine's turn to gasp.

Austin shook his head. "We go on and keep our eyes open. Be alert for anything at any moment. Keep our guns loaded and beside us at all times. If any of the men make a wrong move, don't hesitate to shoot."

"There's a good part to this, I suppose," said Will Drake. "The Indians won't bother us while these men are along."

"Then you'd rather have a viper in your hand than a nest in the jungle," said Ormond Blaine. "I, for one, would not."

"Like Bourke said, we'll be able to watch them. They aren't the harmless traveling men they'd like us to think they are, only they don't know we know it, so we've got something on them, don't we?" Will spread his hands to make his point.

"I say we tell them no, they can't travel with us," said Ormond Blaine. "We thank them for their aid, but tell them we're fine on our own. Besides, we don't have enough food for three more men."

"Three pigs, you mean," said Kora Blaine. "Did you see the way they ate my bread?"

"We have no choice," Austin told them. "If we tell them no, they'll only trail us and ambush us somewhere along the road." He turned to Quint Corle. "Is your father able to drive his wagon?"

"He says he is. He's a hard man, Mr. Bourke."

"He'll have to be. But for the moment I'd feel better if Mr. Drake handled his team."

"Wait a minute," said Will. "I'll need my hands free in case of trouble. I think—"

"You'll have two rifles in the wagon within reach," said Austin. He looked at Danni then and nodded, as if to say it was her turn.

She clasped her hands together and said, "I'm going to keep Kiowa hidden from these men. If they shoot Indians on sight, it won't make much difference that he's half-white. I'm asking everyone here to refrain from talking about him, not to use his name at any time."

All the women nodded. Danni eyed the men and saw that Kiowa was the least of their worries. She was satisfied everyone had heard her, however, and the message was what she considered necessary at the moment.

Austin asked everyone to go and get ready to move while he told the men of their decision. Danni returned to her wagon and climbed inside. Kiowa got up on one elbow and looked anxiously at her.

"It's all right," she told him. "Mr. Bourke knows everything. They asked to travel with us for a while, and we had no choice but to say yes. We're all going to be watching them closely. And no one will breathe a word about you."

His face pale and worried, Kiowa sank down to the mattress beside Jack. A fine sheen of perspiration covered his brow. Danni moved worriedly through her things to him and pulled a blanket over his shivering body. "You can't have fever already," she murmured. But he did, and it was a fierce heat that left the skin of his torso hot and dry to the touch.

"The Indian must have dipped the arrow in dung," Kiowa uttered weakly. "Bill Ottleway said they do that sometimes."

Danni turned her head in disgust and rummaged for the small valise in which she kept her medical supplies. She had herbs for fever, but she had no time to make a poultice for the infection. The cleaning she had done earlier would have to suffice until she could get to him later that day.

"I can't hide here," Kiowa said, and Danni put a hand over his mouth.

"You can and you will."

"Who's going to grease the wheels? Who's going to drive when you can't drive anymore?"

Danni lifted a shoulder. "Perhaps my new husband will. Mr. Bourke claimed me as his wife in front of those men."

"He did it to protect you."

"I know."

She found the herb she was searching for and placed it under the tongue of the shaking Kiowa. Then she heard Austin Bourke call for everyone to move out. Quickly she put her valise away and headed for her seat and the reins. She glanced around herself as she clucked and called the oxen into motion and saw the three men riding together on the north side of the wagon train. Luther tipped his hat and smiled when he saw her looking. Danni turned away. Already she loathed the man.

Austin rode by to check on her several times that day, staying to eat lunch during the brief stop around noon. He climbed into the wagon as Danni was finishing with the poultice and frowned when he saw Kiowa's fevered cheeks.

"Bad arrow," Kiowa said with a tired smile, and Austin briefly laid a hand on his shoulder.

Jack awakened then and Austin spoke with him for several moments before leaving the wagon again. Danni took the opportunity to check Jack's wound, fearful that he too had been struck with a fouled arrow. The wound looked good thus far, with Jack experiencing no fever. He was in pain, however, and he complained of it until Danni gave him a willowbark preparation given to her by the sagacious Bill Ottleway. Soon Jack relaxed and lay back, his eyes open and staring at the stained cover above him.

Danni returned to her seat and drove the team for the rest of the day until Austin called a halt. When she climbed down to unhitch the team she discovered aches in every part of her body and even found walking difficult for the first few minutes. She groaned to herself in pain when she realized she would not be able to sleep in her bed in the wagon. She looked longingly at Eve Blaine's wagon, and while her patients and pretend husband were eating their supper, she wandered over with the intention of asking Eve if she would mind sharing her sleeping space for the evening.

As she approached the wagon she heard Eve's voice, low and angry, and the silky southern tones of Robert McCandliss.

"I am merely making a statement of fact, Mrs. Blaine, and commenting on the disparity here. One man with two women hardly seems fair."

"That's just the way it is, Mr. McCandliss."

"It may not always be that way."

"What are you saying?" Eve demanded. Then her voice became louder. "Shall I call my husband? Or would you prefer to deal with Mr. Bourke?"

"Call them if you wish. I'd like to complain to your husband about this. Perhaps he'll be angry enough to be drawn into gunplay. And then perhaps I'll kill him and claim you for myself. You're a most beautiful woman, Mrs. Blaine. I think I'm in love."

To Danni's complete surprise, she heard Eve laugh. Danni was shocked into looking carefully around the wagon. She saw Eve saunter forward and put her arms around the man's neck.

"So it's a little fun you want?" she asked. "Just a tumble in the tall grass?"

Robert McCandliss lifted his hands. "What more would I ask of you?"

"All right," Eve said, and she whispered something in his ear. McCandliss looked at her with a smile and nodded. "I shall be counting the minutes, I can assure you." Then he swaggered away.

Danni couldn't believe her eyes. She walked swiftly away from them and returned to her own wagon to check on Jack and Kiowa before going back to the cooksite, where Austin sat apart from the others. She went to him and sat down. He glanced at her face and said, "What's wrong?"

"Nothing." Danni couldn't bring herself to speak. She was sickened by what she had seen and overheard. Eve was actually going to make herself available to that horrible man.

Austin took a forkful of beans and chewed a moment. After he swallowed he took a sip of coffee and said, "I want you to sleep on the ground beside me tonight."

She looked at him. "What about the watch?"

"You'll take it with me. Have some coffee, we're on first watch."

Danni sighed in exhaustion. She didn't know if she'd make it. She wondered if she should tell him about Eve and Robert McCandliss. Then she decided not to. It might color the way he treated Eve.

When the flesh on the back of her neck began to prickle she sat up and turned her head. Luther McCandliss was grinning at her over the top of his coffee cup as he sat with the others around the cook fire. Danni moved closer to Austin and reached for his coffee cup. When he casually put his arm around her waist she settled gratefully against him.

"I hate that little bastard," Austin muttered.

Chapter Eleven

Eve slipped out of her wagon during Will Drake's watch and went to stand under the large cottonwood just south of the camp. She was surprised at her lack of nervousness. She kept waiting to feel trepidation or fear, yet she felt nothing but self-loathing for having been frightened into doing what she had no reason to do. She should have screamed for Bourke. McCandliss would have had no choice but to back off.

But she hadn't screamed. She had followed instinct born of panic and now she had no choice but to meet him. If she didn't, he would come looking for her.

As she waited, she swayed with a weariness both physical and emotional. Eve was tired of conflict. These men were threatening harm to other men, and women and children. Men had been threatening harm to other men since the beginning of time. An entire war had just been fought because one half of the country's way of life had been threatened by the other half. It was nothing new.

A revelation had come to her earlier while listening to Mc-

Candliss. She would always pay for the hatred among men. She would always be treated as a possession, to be used at will. Any voice she had would be drowned in the sounds of men satisfying their lust—for woman or for blood. She was merely chattel.

Now she was waiting to become a murderess.

She didn't have long to wait. A hand on her arm made her gasp and spin around. Robert McCandliss pressed a kiss against her mouth. Eve took it as long as she could before breaking away. Feigning breathlessness, she asked, "Did you tell your brothers?"

"Why?" he said, and slid one hand over her breast. "Did you want me to?"

"I thought you might want to share your good fortune," she told him. "Brothers usually do, don't they?"

"Not this time, sweetness. You're all mine." He was pulling at the front of her gown now, eager and insistent. Eve took him by the hand and led him behind the tree. There she undid her buttons, opened her nightgown, and as he brought his face to her breasts, she removed a knife she had concealed along the folds at her waist and shoved the blade into the skin above his left hip. He groaned in pain and staggered back, his face contorting with rage. Eve turned to run and came up against two dark-skinned Indians, both of them holding long rifles in their hands and looking at her with black eyes full of excitement.

She shrieked faintly and heard McCandliss curse at her. He straightened in pain and jerked the knife out of his side. "You don't know what you've done," he said on a whistling breath. He came to her and held the knife to her throat. "You're going to help me. You'll go to your wagon for bandages. One of my friends will go with you, and he'll stand over the Blaine boys with his rifle until you finish. You make one sound, and he will shoot the children."

He shoved Eve in front of him, almost knocking her down. She stumbled forward and ran to her wagon to get her first aid supplies. She didn't look to see if the Indian was carrying out his threat. She took the bag and hurried back to the cottonwood tree, praying for once in her life something would go right and Robert McCandliss would die.

One look at the wound under a lantern was enough to disappoint her. The blade had gone directly through his side, piercing nothing but muscle on its way to his back. He would be sore for a few weeks, but he wouldn't die.

Eve cursed under her breath and he struck her hard across the face. "Yankee bitch. You've made a mistake, Mrs. Blaine. All I asked of you was an hour on your back."

She tossed her hair out of her face and barely glanced at him as she took bandages out of the bag. Once again, he held the knife to her throat. "Make one noise and I will remove your head at the neck. My friends have taught me well."

Eve looked up at the two Indians, who were now smiling at her. He didn't have to worry. The watch was Quint Corle's, and he was fast asleep against the wheel of his wagon. Again, she thought of opening her mouth to scream, but it was only an impulse. She was surprised to feel nothing but defeat and resignation. At that moment, she didn't care what they did to her.

Her face must have conveyed this to McCandliss, because he slapped her again and grabbed her by the front of the nightgown to bring her up close to him. "Nothing can touch you, is that it? You have much to learn, lady. Suppose I let my Sioux friends teach you? They're very fond of pretty white women. They kept the last one we had for almost six weeks. They put a collar around her neck and made her run beside the horses. Come night, when she lay exhausted, they took turns with her."

Eve's impassive stare seemed to infuriate him. He shoved her back with one hand and struck her with the other, his fingers curled into a fist. Eve took the blow on her jaw and the world dimmed as she heard rather than felt the impact.

Fight, she told herself. *What's wrong with you? Fight him.*

Another, colder part of her answered, *Toward what end? You'll only be beaten by fists twice as big as yours. Let them do what they will. They can't hurt you, Eve. They can only kill you.*

Death was almost preferable to life with the Blaines and their particular brand of misery and torment. And if she was really honest with herself, there was nothing in California for her. No one waiting to see her. No one eager for her arrival. She had nothing and no one.

If she were dead she could at least be with her parents, and once again she would know that special, wonderfully warm feeling of being cherished by someone.

The faint smile that curved her lips earned her another blow to the head from Robert McCandliss. This time she lost consciousness.

She awakened to find herself being assaulted by one of the Indians. Her mouth was bound with fabric; her hands were tied behind her back. She was somewhere deep in the brush, with cool grass and damp leaves all around her. She craned her head and saw nothing of McCandliss. Instead she saw the other Indian sitting and watching, awaiting his turn with her.

She closed her eyes again and willed herself away from what was happening to her body. The stench was powerful, the pain searing, but her mind found a tiny beam of light and clung to it. Soon she was no longer on her back on the floor of a brush thicket, but seated at the feet of her father and inhaling the comforting smell of his pipe as he read aloud to her.

Eve reached out with her mind as she imagined the tremor in her father's voice. One part of him lived and breathed the torrid emotions inside the poems he read, the passions that raged and the sorrows that stormed. While another part of him was still, as always, her sweet, loving father, whose hand was ever warm and gentle as it stroked her hair. . . .

Her reverie was interrupted as the man on top of her lifted himself away and gestured for his friend to approach. The second man fell on top of her, spat in her face, and shoved himself violently inside her, making Eve nearly bite through her lip to keep from crying out.

The beam of light was gone, not to be recaptured.

Eve forced herself to lie absolutely still, and when the violent man was finished, she waited until he gestured for her to sit up before moving. Once she was sitting up, he planted a moccasined foot in the center of her chest and shoved her down again. His partner snorted with laughter as Eve stayed flat.

They conversed briefly, then Eve was dragged through the

brush to a small camp with two horses. The violent one kicked her in the thigh and said something that sounded like a warning to her. Eve watched his face closely and saw his hatred for her in the very lines of his face. She kept her mouth closed and lay where she had been left, uncaring what would happen to her next. The violent one spat at her again, kicked her in the face, then walked away.

Eve's eyes teared in pain, and she felt blood course down her throat from her throbbing nose. She swallowed and began to cough, and the other Indian came to jerk off her gag.

Even as Eve struggled to breathe, she began silently to pray for death. It was something to do while they watched her and she watched them.

They weren't far from her own camp, she knew. But she wouldn't call out. She was beyond rescue.

Not that anyone would try, Eve reminded herself. She was certainly expendable, as far as Ormond Blaine was concerned.

She began to pray again, her mind putting the prayers in a song, and she allowed her lids to close, the better to concentrate on the tune.

The next time she opened her eyes it was dawn, and she was alone in the camp. Her head swiveled all around, craning to see in every direction . . . and then she breathed out in disappointment as she saw the violent Indian standing with his back to her. He was urinating against a tree. The other was farther beyond, hovering in a squat over the ground as he defecated.

Eve coughed loudly and both Indians jumped.

She had to laugh. It came sharp and ripe, a raucous sound that carried through the brush and over the trees.

The violent Indian immediately started toward her, his face mottled with anger. His strides were long and Eve sucked in her breath in anticipation of the pain that was to come.

Her eyes rounded in disbelief as an arrow struck the man in the throat. His hands came up to his neck in a silent, frenzied effort to remove the arrow, but the blood from his jugular was already pulsing out.

His companion came after him and stopped in shock at the arrow protruding from his friend's neck. He backed away too late; another arrow came singing through the brush to strike him in the center of his chest, directly through the heart. The two of them stood for several moments, both of them swaying like willows. Then, one at a time, they fell face-forward to the ground.

Eve struggled to sit up and see the face of her rescuer. When she saw him, she felt the first genuine emotion she had experienced in months: a rush of joy.

"Kiowa!" she called.

His face was ghostly white as he came to her. His fine black hair was plastered to his head with perspiration. As he came and knelt over her, she realized he was deathly ill.

"How did you find me?" she asked as he untied her hands. "Are you all right?"

He could only shake his head and stare at her.

"What?" she asked. "What is it?"

"Your face," he said finally. He began to say more, then he firmly closed his mouth.

When her bonds were untied, Eve put her arms around him and hugged him tightly to her. "I can't believe you came."

The color returned in a rush to Kiowa's face. Eve removed her arms and looked at him. "You're ill. Where are you wounded?"

His blush deepened and he half turned away from her. "I saw you leave your wagon last night. I slipped out and followed you. I saw everything. I saw you try to kill McCandliss and I saw what he did to you."

Eve looked away. "You saw everything?" she asked uncomfortably.

Kiowa nodded. "I know what you were trying to do. I went back to the wagon to get my bow, and when I returned you were gone. It took me most of the night to find where they'd taken you."

"What about McCandliss?"

"He went back to the others."

Eve rubbed her reddened wrists. "What do we do now?"

Kiowa glanced at the two dead men. "I can't go back to the wagon train. You can't either. He'll know something went wrong. We'll trail them, just like these two did, and I'll kill them when I have the chance."

Eve looked at him. "Why do you want to kill them?"

"For the same reason you wanted to. Are you coming with me?"

She glanced at the Indian ponies before looking at Kiowa again. "You're sick. You need rest."

"Rest isn't what I need," said Kiowa, and the vengeful note in his voice made Eve wonder at his determination. She looked painfully around.

"Is there water somewhere near? I need to bathe."

"There's a small stream a hundred yards away. We have to hurry, Eve, the wagons will already be moving."

The sound of her hoarsely spoken name stopped her.

"What made you do it?" she asked. "What made you come after me, Kiowa?"

Splotches of color stained his fevered cheeks. He turned and walked away from her. "Come on," he called over his shoulder. "I'll take you to the stream."

Eve hurried after him.

Chapter Twelve

Austin rubbed his neck with a weary hand and tried to sit up straighter in the saddle. Exhaustion and lack of sleep were about to overtake him. Still, he had to admit he had slept better the night before than he would have believed possible. The first hour had been bad; he'd been restless, worried, and watchful, not trusting the camp to Will Drake. But once Danni started breathing evenly beside him he was hypnotized by the easy rise and fall of her chest. Soon he was asleep beside her, and when he awakened three hours later, his arm was around her and he had nestled her against him, as if to keep warm. Quint Corle was on watch by that time, so Austin allowed himself simply to lie still and look at her.

In time her lashes lifted and she gazed sleepily at him. Then her cheeks pinkened and she pulled away from his grasp in embarrassment. Austin let her go and saw her golden hair tumble about her face as she struggled with the blanket around her. Finally she freed herself and pushed her hair back with both hands. Austin handed her the ribbon beneath his arm and she tied her hair up.

He watched her stand and reach for her blanket before sitting up himself. She shook out the blanket and folded it before hurrying over to the wagon. Seconds later she was back, touching him on the shoulder as he pulled on his boots.

"He's gone."

Austin looked up at her. "Jack?"

Danni shook her head, and he knew she was talking about Kiowa.

Half an hour later a similar note was struck by the Blaines. Eve Blaine was missing. Her wagon was empty.

Austin checked both wagons carefully and asked Danni if anything belonging to Kiowa was missing along with him. She thought for a moment, then returned inside the wagon. Finally she came down and said, "His bow is gone. He must have taken it with him."

Now, as Austin rode wearily down the trail, he thought about Kiowa and Eve Blaine, and wondered what had happened. A look at the face of Robert McCandliss told him something was wrong there. His skin was a pasty white, and he kept holding his left side as he rode. The smirk that played around his lips when the talk turned to Eve Blaine made Austin immediately suspicious. But Austin could prove nothing. Nor could he accuse the man.

Luther suggested the same Indians who had hauled off the first woman had probably come for another—just sneaked right in and took her out from under their noses.

Ormond Blaine blustered and snorted and carried on for more than an hour, while Kora Blaine seemed pleased about her rival's disappearance.

Susannah now drove Eve's wagon, and Will Drake rode beside her, protecting her, he claimed, from the amorous advances of the McCandliss men.

No one but Danni and Austin knew Kiowa had disappeared as well.

When Austin halted the train at noon, he was pleased to see

Jack awake. He helped the man out of the wagon and supported him as he took a few tentative steps.

"Tired of peeing in a can," he told Austin. "A soldier doesn't pee in a damned can."

Luther McCandliss's ears perked up. "What kind of soldier?" he came to ask Jack.

"Infantry," Jack replied, and he peered at Luther suspiciously. "You a soldier?"

"Virginia artillery," said Luther, and he spat on the ground at Jack's feet. Jack looked at Austin and blurted, "Shoot this man. He's a traitor."

Austin reached for Jack's shoulders and grabbed them firmly. "Look at me, Jack. There's no more war. Do you understand? It's over."

Luther's nostrils were flaring. "I get it now. He's one of them crazy men, ain't he? Hey, Bob, come over here! Bourke's carrying around a crazy man. Mr. Infantry here thought I ought to be shot for a traitor."

"Did he now?" asked Robert softly as he approached. His face was still pale, Austin noted.

"What about you, Mr. Bourke?" Robert continued. "Bourke's a fine Irish name. Were you in one of those northern Irish regiments that made such a name for themselves?"

"No, I was not," said Austin. "You'll have to excuse my brother. He's not himself these days."

"Brother?" Jack said. "Whose brother?"

Luther snorted. "Guess he ain't exactly all together, now is he?"

Austin looked past them to the wagons. "I suggest you men have something to eat while we're here. I want to be on the move again in half an hour. We should reach Fort Harker within the next twelve hours or so."

Whatever they were planning was likely to happen before then.

He helped Jack back to the wagon and along with Danni managed to get him in a sitting position on the seat next to her. Jack was still muttering under his breath about the Virginia artillery and men who ought to be shot when Austin gave the signal to move out. Danni still looked anxious, he noticed, and he was tempted to tell her not to worry. Kiowa with a bow could take care of himself. His choice of the bow over a rifle told Austin the youth was going to be doing some shooting he wanted no one to hear, which made Austin think perhaps Kiowa was not far away.

Later that day as he rode back to check on Danni and Jack, she called him over and signaled that she had something important to tell him. Austin motioned for her to stop the wagon. She slowed the oxen to a halt and Austin waved everyone else on and tied his horse to the back of her wagon while the other wagons plodded on ahead of them. He helped Jack into the back, onto the mattress, and he asked Danni to move over so he could drive the team while they talked. She handed the reins over in relief and they started moving again.

When they were in line behind the others, Danni told him about the conversation she had overheard the night before between Eve and Robert McCandliss. Austin kept his gaze straight ahead as she talked. When she finished he said, "Why didn't you tell me this last night?"

Hearing the anger in his voice, she looked at him in surprise. "I didn't want you to think ill of Eve."

Austin exhaled loudly through his nose. "What do you care what I think of her? I'm in charge here, Danni. I need to know what goes on, no matter what it is. I might have been able to help her last night."

Danni looked at her hands. "So you think he did something to her?"

"Don't you?"

"Yes," she said. "I do. I think she tried to hurt him and he killed her. He's got a wound in his side. I saw the blood."

Austin drove silently for a moment. Then he said, "He might not have killed her. He might have given her to his friends outside the camp."

"Indians?"

"Yes."

"Won't they kill her?"

"When they're finished with her." Austin hesitated, then

went on. "I think maybe Kiowa went after her. He's romantic over Mrs. Blaine."

Danni turned to stare at him. "Don't be silly. It's Susannah he likes. I see him watching her all the . . ." She paused then and her fine blonde brows met in sudden comprehension. "Oh, no. How could I have been so stupid? It wasn't Susannah he was watching all that time. It was Eve."

"He was watching her bathe at the stream the day Mrs. Corle was taken."

"Did he tell you that?" asked Danni.

"He didn't need to."

Danni shook her head and put her hands to her face. "My goodness. I never considered Eve. She's older."

Austin clucked at the oxen. "So are you."

"I'm not . . . we don't . . ." Her face colored and she turned her head away. "Kiowa and I have never had the sort of relationship you're suggesting."

"I'm not suggesting anything. But it wouldn't be unusual if you had, and it wouldn't be unusual if anything happened between Kiowa and Mrs. Blaine."

"It might not be unusual," said Danni, "but neither would it be right."

Austin glanced at her. "Right for who? You and Kiowa, or Kiowa and Mrs. Blaine?"

Danni's mouth trembled. "We're both married women, Mr. Bourke."

"And you're both, in a manner of speaking, unfulfilled."

She stared at him again. "I'm what?"

Austin didn't know why he kept talking. He was angry with her for keeping things from him, but it wasn't the only reason he wanted to upset her. She was sitting beside him with her tough little exterior and her clear gray eyes and he wanted to damage her somehow, punish her for being so innocent and determined and for making him feel he had to play her husband and protect her and possibly put his life on the line for her.

"Your own husband told me he hasn't touched you in ages," Austin said. "He said he'd been hoping you and Kiowa would become lovers, but it hadn't worked out. He thought I might do."

Her face seemed to change as a flush crept over her cheeks. "No. Jack wouldn't say that."

"He did."

"Then I . . . I apologize for him. I apologize for both of us." She glanced into the back, where Jack lay sleeping. "I didn't know he had unburdened himself to you."

An apology wasn't what Austin wanted to hear.

"I've just insulted you, and you apologize to me."

She turned her face resolutely toward the sun. "I'm not angry with you. I'm not angry with anyone, Mr. Bourke. I'm too tired to be angry."

He put the reins in one hand and reached over with the other to grab her chin and make her look at him.

"I'm going to insult you further, Mrs. Coopersand. I told him I wasn't interested. Don't get the idea I like claiming you to fool these men. I'd do the same for anyone."

She jerked her face out of his grip and rubbed at her chin with shaking fingers. "I haven't gotten any ideas, Mr. Bourke. I thank you for your gallantry and your consideration. I fully understand the reason behind the ruse."

Austin's breathing became uneven. His teeth ground against each other in his mouth.

"I'm beginning to wonder if it was the war or you that made Jack so crazy," he muttered, and he hauled back on the reins. The oxen came to a slow, shuffling halt. Danni looked straight ahead, her spine stiff, and held out her hands for the reins. Austin shoved them at her, then jumped off the wagon. He walked to the back, and as he was untying his horse, Butcher bared his teeth and nipped him between the shoulder blades. Austin turned with a furious growl of pain and instinctively drew his revolver.

It was a struggle to keep from pulling the trigger. The animal looked at him with what appeared to be a smile on his long, equine face.

Austin cursed and shoved his revolver back into its holster. He slapped the horse in the face with his reins and then climbed into the saddle. Butcher fell easily into stride with a kick of the heels, as though nothing had happened. Austin didn't look back at Danni.

As he rode away, it occurred to him that he was like the black horse. He had nipped and goaded, trying to get a response from her so he could justify his unreasonable anger.

It hadn't worked.

Chapter Thirteen

Kiowa rode beside Eve on the taller of the two Indian ponies and watched her hands clench and unclench the reins. It hurt him to look at the terrible bruises and swelling on her face and know the pain she must have suffered. He wished he had made the Sioux suffer the same torments. His hatred and anger for the men responsible kept him from dwelling on his own pain and sickness. It made his teeth clench and his jaws throb, but it kept him upright in the saddle.

He had been planning the death of Robert McCandliss for so long it seemed unreal that it was about to happen. But happen it would. After what he had seen the night before, nothing on earth would stop him from killing the man he had called brother. The man who had slit his throat and left him to die in a bloody farmhouse in Illinois.

Robert McCandliss and his brothers had led charmed lives thus far, raping and murdering at will, escaping uninjured each time the threat of capture loomed. Their luck had been the luck of rogues. But with a little luck of his own, Kiowa intended to change that pattern. He had a plan of attack in mind, one that would depend completely upon surprise. But surprise or not, he would not fail. He *would not,* he promised himself as the vision of Robert McCandliss raping the unconscious Eve returned to torture him again.

He had to tell her when to stop. Around noon he called to her, and in a daze she kept riding. He called again, louder this time, and still she rode on, her expression trancelike. He rode up to her and caught the reins in one hand, jerking her mount to a halt. She looked at him in surprise and blinked. "Kiowa?"

"We'll stop for a time and let the animals rest. Take some water."

He winced as he slid off his pony and saw her do the same. When she stood where she was, not moving, he went and took her by the arm. "Let's walk. Are you thirsty?"

"Yes," she said, and she put a hand to her swollen, torn mouth.

Kiowa removed his water pouch and let her drink deeply from it. Then he took a long drink himself and replaced the pouch.

She reached for his arm again and leaned heavily on him. "You should be leaning on me," she murmured.

Kiowa said nothing. He began to walk her slowly across the grass. He felt her look up at him and out of the corner of his eye he saw her mouth curve.

"You're tall for seventeen. You must be an inch or more over six feet."

"Yes," was all Kiowa said.

"With arms as big around as any spike driver on the railroad. You've worked hard in your life, Kiowa."

He couldn't look at her. She was too close to him. It made him almost dizzy when she was so close.

"I'm thinking you want to kill the McCandliss brothers for a different reason than mine," she said softly, still looking at him. "I'm thinking it has something to do with the scar at your throat."

Kiowa stopped walking. "The reason doesn't matter. They need to be stopped."

Eve's face grew solemn. "It should matter, Kiowa. As sure as I matter to you, it should."

He finally looked at her.

"I know I matter to you," she went on. "It's in your face. It's in your eyes. And while a part of me is worried about disappointing you, another part of me is thrilled to be cared for by someone."

"Even if that someone is half-Cheyenne?" Kiowa said and held his breath.

She squeezed the arm she was holding. "Something tells me you're more of a man at seventeen than most white men I've known."

Kiowa's dark eyes probed hers. He searched her face to see if she was teasing him or playing a game. He saw nothing but honesty and perhaps a touch of fear in her green gaze. His hands tightened on her impulsively.

"I would never do anything to hurt you," he told her in his hoarse voice. "I would never touch you without permission, or attempt to restrict you in any way. I want only to be with you for as long as you'll let me. When you tell me to go, I'll go."

Eve's lids lowered. "Kiowa, I'm touched that you feel so deeply for me. But I'm not just a Mormon's extra wife, and when we rejoin the others I'll ask you to go on as before."

He stared at her, the rejection piercing him as deep as any arrow. "I've just told you—"

"I know what you've just told me. And I'm honored beyond measure, Kiowa." She wrenched her arm away from him suddenly and stood up as straight as possible. "Don't look at me that way. I know the same feelings as you. Since the night you recited Byron I haven't been able to stop thinking of you. But I'm not what I seem. I've done terrible things in my life, and I'm still doing them."

Kiowa began to shake his head. "You're not," he said.

She swiveled her head to stare at him. "I'm not *what*?"

"You're not . . ." He couldn't finish.

Eve's laugh was short and bitter. "You know what I am, what I've been, and you say I'm not? How could it not be so if you can merely look at me and tell? You know why I led McCandliss to that tree last night. You know what he thought he was going to do, don't you? He thought I was going to give him willingly what his friends took by force. And he thought so because I told him I had done it before, during the war."

"Did you?" Kiowa asked, his hoarse voice a croak of pain.

Eve put her hands to her face as if to shield her swollen eyes. Her head throbbed with a terrible pounding. She wanted to lay down in the grass and cry at the hurt and disappointment in his face. "Yes, my sweet Kiowa. Yes. And now do you no longer care for your dear Maid of Athens?"

Kiowa was silent for several moments, long enough for her to open her palms and look at him. Slowly he reached out with one rough and calloused hand and touched her cheek. He lowered his head to hers and brushed her lips gently with his own. His voice a whisper, he murmured,

By that lip I long to taste;
By that zone-encircled waist;
By all the token flowers that tell
What words can never speak so well . . .

Her eyes welled up again as she looked at him. Then she turned abruptly and stumbled toward her pony.

"I won't let you do this to me," she muttered as she went. "No one who handles a bow like you and talks of death and killing so easily should be able to kiss so sweetly and recite the poems of Lord Byron."

His heart in his throat, Kiowa watched her. He didn't know what to say.

She didn't speak to him the rest of the day. She rode ahead by herself and glanced back occasionally, but she never really looked at him. Around four o'clock they overtook the wagon train. The wagons had stopped. Fearing the worst, Kiowa rode up through the brush until he could see everyone. He breathed more easily when he saw Austin and Danni standing beside her wagon and talking to each other. One of the wheels had buckled slightly, which made the wagon lean over like an old dog with a bad hind leg.

Robert McCandliss and his brother Luther were sitting on their horses nearby. Luther was smiling at Danni, his face nearly splitting with mirth. Obviously neither man had offered help. Kiowa wiped at his fevered brow and wished he were able. One look at Danni's face told him she was struggling to maintain her composure.

As Kiowa watched, Will Drake strode up and knocked the dust from his hat. He spoke with Austin and together they bent to examine the wagon. Soon Quint Corle came, and the three of them apparently reached a decision. Quint and Will got under the wagon and attempted to heft it up enough for Austin to get in and straighten the wheel. They would probably use temporary measures to strengthen it until they reached Fort Harker that evening, where more permanent repairs could be made.

Kiowa trained his attention on the McCandlisses again. Why not now? he thought as he studied them. His chances might be dwindling. The closer they came to Fort Harker, the better the odds his stepbrothers would strike and leave the others in camp dead.

His bow was in his hands before he realized what he was doing. His movements were fluid and natural as he nocked an arrow and drew back the bow to take aim. . . .

Then he saw Eve. Austin Bourke twisted and drew his revolver as she rode boldly up to the men around the wagon and slid off the back of her Indian pony. The mouths of the McCandliss brothers went slack in surprise as the men straightened and stood back. Kiowa clearly heard Danni's gasp. "Eve, what's happened to you?"

"Indians," Eve said loudly. "I was captured by two Sioux, and they were killed by another Indian. While he was busy murdering my captors, I escaped."

She turned to point a finger at Robert McCandliss . . .

. . . but he was already gone. He and Luther had wheeled their horses around and galloped away from the wagons at a dead run.

Kiowa felt his limbs begin to tremble. Anger clouded his vision and left him temporarily blinded.

She had done it on purpose. She had warned them on purpose.

Eve turned in his direction and began to call for him. "Kiowa, come out now. Please."

At that moment, George McCandliss rode up to the small group. When he saw Eve, his eyes rounded. He opened his mouth and said, "Where's my brothers?" He looked around the suspicious group then and saw Austin Bourke with his revolver. His hand hovered over his own gun as he turned to Eve. "Did I hear you call for someone named *Kiowa*?"

Kiowa took aim with his bow and let the arrow fly, striking George McCandliss in the middle of the back. He fell forward off his horse and hit the ground.

"Kiowa!" Eve shouted, while everyone around her dropped to the ground and took cover.

Kiowa jerked his pony around and dug his heels into its sides, galloping as quickly as he could away from the sound of her voice and the sight of her face. She had no idea what this had meant to him. She couldn't. If she had, she would never have betrayed him.

Killing George was the only way to ensure Robert's and Luther's return. They would come for revenge, and Kiowa would be waiting, same as before. Eve's efforts to thwart him had been for nothing.

But perhaps they had been for something after all. He couldn't trust her. Not with his heart or anything else.

He rode until he couldn't hear the sound of her shouts anymore and leaped off his pony near the river, where the animal plunged its snout in the water and drank deeply. He dipped his bandanna in the water and laid it across his still feverish forehead. He knew he should eat something, but he couldn't at the moment. He couldn't do anything but think of Eve. He had foolishly allowed her to learn his feelings, and she had succeeded in using that knowledge to crush him.

Kiowa got down on his knees and plunged his face into the icy water just long enough for the cold to hurt. When he came up, a piece of rawhide was suddenly looped around his neck. He grabbed the strip and was jerked upright into a sitting position; then he was tugged onto the ground, where a booted foot was placed against his throat.

He looked up into a face he knew well. Robert McCandliss leaned over him and frowned as recognition set in. The breath whistled through his teeth, and he smiled suddenly. "Hello, Kiowa."

Chapter Fourteen

Danni helped Eve to the Blaines' wagons and heard Susannah complain in a loud voice that Eve's wagon was hers now, and she shouldn't have to give it back just because Eve was alive. Danni marched over to the wagon and told the girl to be quiet and get down, and when Kora Blaine opened her mouth in protest, Danni told her to be quiet, too. Ormond Blaine finally came and shooed the two angry redheads away. He cautiously asked Eve how she was feeling, and when all Eve did was glare at him, he backed away, his face cold. "I'll come back later," he said stiffly.

"You do that," muttered Eve.

Danni looked at her in confoundment once they were inside the wagon and alone. "Shouldn't your welcome have been a bit warmer? They all behaved as if they were disappointed to see you alive."

"I'm sure they are," Eve replied. "Particularly Kora."

Danni wanted to ask what she meant, but Austin Bourke was

waiting. "We have to get you cleaned up. Mr. Bourke wants to speak with you."

Eve's laugh was derisive. "I don't have anything to say. I thought I was doing the right thing."

"The right thing?"

"For Kiowa. He came after me, Danni. He saw McCandliss attack me and he came to save me."

Danni lifted a brow. "Robert McCandliss? Eve, I have to tell you I saw you make arrangements to meet him. Not many will believe—"

"It was a foolish thing to do," Eve interrupted. "You don't know how afraid I was when he cornered me. I couldn't think what to do. Later I stabbed him, and he forced me to tend his wound. Then he gave me to his friends. Kiowa found me and killed them."

Danni sat back and blinked. "Kiowa?"

"Yes. The same as he killed George McCandliss. He intends to kill all of them. I thought I could stop him."

"Why?" said Danni, suddenly angry. "They slit his throat and left him to die. Why shouldn't he kill them?"

Eve winced in reply as Danni roughly applied a damp cloth to her bruised and still-swollen face.

"Who did this to you?" asked Danni.

"The Indians."

"Did they . . ." Danni couldn't go on.

"Yes, they did."

"I see. You're all right? Is anything broken?"

"Just bruised." Eve grabbed Danni's wrist then. "Don't blame me for trying to save him from himself. Revenge has become his purpose in life. You'd know I was right if you could see his face when he speaks of them."

Danni eyed her. "When this is over perhaps he'll find a new purpose."

"You mean me?" Eve smiled bitterly and filled her hands with her black hair. "I'm tainted, Danni. I'm the property of that Mormon monster out there with the pale white hands and the sickly grin. As soon as I can, I'm going to—"

The puckered flap cover was ripped away from the wagon.

Ormond Blaine stood trembling before them, his pinched nostrils flaring red and his chin quivering.

"Madam," he said evenly, "you will remove yourself and your belongings from my wagon this instant. Consider yourself divorced from me and my family. I will see to it properly with the Church as soon as I am able."

Danni tore her gaze from his blistering fury to look at Eve, who cackled hysterically into her hands and then threw her head back. "The Church?" she cried. "You're a liar, Ormond Blaine. We were never married within the Church, and the only reason you're taking this route rather than the Oregon Trail is because the elders in St. Louis threw you out of the Church and most of the other Mormons traveling west know it."

Blaine's white face turned scarlet. "You lie, woman! How dare you speak such filth to me?"

"Filth?" Eve echoed, her own face changing color now. "You want to talk about filth? What about the things you do to your own daughter, Ormond Blaine? How's that for filth? Come out here, Susannah! Tell everyone about the games you play with Daddy at night!"

From beside the wagon Danni heard Susannah shriek in mortification. Kora Blaine roared like a lioness and tried to come through the opening at Eve. Ormond pulled her off and attempted to come in himself, his eyes red with hate. Danni threw herself over Eve, shielding Eve with her own body. Hard fists pummeled at her back and neck, knocking the breath out of her. She held on to Eve and tried to swing her legs around to kick the fists away. Abruptly, they stopped.

Austin had taken the flailing Ormond Blaine by the collar and tossed him out of the wagon. He tossed him right into Will Drake, who pushed him down to the ground and stood looking at him in disgust. He lifted his gaze to Susannah then, and Danni heard him ask if what he had heard Eve say was the truth.

"No," Susannah shouted. "Don't believe her. She's a whore and a liar. We found her at a hospital in St. Louis, all sick and diseased and half out of her mind. It's never come back, Will.

Her mind has never returned. She's still half crazy, just like Jack Coopersand. You can't believe a word she says. She's always making up crazy stories."

"Susannah," said Ormond Blaine in a stern voice. "Why are you making excuses to this man? What is he to you?"

When Susannah didn't answer, Ormond got to his feet and stood toe to toe with Will. "What relationship do you have with my daughter, sir?"

"A carnal one, *sir*. And I obviously wasn't the first."

"Why, you . . ." Blaine stepped back and swung wildly at Will, who simply ducked and watched Blaine turn a complete circle. Will lifted his leg and planted a booted foot in the seat of Blaine's pants and sent him to the ground again. He went after him, but Austin grabbed him by the arm then and said, "Enough. Mr. Blaine, get up."

"I'll get up," he shouted, red-faced. "I'll have my satisfaction from Mr. Drake here."

"You'll get up and get in your wagon. Eve, leave your things where they are and we'll talk about everything later. We need to get moving. I want to reach Harker by nightfall, and I don't want argument from any of you. We don't have time for it."

Danni hurriedly finished administering to Eve, who climbed down out of the wagon, spat in the dust, and walked over to her Indian pony and climbed on its back. Ormond Blaine's lip curled as she rode proudly past him.

"God will curse you for your lies!" he hissed.

"He'll curse you for the truth," she replied.

Danni ran over and checked her hastily repaired wagon wheel once more before climbing onto the seat and grabbing the reins. Jack was in Mr. Corle's wagon now, so the load was lighter. She crossed her fingers and hoped the wagon would make it to Harker. Several of the spokes and felloes had rotted and given way. She didn't know how she was going to manage the cost of repairing the wheel.

Austin rode up once they were on the move again and asked if Mr. Blaine had harmed her.

"No," Danni told him. "It's Eve who's been harmed. And possibly Kiowa."

He brought his black horse alongside her. "Meaning?"

"He killed the two Indians she spoke of, as well as George McCandliss. He intends to kill all of them."

Austin's brows lifted slightly. "You say he's been injured beyond his arrow wound?"

"He saw McCandliss attack Eve. He went to her rescue and I believe she rejected him."

"He may have expected rejection," said Austin. "What he might not have expected was her ruining his plans to ambush the McCandlisses. I'm fairly certain that's what he intended, until she rode into camp and caused them to run. He's probably hunting them now."

"So you're not worried?"

"On the contrary. I feel better knowing he's out there."

Danni said nothing further and he rode away from her, back to the trail ahead. She watched him as he went and was both strangely saddened and relieved by the knowledge that they would no longer be playing man and wife. His steady arm had been a comfort to her, as had his very presence. When he was gone she found herself looking for him, and when he was there she was unquestionably happy. Now he was back to his old self again, brusque, short-tempered, and seemingly angry with her most of the time.

He was different with Jack. He was patient and kind and helpful, and he listened to Jack's ramblings long after any other person would have thrown up his hands and walked away. That was how Danni knew the kind of person he was; not from the way he was with her, or with Will Drake or any of the others, but the way he was with Jack.

With Kiowa it was the same. Austin had made fast friends with the quiet youth, and now he trusted Kiowa to do the right thing, even when Danni was worried and unsure. She knew in her heart the McCandliss men deserved to die. But she wasn't sure she wanted Kiowa to be the one to kill them, in spite of what she had said to Eve.

He wasn't a killer, she kept telling herself. Though he had already killed three men, Kiowa wasn't a killer.

She thought of his quick defense of Austin, and his own kindness and patience with Jack, and decided they were two of a kind. Only she didn't feel tingly or pleasantly warm around Kiowa. Danni lowered her face and looked at the reins in her red and roughened hands. She was probably falling in love with Austin Bourke.

She had known she would the first time she saw him with Jack in that store. He had become a hero to her in those tense, emotional moments. Austin Bourke had stopped to aid a man he didn't know, wasn't kin to, and had no reason to help, and that made him special to Danni. The moment he said he was to be their guide, he became more than special. He became a dream out of a dime novel. Someone to fall madly in love with.

And she supposed she had, if the tingling was anything to judge by. But it would all come to an end—just like the dime novels—when the journey was over and she was settled. Everything she had ever read about love brought her to the conclusion it was best left unrequited. This made sense to Danni, seeing as how Austin was more exasperated than infatuated with her, and she could never see herself telling him her feelings. She couldn't see herself telling anyone, mostly because of the pain involved. She thought she knew now what Kiowa had been putting himself through over Eve; the sadness and longing and secret ache that had become an everyday part of living.

Jack sat up in the wagon in front of her at that moment and waved. Danni waved back, and the wistful smile slowly faded from her face.

There had been times in the last few years when she wished desperately to be touched as a woman again. Times when she held onto Jack and wished for all the world she could bring his manhood back to him, if only to feel, for a few moments, like a warm, vital woman. But the ache always passed, and she went on as before, looking ahead to the next day and what it might bring. Her grandmother had taught her never to worry about what might have been but to concern herself with the here and now, and that's what Danni did.

Someday, when this trip was just a memory, she would take out her feelings for Austin Bourke and dust them off and cherish them anew. She would laugh as she remembered the way her heart galloped when he was near. She would sigh to herself over the memory of his smell, the secrets hidden behind his hazel eyes, and the value of his rare smiles. She would recall the sound of his voice, the touch of his hand, the warmth of his body, and she would smile and tell herself it was good to have known such feelings.

There would be little else for her. No children or grandchildren, no kinfolk. No one.

A long, unconscious sigh escaped from Danni. When she heard the sound of it, she was surprised. She had never believed she would miss having children. After her two miscarriages, she rarely dwelled on the subject.

When Eve rode up to her wagon just before dusk, Danni looked quizzically at her and asked, "Do you know how a woman is made pregnant?"

Eve blinked.

"Pregnant," Danni repeated. "How does a woman become pregnant?"

"You don't know?" Eve asked, shocked.

Danni stared, confused, and then she grew irritated. "Of course I know that part. I meant what happens with the body. How do you know which time will make you pregnant?"

Eve went on looking at her. "Which time?"

"For pity's sake," said Danni angrily. "I grew up on a farm in Illinois with my grandmother. She didn't talk of such things."

"What about other girls in school?"

"I didn't go to school. I worked on the farm. My grandmother was a teacher and she taught me from books she had. I can read and write as well as anyone. I've even read Shakespeare."

"But you don't know how to go about getting pregnant."

"I've asked, haven't I?"

Eve looked speculatively at Jack, riding in the wagon ahead of them. "I don't mean to be personal, but is he capable . . . ?"

Danni held the reins and looked straight ahead. "That's none of your business."

Eve nodded. "I'm sorry. You're right. When was your last menses?"

Danni's head turned. "My what?"

"Your monthly," Eve clarified.

"Oh. Well, it's right now."

"Today? You're having it today?"

"Yes."

"All right. I'll teach you what my father taught me." Eve quickly told her all that her father, the professor, had shown her from his books on biology. Then she looked at Danni again. "Were you just curious, or are you trying to get pregnant?"

Danni lifted a shoulder and sighed. "I've been thinking a life without children will be a lonely one."

She was contemplating asking Kiowa for his help when the time came. She loved Kiowa, not in a romantic way, but she thought he would make fine, strong babies. Providing he came back and rejoined the wagons.

"Eve," she began, and the black-haired woman looked expectantly at her. "I don't know how to put this," Danni continued, "but did Susannah speak the truth about you?"

"Yes," Eve said flatly. "I was a sick whore in a hospital when they found me." She looked defiantly at Danni, waiting for her to pronounce judgement.

Danni only gazed at her. Finally she said, "You're a mystery to me, Eve. You're very hard and very wise and also very sad. You appear to take no joy from life, yet you live as if in defiance of death. I can see why Kiowa is so enamored of you. You're a beautiful woman. But your anger and sadness seem to have overwhelmed you."

"Have they?" Eve said coldly. Then she kicked her pony in the sides and rode off, her back rigid.

"I'm sorry," Danni murmured after her. She hadn't meant to anger the woman. But perhaps she had, a little, she acceded. For making Danni feel like such a fool.

In the space of fifteen minutes the previously clear sky clouded up and turned that day's dusk into an ominous one. An hour after nightfall they reached Fort Harker, and the rain came. Danni watched from inside her wagon as Austin talked his way into the fort. He was gone for what seemed like an hour as she peered through the pelting rain to see him come out again. When he emerged he had someone with him. He brought the man to Danni's wagon and together they looked at the wheel. There was much shaking of heads and nodding, and finally they shook hands. Soon the man returned to the fort and Austin came to see Danni. One look at his face told her the news wasn't good.

"The nearest wheelwright is in Ellsworth. That man was a teamster. He said you need a new wheel and possibly a new axle assembly. You won't get twenty miles with it this way."

Danni's mouth worked, but no sound came out. With an effort she pushed the words forth. "Can he do it here? How much did he say it would cost?"

"He offered to fix it for fourteen dollars."

"Fourteen?"

"He doesn't usually work on civilians' wagons. And he'll need some money to give the blacksmith."

Danni felt the blood drain from her face. Her hands and her feet went numb. Fourteen dollars.

Suddenly she remembered herself. She looked at Austin and nodded. "All right. Thank you for asking."

"Well?" he said.

"Pardon?"

"What are you going to do?"

Danni looked out of the wagon. "I might just find myself homesteading around Fort Harker, Mr. Bourke. Fourteen dollars is a lot of money when you have none to spare."

Austin stared at her. "You mean you're going to pull out and stay here?"

"I think that's what I mean, yes."

"This country . . ." He gestured with his arms. "You approve of this country?"

She frowned, unsure of what he meant. There was nothing wrong with the country around them. It was as green and fertile as any she had seen on the journey so far.

"I don't understand," she said.

"How much money do you have, Danni?"

"Not enough, Mr. Bourke. That's what I've been trying to tell you."

"Can you spare seven dollars?"

"But you said—"

"I know what I said. Can you give me seven?"

"No," Danni said abruptly. "I won't have you paying the other half, Mr. Bourke. I will not."

"I've eaten supper with you nearly every night, Danni. Don't you think that's worth seven dollars?"

She thought for a moment, then said, "Do you think I'll be happier in country farther west?"

"Yes, I do. West and a bit south. There's a place I've got in mind to show you. No one has claimed it yet."

Danni's face lit up. "You know of a place? Does it have good water and some timber? Is there a settlement within fifty miles?"

"It's a hundred or so miles this side of Fort Wallace. A good walk from the river. There are a few trees, but no settlement. Just the fort."

Her excitement deflated a little. "How would I get supplies when I need them? I can't leave Jack alone for so long."

"There are other settlers in the area. You could ask one of them to bring back your things. Just last year someone was thinking of opening up a store between Fort Hays and Fort Wallace. If it came into being, it would be within a day's ride of the place I had in mind."

"A store?" Danni said in excitement. "Oh, I never dreamed of having one so close. I do hope it happens. I hope I'll be able to—" Her mouth closed at the look on his face. She had never seen him look at her in such a way and it made her mind go momentarily blank as she stared back at him.

"You hope you'll be able to what?" he prompted.

"To see it some day," she finished. Then she asked, "Did you have somewhere in mind to show Mr. Corle?"

"Yes," he said. "In the same area."

"Oh." After a twinge of disappointment, Danni forced herself to smile at him. "You're very kind, Mr. Bourke. We've been very lucky to have you as our guide."

He drew in a deep breath and let it out again. "About the money . . ."

"Shall I get it for you now?"

"If you don't mind. We'll have to unload your wagon in the morning."

Danni nodded and got the money for him. She handed it to him, still smiling, and asked if he'd had his supper.

"I haven't talked to Eve Blaine yet," he replied. "Keep something warm for me?"

She looked at him in surprise and nodded. "Yes, of course."

As he departed, Danni smiled happily to herself. Then she looked around her cluttered wagon and thought of everything to be unloaded. She certainly hoped it wouldn't be raining in the morning.

CHAPTER FIFTEEN

IT WAS still raining at dawn, and Eve looked worriedly out the back of the wagon as she thought of Kiowa. He probably hated her now. She had hurt him and betrayed him, and she wouldn't blame him if he despised her. She watched the steady rain and wondered where he had slept the night before, if he had been cold. She had been cold. She had tossed and gotten up a dozen times at hearing sounds in the darkness. She didn't know if it was Ormond Blaine coming, or Robert McCandliss, or even Kiowa. All of them had reason to kill her.

She had told Austin Bourke the whole story and waited for his reaction. Like Danni, he appeared undisturbed by her past. He called her a fool for trying to take on McCandliss with nothing but a knife, but there was a grudging admiration in his eyes just the same. Later he told her to leave her belongings where they were until he could talk to Ormond Blaine. Eve told him not to bother. When she went, she would take nothing but the clothes on her back, which was all she could rightfully call her own. Austin told her to stay put anyway—unless she wanted to sleep outside in the rain.

Eve didn't want to sleep outside. She thought of going to Danni's wagon, but decided she wasn't ready to face her again so soon. The smiling little fool. The woman was unbelievably pleasant and good-natured. Eve decided Danni Coopersand had led an incredibly sheltered life thus far, with little introduction to the pain and misery of the real world. No one who had been introduced to despair would be so relentlessly cheerful and kind. It was hard not to smile back at her, and it was harder yet to stay angry with her. Eve had to smile when she thought of the way Danni spoke to Susannah and Kora, and the way she later threw herself over Eve's person when Ormond Blaine attacked. She was a feisty one.

Eve left the wagon and stepped out into the rainy morning to find out what was happening. She passed the Blaines' wagon and the flap was immediately pulled shut, as if they couldn't bear the sight of her. Eve shook her head and walked on, her feet sticking in the mud.

Everything about the Blaines had come spilling out yesterday, and in her anger and guilt over Kiowa, she had been helpless to stop it. Now she was glad she had said what she did. She was glad it was out, because now she was free and beholden to no one. She was also penniless and had nowhere to go. She couldn't go to California by herself on the back of an Indian pony.

"Danni," she called, as she saw the blonde woman emerge from her wagon carrying a bundle. Danni waved and Eve went to help her down from the wagon. "What are you doing?"

"Unloading some things before the wagon goes inside to be fixed. Mr. Corle said I could store some of my smaller items in his wagon until the rain stops. The bigger items will be unloaded inside."

"Can I help?" Eve asked, and Danni nodded.

"You can see to Jack's breakfast, if you would. He's still sleeping, but he should be up shortly, and since he didn't eat much last night he'll be hungry today."

Eve nodded; then she paused. "Has there been any sign of Kiowa?"

"No," Danni told her. Then she smiled and squeezed Eve's shoulder. "I'm worried, myself. But Kiowa is extremely bright and an excellent shot. I have to believe he's all right."

"I want to believe it," said Eve. She gazed into Danni's clear gray eyes and forced her lips into a smile. "I apologize for my behavior yesterday. You were right in what you said to me."

Danni looked at her soggy bundle. "I'm glad you're not angry. Have you decided what you're going to do?"

Eve shook her head. "I don't have a notion."

Danni opened her mouth, then closed it again. "We'll talk later. I've got to get these things out before Mr. Bourke comes back. Come and I'll show you where my fixings are."

After showing her where she had stored her food, Danni grew busy removing the rest of her smaller belongings from the wagon. Eve put together a plate of cold biscuits and ham and took it to Mr. Corle's wagon, where Jack Coopersand had just awakened and was looking around himself with a blank expression.

"Mr. Coopersand?" Eve said. "I've brought you some breakfast."

"Nurse, come here," he answered. "My bed's wet. Why is my bed wet? What kind of hospital is this?"

"It's not a hospital at all, Mr. Coopersand. It's a wagon, and it's raining outside. That's why everything is wet."

"A wagon? Are we still on the field?"

"We're at Fort Harker." Eve climbed into the wagon and held the plate under his nose. "Are you hungry?"

Jack smiled at her and raked a hand through his dark hair. "Starving. Sakes, but you're a pretty thing. Did you make these biscuits?"

Eve shook her head. "Danni made them."

"Danni? I should have known. She always was a most wonderful cook." Something in his eyes changed then, as if a window had slammed shut—or open. "Where is Danni? Are we to Harker yet?"

"Yes, we're at Fort Harker. Your wagon is being taken inside so the wheel can be repaired. Danni is trying to lighten the contents."

"By herself?"

"No. I believe Mr. Bourke is helping her."

Jack leaned back and chewed on a biscuit, his face growing thoughtful. Suddenly he looked at Eve. "Tell me," he said, "does Mr. Bourke appeal to you as a man?"

Eve lifted her shoulders. "I suppose so. He's kind enough."

"But you wouldn't think of sparking?"

"Mr. Bourke? No. No, I wouldn't, Mr. Coopersand. Why do you ask?"

"Curiosity," he said. "Why wouldn't you think of sparking?"

"I don't really know," Eve said honestly. "He's fair and decent and good-looking, but there are no . . . sparks."

She hadn't felt a spark in ages. She hadn't felt a spark since . . . since Kiowa had kissed her on the lips and recited lines from "Maid of Athens."

A sudden warmth in her cheeks and on the back of her neck surprised her.

Jack emitted what sounded like a chuckle and Eve looked at him again. "Why are you curious, Mr. Coopersand?"

"I want Danni to like him. He's a fine man, our Mr. Bourke."

"But . . . she's married to you."

"Oh, I won't stand in her way. Not for a minute. I want Danni to be happy. She deserves that much. Only I don't want her to think I don't want her. You see what I'm saying?"

Eve wasn't sure. "I think so."

"Her family didn't want her. Her mama died after she was born and her daddy left her with her grandma rather than come for her, so she's got a whole family of brothers and sisters that never cared to meet her. Grandma did her best, but they never had anything to speak of, and then I came along and saw her lose two pregnancies before I left to join my regiment. While I was gone she lost the farm and damn near everything on it.

"I wanted to come back and help her. I was killed in that damn war, only my body doesn't know it. Being this way, you can't blame me for wanting a little happiness for Danni. I think she'd be happier with one of the living."

Eve fixed her gaze on him. "I don't know Danni very well, Mr. Coopersand, but I know she'll never leave you. Danni wouldn't."

Jack picked up his fork and speared the ham on his plate. "Maybe she won't have any choice."

Eve opened her mouth to ask what that meant, but Jack's eyes were already changing again. He was already slipping back into that other world he inhabited and no longer responded when she spoke to him.

When he finished his meal she climbed out of the wagon and went in search of food for herself. As she walked she thought of Danni, who had suffered more than Eve guessed, not having even the love of parents to sustain her.

As she approached her wagon she saw a rumpled Ormond Blaine jump down and run to stand in front of her.

"You stayed the night," he said. "Now you'll have to make other arrangements. This wagon and its contents belong to my daughter."

Eve turned on her heel and strode away. She returned to where Danni was and stood beside the other woman as she watched the men from the fort pull her wagon inside the gates.

"Where are you sleeping tonight?" asked Eve.

"I don't know," Danni admitted. There wasn't room for another person to sleep in the Corles' bulging wagons.

Eve pointed at Austin Bourke. "Where did he sleep last night?"

"I don't know. I don't think he slept. Mr. Drake slept under Quint Corle's wagon last night."

"I've been kicked out of my wagon," Eve informed her, and Danni turned to smile sympathetically. She wiped the rain from her face and said, "So we're both out in the cold."

"Looks like it. Unless the fort is willing to accommodate us."

Danni shook her head. "Austin asked. They told us civilians weren't allowed on the post."

"Austin?"

"Mr. Bourke."

"Did he tell them about the McCandlisses?" Eve asked.

"No, he didn't. I waited for him to say something, but he remained quiet on the subject. I think he's protecting Kiowa."

Eve nodded. Then she thought of something. "The cover of your wagon—they don't need the cover to repair it, do they?"

Danni's smile lit up her face. "A tent?"

"A tent. We'll ask Mr. Bourke to help us."

The two women looked at each other and reached out to clasp hands.

Later that night, as the wind whistled and the rain pelted away at the roof of their flimsy tent, Eve curled up beside Danni and felt her eyes grow moist when she heard the other woman struggle through a prayer that asked for everything to be all right. For all of them.

Under her breath, so low no one but she herself could hear the word, Eve said, "Amen."

CHAPTER SIXTEEN

THE MCANDLISSES assumed the worst when their brother's riderless horse appeared at the river. Luther grabbed Kiowa by the hair and bloodied his face with his fists in an effort to find out if it had been Kiowa who ambushed George and the Sioux. Kiowa said not a word. Eventually he fell into unconsciousness, and Luther gave up. When Kiowa came to, Robert took the reins of George's horse and in the same motion drew his revolver and put a bullet through the brain of the Indian pony Kiowa had been riding. Kiowa's teeth nearly bit through his lip with the rage he felt. Robert smiled at seeing the smoldering anger in Kiowa's eyes.

"Rather a waste of good horseflesh, isn't it?"

The brothers picked Kiowa up and tossed him across George's saddle. The rain glued his black hair to his head and ran off the tip of his nose in a steady stream. The tight rawhide strips holding his arms and legs had begun to stink. As they moved forward, his stomach immediately began to ache from the constant grinding and sawing motion of the saddle beneath him. He began to heave repeatedly as they rode west to pick up the trail of the wagons.

Just before dusk they came across George. He was slumped over in the middle of the road, the arrow gone from his back. Kiowa figured Austin Bourke had planted him there. Luther got off his horse and cursed and shouted and pounded the ground with his fist, while Robert simply sat astride his horse and watched.

When Luther finished braying and sobbing over George he walked over and jerked Kiowa onto the ground. He cut his bonds and told him to dig a grave and find enough rocks in the stream bed to cover it. Kiowa's stiff muscles screamed at first, but he was glad to have the opportunity to stretch and loosen their cramped condition. He was also glad to bury the man he had killed. It was all he could do to keep his expression free of the satisfaction he felt.

The rain made the digging sloppy, but Kiowa was eventually able to finish his task. He took large stones from the stream and gathered bark and branches from the poplars, cottonwood, and osier that made up the brush, and added some wild onions he had found. No animal would be fooled, but the preparations made Robert nod in tacit agreement. The weepy Luther stood over the grave and mumbled and stuttered through a psalm; then he gave up and walked away. Bob came and put a leather collar around Kiowa's neck. The collar was attached to a long lead of approximately twelve feet. Kiowa knew what came next. He would be expected to run alongside Bob's horse.

After the first hour, his legs lost sensation and his entire body felt numb. He stumbled on, his flesh burning. Kiowa kept his eyes trained on Robert's back. He focused on the hatred he felt for the man, and the tide of revulsion that came over him each time he saw those grinning yellow teeth. He thought of how much he wanted the man dead and rotting in the ground. He tried to think of how, even now, he might bring that state of affairs about. There wasn't much he could do with his hands tied. He couldn't *will* the man dead.

But he wasn't giving up. As long as he lived and breathed, he wasn't giving up.

He had no idea what the McCandlisses' plans for him were. He had expected to be killed immediately, and it surprised him when he was taken captive. Perhaps Robert intended to use him in some way to harm the people in the wagons.

When they stopped and made camp, Kiowa knew they were close to Fort Harker. He collapsed near a large cottonwood and Luther got off his horse and walked over. Kiowa lay limp and motionless, unable to move.

"Is he dead?" asked Robert, and Luther grabbed Kiowa's hair to peer into his face. "Naw, he ain't dead. Too bad. Just have to try again tomorrow." He chuckled at his joke, then said, "Shoulda had the sense to die the first time Bob tried to kill you. That's a hell of a scar you got there. You got a powerful yen to kill us, is that it? You're wantin' to kill us 'cause of what happened back in Illinois? Is that why you followed us out here?"

Kiowa only looked at him.

"Hey," said Luther. "I think I know what the problem is, Bob. I think you cut his talk box when you slit his throat. He probably *can't* talk no more."

Robert looked at Kiowa. "Is that true? Are you dumb?"

Kiowa blinked and gave a short nod.

"Well, I'll be damned. Why the hell didn't you say—" Luther stopped when he realized the ridiculousness of what he was saying. He slapped Kiowa on the back and then grabbed him by the chin to lift his head. "Yessir, that is some scar. Someone did a real good job of sewin' on you. Was it one of them little ladies with the wagons? Eve, maybe? She's a pretty one, that Eve. God, yes, Bob had his hands full with her. Hell, he had his hands full *of* her." Luther roared with laughter.

Kiowa's face remained expressionless.

"Mercy, but she was mean, though," Luther said when he stopped laughing. "You see where she stuck Bob? Shoulda killed her himself instead of givin' her to them goddamned renegade savages to play with. Them two was so mean their own people wanted nothin' to do with 'em, so how do you figure the little wildcat got away?"

Too bad she hadn't aimed a few inches to the left, Kiowa thought as he eyed the bloodstain on Robert's shirt.

"We'll get her, though," Luther continued. "You and me, little brother. You'll lure her, and I'll grab her. Bob ain't finished with her yet. We ain't finished with any of 'em."

Kiowa heard something then, and he knew Robert heard it too from the way he suddenly leapt to his feet and drew his revolver.

Soon Kiowa heard someone halloo the camp. Robert gave answer and a soldier rode into view. He looked at Robert's and Luther's drawn guns and smiled. "Easy, boys. I ain't lookin' for trouble." Then he saw Kiowa. "Well, looky here. You takin' the Indian to Harker?"

"That's right," Robert said smoothly, and he holstered his revolver. "Are you going to Harker?"

"Yessir. Took some mail to Riley and now I'm on my way back. I was due back earlier but this damn rain is slowin' me down considerably. Mind if I have a cup of your coffee?"

"Go ahead," said Luther, and he shoved a cup at the man.

The soldier was older, Kiowa saw. A grizzled veteran at home in his uniform. He took the cup of coffee and sat down across the fire from Robert and Luther. "You two kin?" he asked. "You look alike."

"Brothers," Robert told him. "Are you from Harker?"

"That I am. Before that I was at Riley, and before that I was at Leavenworth, and before that I was ridin' under Custer and Phil Sheridan. Before that I fought in the Mexican War, and before that, I was kissin' girls and gettin' drunk every Saturday night."

Robert and Luther exchanged grins and laughed. "You fought under Custer?"

"For a time, yessir. I hear he's at Fort Hays now."

"Custer is at Fort Hays?"

"So I'm told. Appears to be a different man from when I knew him. Course the terrain is different. Ain't too much glory to be found out here. What'd this one do?" He pointed at Kiowa.

"Raped and killed a woman from a wagon train on the Smoky Hill Road," said Robert.

"Is that so?" The soldier looked at Kiowa with narrowed eyes. "Is that the party led by Austin Bourke?"

"It is." Robert sat up. "You know Bourke?"

"A damned fine officer. Best I ever served under. I heard he'd be comin' through. Y'know I'll never understand why he left the army when he did. He would've made a hell of a career man."

"Bourke was an officer?" asked Luther.

"A lieutenant. He answered to Wesley Merritt, Custer's rival of sorts. I fought with the Wolverines at the Battle of Yellow Tavern, where Jeb Stuart was brought down. Sad to say, so was I. When I recovered from my wounds I was sent to fight under Bourke and Merritt." He stopped talking then and smiled at the brothers. "You boys see any fighting?"

"Yes, we did," Robert said. "I was in the Virginia artillery and my brother there was also an artilleryman. Brother George, God rest his soul, was a fighting infantryman."

The soldier didn't look at all uncomfortable. "Some of the best damned fightin' men I ever saw came out of Virginia. You boys should be proud."

Robert nodded. "Did you do any fighting in the Shenandoah Valley?"

Kiowa sucked in his breath. *No,* he silently told the soldier. *No.*

"We did," the soldier said. "Lieutenant Bourke was taken prisoner at Cedar Creek and sent to Salisbury, North Carolina. I went with him. Everyone talks about what a hellhole Andersonville was—well, mister, I'm here to tell you the men who died at Salisbury died just as horrible. Filth, disease, and starvation. My God, the things we do in the name of country." He lowered his head over his coffee cup and drank. Then he looked up and smiled. "You boys don't hold no hard feelings, do you? Here I am, an old soldier just a ramblin' on like a fool, never thinkin' there might be some bad feelings yet."

"No, there are no bad feelings," Robert told him. Then he calmly drew his revolver and shot the man through the heart.

The soldier stared in dismay, his eyes round and full of shocked surprise. Then he fell forward into the fire Luther had built. A choked scream issued from his lips; then there was silence and the smell of charred flesh.

Luther watched a minute before leaning forward and dragging the old man out of the fire. "Damn if he didn't put it out. Hell, it got all wet. You start the fire this time, Bob. You know I can't do it so good when it rains."

Robert ignored him and got up to drag the old soldier into the brush. He came back a moment later for a knife. He started off again, then he stopped and looked at Kiowa.

"You," he said, "get up and come here. I want you to see what your people do to the whites they capture."

A cold ball of dread rolled in Kiowa's stomach. He stumbled to his feet as Robert came and jerked on his leather collar, and he reluctantly followed him to where the body of the soldier lay. Robert slit the leather ties on Kiowa's wrists and put the knife in his hands. Then he drew his revolver. He placed the revolver against Kiowa's head and said, "Cut off his hands and feet first."

Kiowa lowered his head. His fingers trembled on the hilt of the knife.

"Do it," Robert ordered, "or you'll be on your way to visit your dead whore of a mother. Go on and cut him."

"I'd rather cut you," Kiowa said hoarsely, and he took advantage of Robert's surprise at his speech to turn swiftly and sink the knife into the man's middle. Robert staggered back and the revolver went off, grazing Kiowa in the side of the head and causing blinding pain. He fought back from the threatening darkness and scrambled to get the revolver out of Robert's hand. From camp he heard Luther shouting. He wrestled the revolver away from the snarling Robert and crawled on top of him until he was sitting on his chest, his legs around the buried blade. "This is for the soldier," he said as he yanked the knife out. Then he cocked the revolver and said, "This is for Eve," as he pulled the trigger and fired into Robert's open mouth.

He whirled as Luther came running. Luther slid in the slippery mud and fought to come to a stop and run the other way when he saw the revolver in Kiowa's hands and the wild gleam in his eyes as he sat atop the dead Robert McCandliss.

Kiowa aimed the revolver and fired, but he missed the fleeing Luther. He cursed and jumped up, and he reached Luther as he vaulted onto his horse. Kiowa took hold of his leg and jerked, but Luther twisted away and came back to kick him solidly in the head, where Robert McCandliss's bullet had plowed its path. There was no fighting back the darkness this time, as Kiowa felt his knees buckle beneath him. The last thing he saw before losing consciousness was Luther riding at a gallop away from the camp, his hair wet and streaming behind him.

When Kiowa opened his eyes, he saw a man with a face brown as leather and hair black as a crow leaning over him. Buckskin covered the lower half of his body, but the upper half was wet and glistened with rain.

The man pointed at him and said something Kiowa didn't understand.

Kiowa frowned and moved his lips, but he thought better of speaking. Better to play the mute again. He pointed to the scar at his throat and shook his head.

The man grunted and nodded. He turned away from Kiowa and made a sound that soon brought other Indians to him. One by one they came to look at Kiowa, some suspiciously, most of them impassively. There were six men in all. The older man who had found him made some grunting noises and other sounds and pointed to Kiowa's throat.

Then he pointed in the direction of Robert McCandliss and the dead soldier.

More grunting and alien sounds ensued.

Soon a young man stepped forward and leaned down to touch Kiowa's head. Kiowa turned away, but the man spoke sternly to him and motioned for him to be still. The man's hand came away covered with blood, and Kiowa stared at it, aware that the blood was his. The volume of it surprised him.

After more talk, the men seemed to reach a decision among themselves. Two men were dispatched to see to the bodies of McCandliss and the soldier, and two more bent down to lift Kiowa from the ground. He stiffened in fear and thought of everything he had ever read about the notorious Indians who inhabited the plains. The man who had found him drew a knife from a belt at his waist and approached Kiowa with an intent expression.

Kiowa squeezed his eyes closed and hoped the taking of his scalp would be swift and that he would lose consciousness again almost immediately.

The Indian slit through the leather collar at Kiowa's neck and tossed it contemptuously away. Kiowa opened his eyes and saw the man taking a closer look at the scar on his throat. The Indian seemed impressed.

Abruptly the man broke away and motioned impatiently for everyone to move. Kiowa was carried to Robert McCandliss's horse and placed on its bare back. An Indian hopped up behind him and held him upright. The reins of the horses belonging to George McCandliss and the old soldier were held by another Indian, and when all were mounted, the Indian in charge moved out.

Kiowa attempted to look back, to see what the two Indians were doing with the bodies of McCandliss and the soldier, but the rain was too heavy, and he was too sick. After a while he closed his eyes and just let go.

CHAPTER SEVENTEEN

AUSTIN STOOD beside the makeshift tent in the darkness and shivered inside the raincoat he wore. His watch was coming to an end and he was ready to find someplace warm to sleep. He glanced at Will Drake's form, bundled up beneath the Corles' wagon. It was Drake's watch next. He supposed he'd go over and take his place. He wouldn't sleep as well as he had next to Danni, but he would be out of the worst of the weather. It had stopped raining for a while that evening, but it was starting again, light drops that landed with little force but foretold of heavier rain to come. It would slow them down even more, Austin knew.

Neither the Corles nor the Blaines were happy about being detained because of Danni's wheel, and Austin had come close to losing his temper with their petty-minded behavior. He assured them the same hold on movement would have been called for if the wagon had been theirs and not Danni's, and should any misfortune befall them in the future, he would do his best to help them in the same way. He couldn't emphasize enough how important it was that everyone pull together and take an interest in the welfare of the others.

His exhortations toward that end had little impact, however. He had never seen a group of people more unwilling to help each other. Not just the Mormons, which was to be expected, but even the Corles were cold to the cause of Danni and Kiowa and now Eve. Austin wanted to blame the war for creating this selfishness among people, but it was only a convenient excuse for the rudeness he encountered. It was a major concession of the Corles to allow Jack to sleep in their second wagon while his own was being repaired. Their attitude, and the attitude of the Blaines toward the ailing veteran, disgusted and dismayed Austin.

He could see why Danni had the trouble with these people that she did. She was far too good for them. She was always quick to smile and even quicker to share whatever she had. Such traits would automatically be cause for suspicion among suspicious people.

Austin looked at his watch and saw it was time to wake Will. He checked the tent once more to make sure it was sound, and couldn't prevent himself from opening the flap and peering inside. Danni sat up immediately, her eyes round with alarm. "What is it? What's wrong?"

"Nothing." He wanted to kick himself. "I was checking to see if you were still dry."

She relaxed. "Yes, you did a wonderful job for us."

He nodded and would have backed out, but she said, "Is it still your watch?"

"I was just going to wake Will."

"Where will you be sleeping?"

"Under the Corles' wagon."

"Is it dry?"

"Dry enough."

He started to back out once again, and once again she stopped him. "Do you think the wheel will be done tomorrow?"

"I don't know, Danni. I think so. Why don't you try and get some sleep?"

"Maybe we should have gone on to Ellsworth and had it fixed there."

"They would have charged us even more money in Ellsworth. Please go to sleep now. I'm sorry I disturbed you."

He backed hastily out and pulled the flap closed as he went, in case she tried to follow him. Part of him had been afraid she was going to invite him to sleep in the tent with her. He was afraid because he would have accepted.

Austin had thought about it many times in the last few days, but he had no plausible explanation for why he slept so soundly beside Danni Coopersand. In view of her personality, he would have expected just the opposite to be true. But after only minutes of lying beside her and watching her sleep, he himself would fall into deep, restful slumber, something he hadn't known regularly since before the war. It was wonderful when it happened, but thinking about it later and attempting to determine a reason had been worrisome for him.

He supposed it was because she made him feel so tired. All her demands on him. None of them verbal, of course, but they were demands just the same. Every time she gazed at him with her adoring gray eyes he felt he had to be more of a man than he was. He felt he had to be stronger, harder, and better just to measure up to the ideal she had created. It made him uncomfortable, but it also made him try. And it was the trying that annoyed him, since he knew he didn't have to be any of those things for her. He didn't have to be anything but who and what he was.

The fact was, she was making him crazy. The last time a woman had made him so crazy was when he was twenty-five and in love with the girl from the general store in town. She looked like Danni Coopersand, with the same blonde hair, but her eyes had been a bright blue, and her smile had been less open and honest, more secretive than Danni's. She had taken Austin's heart and crushed it between her long piano-playing fingers one summer. He had done everything a male could do to prove undying love for a female, and she had thrown him over for a soldier.

For a long time Austin swore he would never be a soldier, but the time had eventually come when he was forced to enlist. Having raised horses all his life, he was a cavalryman from the start, and from the start, the cavalry had little to do in the war but act as messengers between generals and ride pickets. When Phil Sheridan convinced the army that the cavalry could fight, they fought almost daily from that time on, and Austin had been in the thick of it. He thought of the blonde from the general store from time to time, but only to steel himself against the camp whores and remind himself of the fickle ways of women.

On occasion he had given in and relieved the pressure and loneliness with a luckless follower of the camps, and he had been blessed in escaping disease, a fate which most of the men succumbed to at some point. After the war he met numerous females, but none could bear to look at him in his gaunt, emaciated condition. It was only when his cousin's wife arrived at their stage station and began to throw herself at him that Austin realized he must look like a whole, healthy man again. There were better-looking men. There were men who were taller and broader and who had good cause to like what they saw in the mirror, so Austin wasn't fooled by the attentions of his cousin's wife. Like most women thus far in his life, she had been nothing but a source of annoyance to him, as she obviously was to her husband.

Austin was equally annoyed with Danni, yet another man's wife, but in some part of his mind he was also strangely fascinated by her. All heroic implications aside, no one had ever looked at him quite the way she did.

He wondered if the reason he found her fascinating was because she found him fascinating.

His father would have thought so. Galen Bourke was fond of saying it took two to spark. Which only caused Austin to wonder if that was what he was doing. His version of sparking.

And what about her? he wondered. Was that what she was doing?

No, he quickly told himself. Danni treated everyone with the same kindness she showed Jack, her husband.

Austin dragged himself over to the Corles' wagon to wake

Will. He knew he wasn't being completely truthful with himself about certain aspects of his relationship with Danni Coopersand, but it wasn't something he wanted to spend the night thinking about. He was tired and he wanted to get some sleep. At some point tomorrow the wheel would be repaired and they could move out. Once they were on the trail he would be able to maintain some distance from her and give himself more time to examine his feelings. He wasn't used to thinking so much about a woman.

Will smacked his lips and rolled out of his blanket when Austin nudged him. He sat up, pulled on his boots, and stood without saying a word.

Austin guessed he was still sore about the dressing down he had received over Susannah Blaine. Austin had warned him he would be put on report if he persisted in his attentions to the young girl. Will had laughed at him and asked how Austin was going to put him on report since he was no longer in the army. After their arrival at Fort Harker, Austin had gone to see the commander.

Now Will was sulking and angry. His record wasn't in great shape to begin with, and to have a black mark like this—he couldn't forgive Austin.

"I understand," Austin had said, "but I always mean what I say, Will. Don't test me again."

Will had said nothing to him then and he said nothing to him now as he walked away to begin his watch. Austin shook out his blankets and took off his boots to settle down on the ground. The business with Susannah and her father was difficult and unpleasant, and if Eve's allegations were indeed true, as Austin suspected they were, then the rest of the trip was going to be strained and uncomfortable for everyone.

Ormond Blaine would be the camp pariah, with none of the other men speaking to or even looking at him. Austin knew how it worked. He knew what the whole could do to the few, and the few to the one. Prisoners at Salisbury who had given in to lust and taken advantage of younger and weaker men in the camp had been captured, judged, and hanged within the walls of the prison—by other prisoners. Even in a world without justice, there was justice.

Austin squeezed his eyes shut as familiar images came abruptly back to haunt him. He hadn't meant to think of it. It had come to him only in comparison, but here he was thinking of it again. The pitifully thin faces and skeletal forms of the men in his area who lay helpless and dying in the greasy, crusted tents. The flies. The filth.

Oh, God, he silently begged. I don't want to remember anymore.

But he did, and his fingers clawed at his eyes to take away the horrible pictures there. The agonizing memory of death, death, death all around. Death over a tiny, puny lemon sent in by some kind soul on the outside. Death over a stolen blanket or a pair of boots. Sickness and disease everywhere; vomit flowing in greasy pools on the top of the filthy stream. Clumps of hair coming out with each pass of the comb. Skin turning yellow, falling away from the bone like drapes from a curtain rod . . .

Austin sat up and hit his head hard on the wooden bottom of the Corles' wagon. The sudden pain made him gasp and then curse. He turned over on his side and saw a spreading pool of water coming in his direction. The rain was driving down at an angle now, hard and steady. Austin pulled on his boots and picked up his blanket.

He ignored the smirk on Will's face as he walked to the makeshift tent in the center of camp and opened the flap. Danni sat up again, but he shushed her with a finger.

"It's wet under the wagon," he said in a whisper, and Danni nodded. She moved closer to the sleeping Eve and patted the ground beside her in invitation for Austin to put his blanket down. He hesitated only a moment before tossing down his blanket and sitting down to take off his boots. He felt Danni briefly lay a hand on his back.

"I thought it might be wet out there. It's raining much harder now."

"You couldn't sleep?" he asked as he settled down beneath his blanket.

"No," she said. "But I will now."

Why? he wanted to ask her. Why now? Did she sleep better when he was beside her?

He said nothing. Not once did any of the horrible pictures in his mind return. He thought only of how warm the hand on his back had been and how soft her voice was. He closed his eyes in the dimness and listened to the sound of her breathing. Eve's was slow and rhythmic; Danni's was more uneven. He turned on his side to face her.

"Still worried about Kiowa?"

"Yes," she whispered. "I can't stop thinking about him. How will I know if something has happened to him?"

"You won't."

Danni made a low noise of frustration and on impulse Austin reached over to pat her arm. His palm landed on something much softer, and he realized with a start he had just touched her breast. Before he could open his mouth and start apologizing, she took his hand between the two of hers and held it as she turned to face him.

"Try to sleep," she whispered, and patted the back of his hand with her fingers before she released him.

After minutes of staring into the darkness and trying to make out her face, Austin closed his eyes.

When he awakened five hours later he felt a heaviness on his chest and opened his eyes to find Danni sprawled across him, sleeping soundly. Eve sat up, yawned, and looked at Austin with amusement.

"Good morning."

"Morning," Austin said, and the sound of his voice awakened Danni. She lifted her head, looked at him, and then rolled hastily away. "I'm sorry," she said, her voice still thick with sleep.

"You shouldn't be," Eve said with a wink. "The two of you looked very comfortable."

Danni's cheeks grew red and she looked fiercely at Eve. Austin cleared his throat and reached for his boots.

When he stepped outside the tent he saw the sky was still overcast and gloomy, although the rain had stopped. His eyes roved over the camp, looking for any changes, any sign that Kiowa may have slipped in during the night. There was nothing unusual or out of place. He saw Quint Corle dozing while leaning against his father's wagon. The last watch had been Quint's, and Austin shook his head to think of the stings and harassment an army man would receive for falling asleep on the watch. In wartime a man had actually been executed for the offense.

He walked over and lightly shook Quint by the shoulder. The man's eyes opened wide and he brought his rifle to his chest. Austin knocked his hand away before he could pull the trigger.

"Sleeping on watch near a fort is understandable," Austin told him. "You figure the post is keeping a watch, so why should we. But even forts get attacked, Corle. Don't let it happen again."

Corle grunted something and walked away. Austin watched him crawl inside his wagon before turning to wake up Will Drake.

By mid-morning the rotted spokes and felloes of Danni's wheel had been replaced and the iron outer rim repaired. The wagons were ready to move again. Austin took the lead and rode west, toward Ellsworth. If all went well, they would camp on the other side of the town that night. Austin hoped the skies would clear and the rain would stop. If it didn't, they were in for trouble.

Chapter Eighteen

The farther they moved from the last place Danni had seen Kiowa, the more worried she became. Revenge and rejection aside, he wouldn't leave her and Jack without a word of farewell. With each hour that passed, she became more and more certain something had happened to him. He had been sick and feverish and exposed to the rain, conditions favoring pneumonia. When she closed her eyes she could see him lying in the mud somewhere, fighting for breath.

She shook her head and attempted to shove the morbid thoughts away, but they persisted. For the first time, she was forced to think of a life without him, and she came to realize just how much she had been depending on his help in her vision of the future. Jack would be little use to her on the claim. He could do a bit at a time, but his attention span was never long enough to complete any one task. It would be up to Danni to take care of the building and digging and hoeing and planting. Not to mention the cooking, laundry, mending, and other daily chores. She was going to be one busy woman.

There would be neighbors, Austin had said of the place he had in mind to show her. Perhaps they would help her build her house. Danni had heard of such things before, where the community pitched in and helped build a house in little more than a day. By herself it might take months to put together a suitable place to live, providing she could figure out exactly how to do it. She had a rough idea, and she studied the construction of every home they had passed thus far on the trail. She knew how to mortise and tenon, and she had several tools in her wagon, like an adze, a broadaxe, a maul, and a froe used to split shingles, if they were lucky enough to find timber. She even had an old sod plow, in case there was no timber and she was forced to live in a "soddy." She had tried to think of everything.

Not once had she considered the possibility of Kiowa leaving her and having to do it on her own.

Though she should not have been surprised. He was a healthy young man. She could not expect him to stay around and take care of her and Jack. He had a life of his own to lead, and Danni had no right to keep him tied to them out of any gratitude he might feel toward her. He had done more than enough for them in the short time they had known him. He had been kind and dutiful and more conscientious than any male she had ever known.

A tiny smile tugged at her lips when she thought of the plans she had made for him, including her intentions for Kiowa to impregnate her someday, so she could have children.

What a foolish notion. She didn't know what she had been thinking. The loneliness must have overwhelmed her at the time.

"I hope you're still alive," she breathed aloud. "I don't care about anything else, Kiowa. I swear I don't. I can do it all by myself if I have to. I will do it all by myself. Just be alive."

Eve rode up on the Indian pony then and smiled at Danni as she reined in the animal to walk alongside the wagon. "Were you singing?" she asked.

"No," said Danni. "I was talking to myself. People say you tend to do that on the prairie. I was practicing."

Eve laughed. "I've been practicing myself." Then she grew serious and said, "I've also been thinking. It's beginning to look like we could be friends, Danni."

Danni smiled at her. "I've always thought so."

"I'm glad," said Eve. Then she drew a breath and asked, "Do you have much food?"

"I have enough," Danni told her.

"I notice you feed Mr. Bourke quite regularly."

"He likes my cooking."

"And maybe your company?"

Danni looked at her. "What are you implying?"

"Not a thing," said Eve. "He could eat with any one of us. We're all supposed to provide food for him and Mr. Drake. But so far it's been mostly you doing the providing. The reason I'm asking is because I have no provisions of my own."

Danni looked kindly at her. "Eve, you're welcome to anything I have. Are you hungry now?"

"Bourke says we're going to stop soon. I can wait." She paused then. "I'll work it off, Danni."

"You will?" Danni said with a grin. "You mean you'll wash dishes?"

"No," Eve said quietly. "I mean I'll work it off. I'll stay and help you on your claim . . . that is if you want me."

Danni stared at her. "I thought you wanted to get away. I thought—"

"I still intend to go to California some day," Eve told her. "Just not right away."

"I see." Danni switched the reins to her left hand and wiped her right hand on her skirt. "You must have been reading my mind. I was just wondering what I was going to do without Kiowa."

Eve sighed and rubbed at her eyes. "If not for me he'd still be with you. I'd like to try and take his place, if you'll have me."

"Have you ever farmed before? It's a hard life, Eve."

The black-haired woman looked at her. "I'm trying to tell you I have no choice, Danni. I have nowhere else to go. I have no money, no clothes, and no food. I'm throwing myself on your mercy."

Danni reached out with her hand and touched Eve on the shoulder as she rode alongside her. "I have an extra dress or two that should fit. In the meantime, we'll ask the Corles if you can sleep in the wagon Jack slept in. They shouldn't mind."

Eve smiled gratefully at her. "Thank you, Danni. I won't be a burden forever."

"You won't be a burden at all," Danni told her, and as she watched the other woman ride away again her mood began to lighten. She wouldn't be alone after all. Eve was going to be there to help her.

They stopped for lunch in Ellsworth, and the last of Danni's blues evaporated as she walked arm in arm through the town with Eve. Though they had no money to spend, they looked in the storefronts anyway, and by the time they finished window shopping, Austin was snappish and impatiently awaiting their return so they could move on. Danni and Eve laughed and hurried to the wagon as he rode by and scowled at them.

"It's going to rain again," said Danni after he had ridden past. "That has him worried."

Eve looked at the sky and frowned. "Kora hates the rain. She gets crazy when it stays dark and dismal like this."

Danni glanced at the Mormon's wagons. "Does their herd look smaller to you?"

"Yes," said Eve. "Will Drake used to ride around the cattle and keep them together. He doesn't do that anymore. They're drifting away, one or two at a time."

"Could be Indians," Danni offered.

"Could be," Eve said uncomfortably.

Danni noticed and apologized. "I shouldn't have mentioned it—them."

"No, it's all right. The Indians who hurt me are dead now."

Will Drake rode by and shouted for everyone to get moving, and Danni held up her reins and called to her oxen. Eve clucked to her pony and rode ahead, her hair in a black braid flopping behind her.

"She sure is pretty," said a voice behind Danni, and she turned her head to see Jack sitting up behind her. He was smiling appreciatively after Eve.

"Yes, Eve is very pretty."

"The two of you look like something together, one of you fair, the other dark. Really something."

Danni smiled. "Are you hungry, Jack?"

"No. Mr. Bourke fed me while you women were in town. Some Indians came to the wagons and asked for food while you were gone. Mr. Bourke gave them what was on his plate, but he explained he couldn't give them any more. They didn't seem to understand, so I gave them what was on my plate. They were still hungry afterward. It's very sad, Danni."

"Was it a family?" Danni asked.

"Oh yes. A large one, with several hungry babies and an old man and woman to boot. They asked Mrs. Blaine for some food, and she threatened to shoot them if they came near her. Mr. Bourke grew angry with her and told her to go inside her wagon. He knew they weren't dangerous. They were hungry."

"What sort of Indians were they, Jack?"

"Does it matter?" he answered. "I don't know and I didn't care. It makes me sick to my heart to see what these people have been reduced to because of us. Do we really need so much, Danni? Do we have to take so much?"

Danni looked at her hands. "We're just living, Jack. Trying to get along and hoping for the best. We're not criminals."

"Aren't we?" he said, his voice low. "I tend to believe we are, Danni. We're not only stealing their land, we're stealing their method of living. That makes us the worst kind of criminals. We're committing crimes against nature."

"Maybe," said Danni, still not looking at him. "But if we are, then it must be in our nature to do it. It's not something I'm proud of, Jack. I don't like to hear stories of hungry babies. But where are we to go? What are we to do? We had no choice but to come out here."

"You had a choice," Jack argued. "You could have put me in the hospital like the doctors said and gone it on your own. You could have found a life in Mattoon and done just fine for yourself, Danni. Don't try to tell me otherwise, because I know better. It's me that brought us out here. I'm the reason those poor damned Indians are starving to death. It's me."

Danni heard the anguish in his voice and turned to soothe him. "Jack, please don't. You've been so good these last few days. Please don't upset yourself."

"I can't help it," he sobbed. "Oh, God, I just can't help it. Don't you see, Danni? Don't you see how it's all my fault? I'm the white man, Danni. Me."

Danni had no choice but to move as far over on the road as she could and stop the wagon. As the other wagons passed her she climbed in the back and put her arms around her sobbing husband. "Hush, now," she said. "Hush. It's not your fault the Indians are starving, Jack. It could never be just one man's fault. We'll do everything we can to help them, I promise. We'll share whatever we have."

"Danni?" a voice called from outside.

"In here," she said, and after a moment Austin climbed into the seat of the wagon. "What's wrong?"

"It's Jack. He's upset about the Indians who came to the wagon today."

Austin looked at Jack and a flash of understanding passed over his unshaven face. He left the seat to lead his horse around to the back and tie it on, then he came back and climbed up again. He flicked the backs of the oxen with a switch Danni kept and they ambled forward. Danni held Jack for the next hour and spoke soothingly to him until he fell asleep. When he was breathing deeply she eased him on to his pillow and dragged her numb limbs away. She made her way to the seat again and sat down beside Austin.

"It's all right now. He's asleep. I can drive again."

Austin made no move to relinquish the reins. "What did he say?"

Danni shrugged and told him the gist of Jack's comments. "He feels personally responsible for the Indian's plight."

"All of us do," said Austin. "And all of us are." He looked at her then. "It's going to get worse. More of them will starve. More will die of disease. And we'll all be responsible."

"Because we're white?" Danni asked.

"Because we're here."

"Would you rather we weren't? Would you rather all of us

stayed put in the eastern half of the country? Or maybe you'd rather our forefathers had never even come to America?"

Austin shrugged. "There's no blame to be placed, Danni. There's only what is."

She exhaled through her nose. "You sound like Kiowa."

His eyes flickered and she could tell she had made him think of the youth. She clasped her hands together and sat forward. "Eve has decided to stay with Jack and me on whatever claim we stake. She's going to help me."

"You'll need help."

Danni looked at him. "What about you? What are you going to do after you reach Fort Wallace and collect the rest of your money?"

"I haven't thought about it."

"Will you go back to the coach business?"

"No."

"What did your father do?" she asked, curious.

"He owned a horse farm."

"In Michigan?"

"People in Michigan ride horses, too."

Danni smiled. "Of course. What became of the farm?"

"The bank foreclosed on it when my parents died."

"And you were in the army. Have you ever returned?"

"No," he said.

"Now I know why you went into the cavalry. You were born into it. You'd probably make a very good ranch hand."

"I'd make an even better ranch owner."

Danni smiled again. "Yes, I think you would."

A plop of rain hit her square in the forehead then and Danni looked up at the sky with dismay. Austin cursed and handed her the reins. "Try to keep up, Danni. We won't stop for a while yet. I want to cover as much ground as possible."

She nodded and watched him jump down from the moving wagon. He untied his horse while the wagon was still rolling and swung himself up into the saddle. The rain had him more than worried, Danni saw. As she watched him hurry ahead it made her wonder if he knew something the rest of them didn't.

Chapter Nineteen

When the wagons finally stopped for the day it was near the end of the tracks being laid by men who worked for the railroad. There were makeshift tents pitched all around, and the smell of hot coffee and burned beans filled the air. Eve climbed tiredly off her pony and looked for somewhere to relieve herself. A dozen men watched her, and she turned abruptly away from their eyes and climbed inside Danni's empty wagon to use Jack's pot. When she came out she saw Danni busily making some coffee of her own. Eve went to offer her help, and together they prepared a meal including some prairie turnips Eve had found that day.

As they ate, the eyes of the railroad men were on them. Eve looked at Danni to see if she noticed, but Danni was all smiles. Nor did Bourke appear to notice the bold gazes of the railroad men. No longer hungry, Eve got up to wash her plate. Kora Blaine approached her from behind and in a barely concealed voice said, "You could make some extra money here tonight, Eve. Even with your face the way it is you're still attractive, and these men obviously haven't been around women in months. Does it seem like old times to you?"

Eve turned and looked at her. "Don't worry about me, Kora. Worry about your daughter."

Kora's lips thinned. "My daughter is just fine, apart from being injured by your lies."

Eve stood still. "You know I wasn't lying. If you care about Susannah, you'll get her away from him as soon as you can."

"Care?" Kora repeated in a heated whisper. "Susannah can take care of herself. She's no longer a child."

"Susannah may want to stop him and not know how," Eve insisted. "She needs your help."

The red-haired woman stiffened. "I don't know why you persist in this delusion. I haven't the faintest idea what you're talking about. All I know is you're cheap and tawdry and we're glad to be rid of you. You've been nothing but trouble since the day we found you. I'll thank you to come and get your things from my wagon. I no longer want any part of your presence near me."

"Your husband said all my things now belong to Susannah," Eve told her.

"He was talking about the wagon," Kora informed her. "You may have the clothes he purchased for you. We certainly don't want them. Nothing of yours would fit Susannah anyway."

And the colors are all wrong for her, Eve thought. She had told Austin Bourke she didn't want anything from them, but a few items would be nice to have.

"Fine," she said. "I'll come for them later."

"Come now, unless you want the bundle tossed out on the road."

Eve sucked in her cheeks and followed the other woman to her wagon. Ormond Blaine was sitting on a stool and he sat up straighter as she approached. His eyes were cold as he surveyed Eve, and as she caught the bundle of clothing Susannah shoved at her from the back of the wagon, he said, "The Church did not excommunicate me, Eve, and I won't have you repeating such slander. I want to get that much straight with you before we part ways."

Eve turned her back on him and would have walked away, but he rose from his stool and gripped her arm. "I want you to say you understand, Eve."

She looked him in the face. "What am I to understand? The Mormons asked that you no longer affiliate yourself with them, and that you cease attending any function related to the Church. I was there when they said it, Ormond. I heard every word."

"What you heard was a difference of opinion on Church policy, nothing more. I am now and will continue to be a member of the Church in good standing. They have financed my venture to the west and entrusted me to—"

"They entrusted you with money to help the poorer members of the Church in St. Louis, not to fund your own way out west. That's why they threw you out, because they found out you bought all these cattle and those mules. Rather than give the money back, you left town."

Ormond's face began to turn color. His grip on her arm tightened. "You don't know what you're saying. When I reach Salt Lake I'm going to serve Brigham Young himself. I'm going to be one of the higher ranking members of the Church. I'm going to be a leader of men and—"

"A fiendish plague on children," Eve finished for him. "Your own daughter in particular."

Ormond brought his hand up and struck her hard across the face. Eve cried out and fell away from him, her hands protecting her already bruised countenance. He lurched after her and would have struck her again if Jack Coopersand had not stepped forward with a revolver in his hand.

"Back away from that woman, Sergeant," Jack said in a menacing voice.

Ormond froze, his hand in mid air.

"I said back away, Sergeant!"

"I'm not a sergeant," Ormond told him, his voice high and thin. "I'm a Mormon."

"You're a liar, is what you are. Now back away from her before I shoot you and drag you away."

"I'm backing." Ormond took small steps away from Eve, his eyes round as he looked at Jack.

Eve let her hands fall. She stepped forward. "It's all right now, Jack. He didn't hurt me. I'm fine. You can put the gun away."

"I can't," said Jack in a hoarse voice. "I'm going to have to shoot him. You don't know what he's done to others. There was a woman on a farm last month—he did awful things to her. Awful."

"My God," breathed Ormond. "He thinks I'm someone else. Help me, Kora. Go get Mr. Bourke!"

"Here," said Bourke, and Eve saw him approach, with Danni close behind. "Corporal Coopersand, put down your weapon. That's an order."

"Captain, I can't."

"That's Lieutenant, Corporal Coopersand, and I gave you an order. Put the weapon down *now*."

Jack hesitated another moment, but the command in Bourke's voice was hard to ignore. Slowly, he lowered the weapon. Bourke held out his hand for it, and Jack gave it to him. "I'm sorry, Lieutenant. Somebody has to do it."

"I understand," Bourke said to him.

Ormond Blaine was perspiring heavily. His face was red with anger as he turned on Bourke. "That man could have killed me. He thought I was someone else, and he was actually going to kill me. What are you going to do about it?"

Bourke was unperturbed. "What do you suggest I do about it?"

"*Restrain* him. For God's sake, he nearly shot an innocent man."

Bourke looked at the handprint on Eve's face. "Are you sure about that?"

"Am I—" Ormond blustered and muttered and finally turned away to climb heavily into his wagon. Kora immediately followed him. Will Drake, standing nearby, was laughing so hard there were tears rolling down his cheeks. Danni went to Eve and helped her with the bundle of clothes in her arms.

Bourke took Jack by the arm and led him away from the Blaines' wagons.

They were met by a man from the railroad camp, who took off his hat and nodded to Eve and Danni before speaking to Jack and Bourke.

"The name's Jerry Chaswell," he said as he extended a hand. Bourke shook it briefly and gave his own name.

"Can't believe you made it this far with your cattle, Mr. Bourke. Our own beef shipments have been stolen three times runnin', and we're gettin' awful tired of eatin' beans and hard-tack. Think you could spare a steer or two?"

"I could if they were mine," Austin told him. "They belong to Mr. Blaine. You'll have to deal with him." He turned and pointed. "That's his wagon."

"Much obliged," said Jerry Chaswell. Then he paused. "Where you folks headed?"

"Fort Wallace."

"Homesteaders?"

"Some."

"There's a rumor goin' around about a cholera epidemic out that way."

Eve and Danni both looked up.

"Cholera?" said Danni.

"Yes, ma'am. A terrible sickness, cholera. I'd want to stay away from it."

"Yes," Eve agreed, thinking of her father.

"They say it's killed more than two dozen already."

The women looked at each other, and Jerry Chaswell excused himself and walked away. When he was gone, Danni turned to Bourke. "He said rumor, didn't he?"

Bourke nodded. "We'll find out for certain when we reach Fort Hays."

He guided Jack to the wagon and stayed with him while Danni and Eve cleaned up the supper dishes and put on more coffee. Danni rummaged around in her food supplies until Eve finally asked her what she was doing. Danni pulled out four jars of preserves and smiled at Eve over her shoulder as she walked toward the men in the railroad camp. Eve opened her mouth to tell her not to go, but a circle of men had already closed around the smiling Danni.

When Bourke left the wagon, Eve saw him looking around. She pointed and said, "Danni went that way with her arms full of preserves."

Bourke stood stock still and stared into the railroad camp. "How long has she been gone?"

"Only a few minutes." Eve watched him and smiled to herself. He was obviously smitten with Danni. She wondered if he realized it yet.

Her smile slowly died as she thought of the tangled triangle the three of them made. Jack, Danni, and Austin Bourke.

When another few minutes passed and Danni had yet to return, Bourke left the camp and went in search of her. He came back with one hand on her arm, his face stern. Danni smiled sheepishly at Eve and looked slightly embarrassed.

"What happened?" Eve asked, when Bourke had walked away.

"Nothing. The men were delighted to receive my preserves, and I was telling them about our journey thus far when Austin came and led me off like some naughty child away from home for the first time."

"He was worried about you. So was I. These men haven't been around a woman in a long time."

"I know. That's why I thought they would enjoy the preserves. They thanked me very graciously and behaved like perfect gentlemen . . . most of them, anyway." Her face brightened then. "They said George Custer and his wife Libby are at Fort Hays right now. Wouldn't it be something if we could meet them?"

"Custer?"

"One of the heroes of the war. Surely you've heard of George Custer?"

Eve glanced at her. "I'm not convinced there were any heroes in that war."

Danni smiled. "Not even Mr. Lincoln?"

"Heroes appeal to you, do they?"

"When the heroism is selfless, yes."

"Custer hardly falls into that category."

"Perhaps not. But his wife surely must."

Eve exhaled. "You'll have to forgive my lack of enthusiasm, Danni. I haven't known many heroes in my time."

"Just a seventeen-year-old boy called Kiowa, who risked his life to save yours," Danni responded.

Eve's face colored and she lowered her head, unable to speak. Danni was right. Kiowa had shown true heroism when he came for her that night. And she had repaid him with treachery.

Danni left her alone with her thoughts to speak to the Corles about Eve sleeping in one of their wagons. Eve sat where she was until Danni returned and told her the Corles had agreed. Without further conversation she picked up her skirts and went to Quint Corle's empty wagon. The interior was piled high with bundles and trunks and pieces of furniture. Eve made herself a bed on the same thin feather mattress Jack had used and settled down. Her cheek was tender where Ormond Blaine had struck her, and her head throbbed with a painful headache.

She lay sleepless for several hours, her mind whirling with thoughts of every kind, until Quint Corle poked his head in the back of the wagon and looked at her. Eve sucked in her breath and sat up. "What is it?"

He smiled. "Not a thing. I'm on second watch tonight. I thought I'd see if you were awake."

"I'm awake, but I prefer my own company, thank you."

"It's my wagon," said Quint. "You could be a little nicer."

"If forced conversation with you is a condition of my sleeping in your wagon, then I'll sleep elsewhere." She got up and reached for her blanket.

"Now, hold on a minute," said Quint. "I didn't say anything about any conditions. I just thought you might like to talk is all."

"I've said that I don't care to."

"I heard you."

"Well?" she asked. "Are you going to leave, or shall I?"

He grinned at her. "You must've made one mean old whore."

Before Eve could respond, he was gone. She went to tear open the flap, but she saw him nowhere near. He had vanished. She sank back against the side of the wagon and stared out at the camp, the anger simmering in her. At times she wanted to pick up a gun and start shooting at every male in sight. She wanted to make them pay for the awful things they said and the horrible abuse they heaped not just on her, but on women everywhere.

Then she would see men like Austin Bourke. Or Kiowa. Good and decent men, who treated women with courtesy and respect. She gazed at Bourke's sleeping form near the camp fire and saw him turn restlessly in his sleep. Will Drake was beside him, sleeping like a stone. Bourke tossed once again, and Eve heard him call out something in his sleep, his voice raw and not at all like his normal speaking voice. She frowned and looked around to see if Quint Corle was anywhere near, but she saw no sign of him. Bourke's nightmare continued, and just as Eve was considering getting out of the wagon and moving to shake him out of it, she saw Danni, dressed in a long nightgown, climb out of the back of her own wagon.

Danni walked over and stood above him for several moments before leaning down beside him and placing a gentle hand to his temple. Bourke came awake with a start and sat up to grab her by the throat. Danni fell back in fright and Eve prepared to jump out of the wagon and help when she heard Bourke moan suddenly and tear his fingers away from her neck. He covered his face with his hands and turned away from Danni, who went to her knees and put a comforting hand on his arm. Bourke shuddered and shoved her away from him.

Eve saw Danni get to her feet and stand trembling above him before turning abruptly away. Danni walked stiffly back to the wagon and got inside without a backward glance. Bourke rolled out of his blanket and sat with his elbows on his knees, his head in his hands.

Slowly, Eve returned to her mattress on the floor of the wagon. It appeared demons pursued each of them in some way.

She had just closed her eyes and drifted off to sleep when a sudden cry from the railroad camp awakened her. She lifted her head and tried to make sense of what the man was shouting. Finally she understood. He was shouting one word over and over: *"Indians!"*

A *frisson* of panic temporarily immobilized her, but she forced herself out of the wagon. She saw Danni and ran to clutch her hand as they strained to see what was going on. Ormond Blaine came running up to them, his suspenders flapping around his hips. "My cattle!" he was shouting. "They're taking my cattle!"

Bourke came and shoved both women toward Danni's wagon and shouted for them to get inside. In the distance Eve could hear shouting and whooping and the bawling of cattle. Then she heard the sound of gunfire.

"Danni, get in." She pushed at Danni's back, and together they crawled inside the wagon, where Jack was sitting, round-eyed. He moved not a muscle; he simply stared.

They sat huddled in the wagon for what seemed like an hour, until the shouts and shots faded away and the night grew quiet once more. Danni moved to leave the wagon, and Eve went out after her. Jack was still in a catatonic state and didn't move.

Ormond Blaine was pounding on the side of his wagon in frustrated anger. Eve and Danni passed him and went on, looking around the camp to see what, if anything, had been disturbed. Everything appeared normal.

A thought struck Eve then, and she broke away from Danni to run to where the horses had been tethered.

Her Indian pony was gone.

A sound of anguish escaped her throat. None of the other horses had been taken. Why take only one pony?

"They didn't have time to get to the horses," Will Drake said behind her.

Eve turned. "They got mine."

"That pony? Hell, he was theirs to begin with."

"You can sit with me in the wagon," Danni told her as she joined them. "Or you can ride my horse."

"Thank you," said Eve. But she wasn't mollified. That pony

had been a symbol of her victory, her survival. And, in an odd way, it had made her feel somehow connected to Kiowa. As long as she had the pony, Kiowa was alive. Now she didn't know.

CHAPTER TWENTY

KIOWA SAT up for the first time in two days and looked around himself. He was in a lodge and there was an old woman with him. She nodded and chuckled when he saw her, and he could see she was pleased that he was strong enough to lift himself. He looked past her, to where rays of sunlight were streaming in around a flap of the lodge. If the flap were opened, the sun would flood the lodge with light from the east. His eyes studied the construction of the structure, never having been exposed to anything like it. There was a tripod frame, and many other sticks bound together at the top, all of them covered with stretched buffalo hides, sewn together with what appeared to be sinew. Kiowa had read of such structures, but he was awed to actually be inside one.

Toward the top there were flaps pulled open for ventilation of the smoke that drifted up from the small fire in the center of the lodge. Over the flap that served as a door were a row of roughly fashioned pins that held the hides together over the entrance. Kiowa was impressed.

The woman sitting in the lodge with him said something to him, then she picked up a bowl and handed it to him. Kiowa inhaled the broth and his stomach rumbled noisily. The old woman laughed and left the lodge.

Kiowa held the bowl to his mouth and drank. The liquid was warm as it traveled to his stomach, and he greedily drank every drop. When the bowl was empty he belched loudly and put it down beside him. He got unsteadily to his feet and walked to the flap of the lodge, intent on finding somewhere to relieve himself. The old woman opened the flap as he reached for it and immediately started scolding him. Kiowa backed away from her glare and wondered how to tell her what he needed.

Not knowing what else to do, he pointed to his genitals and then pointed to the door of the lodge.

The old woman frowned heavily at him.

Helplessly, Kiowa repeated his motions, this time squeezing his knees together for effect.

The old woman burst out laughing and came to take him by the arm. She carefully helped him out of the lodge and showed him where he could relieve himself. Then she primly turned her back and waited, like some spinsterish schoolmarm back in Virginia. When he finished, he returned to her and she took his arm once more.

Before they could reach the lodge again, the sounds of pounding hooves and shouting men reached Kiowa's ears. He held back when the woman urged him inside, and he pulled away from her to walk to the front of the lodge and look around himself. The encampment was a circle of sorts, with each lodge opening facing east. Women and children came out of lodges and left their work and play with smiles of happiness on their faces. Even before he saw them, Kiowa guessed the men were returning to camp.

With them came a small herd of cattle and an Indian pony that made Kiowa stare in recognition. He sucked in his breath and scanned the horses of the returning men to see if they had brought any captives with them. There was no one.

If the pony was Eve's, then the cattle had to belong to Ormond Blaine. That meant the wagons had been attacked.

His throat thickened as he stared at the pony. Was Eve dead? he wondered. Danni? Were any of them still alive?

The old woman yanked at his arm again and gestured for him to return inside the lodge. Kiowa took a last glance at the men, who were busy herding the cattle to the other side of the stream that ran through the camp. He recognized the older man who had found him, and at the same moment the man looked up and saw him. His black gaze was fierce as he studied Kiowa. Then the old woman pulled him into the lodge and Kiowa couldn't see him anymore.

Something in the face of the older man bothered Kiowa, and he lay on his side in the lodge for a long time before he realized what it was. It was his own resemblance to the man. They had the same broadness of cheek and sharpness of nose. The same full lower lip and squared chin. Kiowa did the arithmetic in his head and wondered if what he was thinking was possible. Could the old man have been a few hundred miles farther west in his youth?

It was possible, yes.

Could he have been among the young men who had taken Kiowa's mother?

He was the right age.

Kiowa inhaled deeply and forced his eyes shut. Stop, he told himself. You're looking for a reason to hate him because he brought back that Indian pony. He's not the man who fathered you.

The Cheyenne had shown him nothing but kindness thus far, treating his wounds and making him well again with their herbs and medicines. Kiowa knew it was because they considered him one of them, and because the scar at his throat made him out a survivor. He wondered what their reaction would be when he tried to leave.

Before he could examine the possibilities, the flap on the door was opened and the older Indian in question strode into the lodge. His eyes were critical as he looked Kiowa up and down. He lifted a hand and motioned for him to get up. Kiowa got up. The man came to stand before him, and they gazed into each other's eyes, both of them even in height.

The man grumbled something to the old woman, and she left the lodge. He moved around Kiowa then, and while behind him, the old man pulled down Kiowa's trousers and looked at the wound in Kiowa's buttock. Kiowa gritted his teeth and stood still. He was glad he had been allowed to keep his trousers. They had been washed and put back on him in his feverish state. He couldn't see himself in a breechclout or any of the other animal-hide garments worn by the Cheyenne.

He wondered if the man could tell the wound in his backside had been made by an arrow.

The Indian grunted in satisfaction and pulled up Kiowa's trousers. Then he came around and put a finger forward to scrape at the dark stubble on Kiowa's chin and cheeks.

From my mother's side, Kiowa silently told him.

The Indian leaned back again and stared speculatively at Kiowa. After a moment he spoke to him, patted him on the shoulder, and took him by the arm to lead him out of the lodge. They walked through the camp together, and Kiowa had to hurry to keep up. Already he was feeling weak and wanted to rest. They walked to a large lodge almost in the center of the camp and waited outside while the old man announced himself. After a moment the flap was opened and they were invited inside.

Kiowa started to the left but was yanked back and pointed to the right, where it was indicated he should sit to the left of a man already sitting on the ground. The man on the ground—evidently the chief—didn't look at Kiowa. He was busy filling his pipe.

Soon more men arrived and Kiowa sat motionless, his body aching, while they arranged themselves around the fire. Never did anyone walk between a man and the fire, but always behind. Kiowa's eyes were nearly closed when the chief lit his pipe and started smoking. The discussion soon began, and when someone placed a finger in Kiowa's chest, he lifted his head and came to attention. Everyone was looking at him with expressions of expectation, as if they were waiting for him to speak.

Kiowa decided to try and tell his story without words. He pointed to the scar at his throat, and then he held up three fingers. Next he walked the fingers along the ground, to signify three men. He looked up to see if everyone understood. His benefactor nodded at him to go on. This was not their language of sign, but some signs were universal.

Striking his fist hard against his other hand, Kiowa pointed to himself and then held up two fingers in an attempt to tell them that he had already killed two of the men responsible.

The faces watching his were open and understanding. He could see they comprehended what he was telling them.

Next he held up only one finger. Then he pointed to himself and to his scar again and mustered a look of determination that no one in the lodge could misunderstand.

There's one left, he was telling them. *And I want him.*

Then he waited to see what would happen.

Nothing happened. The men smoked some more, looked at each other and at Kiowa, and sat without speaking.

Finally the chief emptied his pipe. Without a word, the men began to leave the lodge. Kiowa looked at the older man and frowned. The older man cuffed him on the arm and led him outside. Kiowa had no idea what had just happened, or what the purpose of the discussion had been. He had a feeling he had failed to communicate his desires after all.

Once in the open air again he breathed deeply and felt the need for sleep nearly overwhelm him. His bones felt as if they would no longer support him as he trudged tiredly after the man who had brought him to the Indian camp. As soon as he reached the lodge and his bed, he fell forward with a deep sigh and went instantly into a sound sleep. The old Indian nodded to his wife and patted her on the arm before leaving the lodge again.

When Kiowa awakened once more it was dusk. He could hear activity in the Indian camp, and he opened his eyes to see he was alone in the lodge. Quietly he rolled off his bed and went to peer through the flap over the door. Several small fires were burning near the center of the camp, to one side of the chief's lodge. Kiowa saw what appeared to be most of the men gathered in loose groups around the fires.

Time to slip away, Kiowa thought as he watched them. The Indians were watching another man, one who stood and began to dance on his own around the fires. In his hand was a stick, which he waved through the air above his head as he danced. Kiowa stood and watched him, unable to force his gaze away from the sight of a half-naked grown man dancing by himself. He had never seen anything like it.

Slowly he emerged from the lodge and inched closer, curious to see the expression on the face of the dancer. He moved as close as he dared and narrowed his eyes to see the man's features. Anger was the best word to describe what he saw in the dancing Indian's painted face. Anger, and perhaps even hatred. Kiowa stared at the man's glistening brown skin and fierce moves and wondered if he was watching a war dance of some kind. Were they celebrating the attack on the wagons?

The Indian danced on, until he reached what seemed to be a frenzied peak of concentration. Then he rushed toward a drum placed near his movements and struck it heavily with the stick. A hush of anticipation followed this action. Men around the circle seemed to be holding their breath and waiting, and Kiowa found himself holding his own breath.

The man holding the stick began to shout, and his emotions were such that a vein stood out in the middle of his angry red forehead. In the next moment, he hurled the stick away from him.

Kiowa jumped with a start as the men around the circle scattered and ran. The stick landed only inches from Kiowa and he bent to pick it up. As he walked forward and held out the stick, the men in the camp erupted into sudden, raucous laughter and began pounding each other on the back. Kiowa frowned and then tried to smile at them. They pointed fingers and laughed even harder.

Finally his stern-faced benefactor stepped forward and gestured for him to throw away the stick. Kiowa threw it down. The men went on laughing, some of them jeering now and saying things in suggestive voices. Kiowa frowned again and lifted his hands to the man as if to say, *What did I do?* The old man only looked at him, his expression showing signs of exasperation. Soon a woman was led to Kiowa and placed in front of him. Her face was hidden by a curtain of black hair. She would not look up at him.

The older man stood beside Kiowa and began to shake his head. He lifted his arms and began to wave them, as if saying no to something that had been suggested. Angry faces stared back at him, and accusatory voices were lifted. Kiowa could see the man was trying to save him from some error that he had unwittingly committed. Kiowa didn't know what he had done, but he didn't like the implications. The woman standing in front of him obviously felt the same.

Suddenly the chief came forward. He lifted one hand, said one word, and immediately everyone fell silent. The chief stepped forward and touched the woman on the shoulder. He spoke low to her, then he turned to Kiowa and touched him on the shoulder. Next he looked at the man beside Kiowa and spoke sternly to him. Kiowa's stomach sank. He wasn't going to get out of whatever he had done. He wished he had crept away while he had the chance.

Abruptly the chief turned his back on them and went to his lodge. The rest of the crowd began to disperse. Kiowa looked at his benefactor and lifted his eyebrows. *What now?* The older man only shook his head. Kiowa started to follow him back to his lodge, but the man stopped him and pointed to the woman. Then he made a shooing motion with his hands.

Kiowa stared. *What?*

The man muttered something under his breath and disappeared inside his lodge. Kiowa stood dumbfounded, not knowing what was expected of him. Finally he felt the woman's gaze on him. He looked at her.

She was young. Her face was scarred as if by fire on her right cheek and temple; otherwise she was an attractive girl. Kiowa smiled tentatively at her and saw her eyes immediately fill with contempt. She turned her back on him and began to walk away. Kiowa watched her, still not knowing what to do. After a moment she paused and looked over her shoulder. Angrily, she gestured for him to follow her. Kiowa let out his breath and rolled his eyes. He wished he knew what was going on.

Inside her lodge she sat heavily on the ground by the fire and looked defiantly at him. Kiowa sat down across from her and looked longingly at the bed to his left. He was exhausted again and ready to sleep. His strength was coming back to him, but he needed rest.

The woman saw him gazing at the bed and her look turned cold. Kiowa sighed and shook his head. He held up his hands to say no.

Her expression turned suspicious. She spoke rapidly to him, and he stared at her in confusion. Her suspicion grew and seemed to change, and she said something further. Kiowa went on staring at her, trying to discern her meaning. Finally she looked at him and said, "You speak English?"

Kiowa blinked. His eyes rounded as he continued to stare at her. Slowly, he nodded.

"You are white after all," she said in perfect English. "Our chief knew this."

Kiowa nodded again.

"Can you speak?" she asked.

He did nothing, only looked at her.

"Making words will not harm you," she said impatiently.

Kiowa remained silent, and she frowned at him.

"Speak if you can. I won't tell the others."

Slowly he opened his mouth. "How do you know English?" he whispered.

"I was taken by whites when young. The Cheyenne traded a white girl to get me back. Now they wonder if they made a mistake."

Kiowa peered at her and asked the first question that came to him. "What happened to your face?"

The look she gave him was weary. "The whites burned everything with fire. They burned my mother and my brothers, and they burned me."

Her flat tone made him sorry he asked. "That dance," he said. "Why am I here with you?"

She lifted her chin. "The man who danced was my husband. Now he is not. He threw me away, like the stick. You picked up the stick. Now I belong to you."

"No," said Kiowa, shaking his head.

"Yes," she told him. "The chief said neither of us belong. He said I am your dog, to whip as you please."

Kiowa fell back to the ground and groaned. He should have left when he had the chance.

Chapter Twenty-One

When Austin led the wagons away from the railroad camp it was with a great sigh of relief. Railroad camps seemed to invite Indian attacks. Though what had happened the night before could hardly be considered an attack. The Indians had been more interested in cattle than in scalps. It made Austin wonder if much of the murder that had occurred thus far in Kansas had actually been committed by Indians or by men like the McCandlisses. There was no way of knowing. What had happened to Ingrid Corle was by no means an isolated incident, but Austin believed a good number of whites and bandits from Mexico had learned how to kill like Indians for the purpose of subterfuge. Many of the Indians he had seen were trying only to stay alive.

With Ormond Blaine's herd of cattle in their camp, there would be no hunger among the Cheyenne for some time to come. Austin hoped that meant there would be no reason to attack his wagons.

On the second day of June they left the railroad workers

behind and started toward Fort Hays. According to Danni, George Custer and his wife were at Fort Hays; Austin wasn't looking forward to meeting Custer again. He had dealt with him on several occasions during the war and found him a showy, ostentatious, unlikable man. While trying to thwart Jubal Early's Confederate infantry troops at Cedar Creek, Austin and several other men had been trapped on a narrow ridge with only a small amount of ammunition. Custer had ridden near them and seen the situation. Austin called to him to send help, but the man rode away without a word of acknowledgement, leaving Austin and the others to be captured and taken away when the troops withdrew that day.

The other men solaced themselves with the idea that Custer hadn't seen them. It only *appeared* he had seen them, they told each other. Austin knew the truth. Custer had seen them. But they served Wesley Merritt and were Merritt's responsibility, not Custer's. Custer had more important things to attend to—like being promoted to major general after the battle at Cedar Creek. Wesley Merritt was made a major general on the same day, a fact that had made Austin smile in his ragged tent at Salisbury when he heard it.

Seeing Custer again was something Austin wanted to avoid if he could. All rational explanations aside, he still harbored malice toward the man, and he thought he might possibly kill him if the opportunity presented itself.

Danni wouldn't understand, he told himself as he rode ahead of the wagons. All she knew was what she had read, and everything she read made George Custer out to be a model among men.

It made Austin sick to see her beam at the idea of meeting him.

If the arrogant sonofabitch laid one hand on her Austin would rip his arm off.

He stopped his horse and forced himself to fill his lungs with air. He couldn't think about Custer without seeing red. He drew in several long breaths and released them while he tried to think about something, anything, else. Will Drake rode up behind him and looked quizzically at his face.

"You eat something that didn't agree with you?" he asked.

Austin shook his head. "I'm fine."

A raindrop hit him in the forehead.

"Dammit," he said.

Will looked up at the sky. "Not again. The road's muck and mud as it is."

"There might not be a road if this doesn't stop."

"The Saline?"

Austin nodded. "It's even with the banks now."

The next day the river looked even more dangerous, and the day after that, when the rain drizzled from the sky all day, Austin for the first time began to wonder if they would make it to Fort Wallace. Raiders and Indians he could fight, but he was no match for nature. If the Saline decided to spill over its banks, there would be nothing he could do, short of running for the nearest high ground, and even that action didn't guarantee their safety.

Austin wanted to be as close as possible to Fort Hays before the river flooded. He didn't necessarily want to be *in* Fort Hays, since it was surrounded by a ravine, at the bottom of which ran a stream that was probably swollen on its own. But if they could get near the post, there would be a doctor available in case anyone was hurt, and there would be help in searching for anyone lost. Austin didn't want to think about such things, but he had experienced more than one flood and knew the devastation would be considerable. The water might take some livestock, and maybe a wagon, and possibly a life or two. He would do everything in his power to curtail their losses, but he was only one man.

The next few days he pushed everyone hard, getting in as many miles as possible and driving them long past dark. Danni hadn't spoken to him much since the night near the railroad camp, and Austin hadn't forced anything. He knew she was hurt by the way he had shoved her away from him. He didn't care. He had finally made up his mind about her and decided she had no business trying to look after him. She had no business touching him and trying to soothe him. Let her play nursemaid to everyone else if she wanted to, but she wasn't going to do it to him. He didn't need or want her to do anything but feed him on occasion. He wasn't one of the walking wounded, like her husband, and he didn't require her particular aid.

It helped, of course, that she wasn't speaking to him or looking at him anymore. He felt nothing from her when he rode beside her wagon or sat down to supper; no warmth, no smiles, no interest, concern, or sympathy. She was blank.

Austin told himself he preferred her that way. Her clear gray eyes no longer looked at him but at the road ahead. When she spoke in the evening it was in a low voice to Eve or Jack; it was never anything for everyone to hear. That was fine with Austin. In fact, his overall concentration had improved. He wasn't sleeping any better, but his worries about the Saline River and a possible flood were enough to keep even the soundest sleeper awake.

That evening he found the highest ground possible and called a halt. As the wagons were brought into a circle he noticed Jack was awake and looking more alert than usual. All through supper Jack was lively and talkative, which, oddly, brought a small frown between Danni's brows. She said nothing to her husband, merely watched him as he nattered on and on, talking about farming methods and politics and anything else that occurred to him, as if he were making up for all the time spent in his other, narcoleptic world.

Austin talked with him and was surprised when Jack remained awake while everyone else bedded down.

"You have first watch, don't you?" he asked Austin.

"Usually," Austin replied.

"Good. You don't mind if I stay with you, do you? I need to stretch my legs."

Austin lifted a shoulder. "You're welcome to walk along with me." He paused then. "Are you feeling well, Jack?"

"Yes," said Jack. "I'm feeling very well."

They walked together in silence for some time, and Austin

could feel Jack watching him. Finally he stopped beside the quiet string of horses and asked Jack what was on his mind.

"Duck," said Jack.

"What?" Austin stared at him. In the next moment he felt a pair of teeth nip sharply at his shoulder. He turned around and swung with his fist, but Butcher was already backing away, his black head bobbing as he went. Austin cursed loudly at the horse and turned back to Jack.

"I told you to duck," he said.

"What's on your mind, Jack?" Austin repeated between his teeth. He started walking again.

"Nothing. Why do you ask?"

"You're acting strangely."

"Am I? Maybe I'm acting normal for a change and you just don't realize it. Danni could tell you."

"So you're feeling like your old self again, is that it?"

"You could say that, yes. How far do you suppose we are from Fort Hays?"

"We should be there tomorrow."

"That close?"

"Yes. If the Saline floods I want to be near the post."

"How much farther is the land you want to show Danni?"

"From Fort Hays? Less than a hundred miles."

"If we pull out and stay there, do you still get your money?"

"I'd better," said Austin with a wry grin.

"What if someone drowns in a flood? Do you still get your money?"

Austin turned to look at him. "I'm going to do my best to see that no one drowns in a flood."

Jack smiled. "I believe you, Mr. Bourke. No wonder Danni is in love with you."

Austin nearly tripped. He forced himself to keep moving. "You're mistaken, Jack."

"I think not. The harder she tries to not show it, the more obvious it is to me. She's not looking at you anymore, that's proof." He sighed then, a long, drawn out sound. "She never really loved me, you know. She only married me because I asked." He held up his hands when Austin would have protested. "Yes, yes, I know she loves me. But it's not a romantic kind of love. It never has been. I knew that when I married her. I thought it might come later, after we had been married a while, but the war came and . . . anyway, the love she has for me is a love for kittens and babies and other helpless creatures. The way she loves you is different."

Austin was staring at him. "I wish I understood you, Jack. One moment you're sane as—"

"Could you love her?" he interrupted. "Could you love Danni?"

"No," said Austin bluntly.

Jack looked at him. "Honestly?"

"Yes."

"You're lying to me, Bourke."

"Jack, she's your wife."

"And to you she can't be anything else?"

"No."

"That's too bad," said Jack. "Eve says Danni will never leave me, and I'm inclined to agree with her. Danni's loyal to a fault."

Austin exhaled through his nose. "I should think that would make you happy, Jack. I know men who would kill to have someone like Danni for a wife."

"But not you," said Jack.

"I have nothing to offer a woman," Austin responded. "Any woman."

Jack chuckled and looked at the hands he clasped in front of him. "Maybe you have more to offer than you think you do." He glanced around himself then. "You can't blame me for trying. I have to do what I can when I can."

No, Austin couldn't blame him. He looked at Jack and said, "If Danni did want to be with someone else, what would happen to you?"

Jack's gaze lifted. "I'd go to a hospital, where most folks think I belong."

"Do you want to go to a hospital, Jack?"

"They might be able to help me."

Austin didn't think so. On bad days Jack would be left sitting in a wheelchair in a corner; on good days he would be allowed to sweep the hospital corridors and spoonfeed meals to the other patients.

"You don't belong in a hospital, Jack. You belong with your wife on your claim."

Jack's eyes reddened suddenly. "Damn you, you're not listening to me. I need you to listen to me now, Bourke, while I'm making sense. She doesn't love me, she—"

"Jack?" a voice called, and Austin turned to see Danni walking toward them. She wore a shawl over her nightgown. Her face was worried.

"Here," he said, and he abruptly turned and walked away from Austin. "I was talking with Mr. Bourke."

Danni looked at Austin. He met her glance and they looked at each other for the first time in days. He searched her eyes for some hint of what Jack was talking about, but he saw nothing warm or soft in her gaze. What he saw was dread.

She turned to Jack. "I hope you're not trying to pawn me off on Mr. Bourke again. He has enough of a burden right now, Jack. We don't need to add to his troubles."

Jack mumbled something to her and she took his arm and led him away without a backward glance.

Austin sighed as he watched them go. He wished he had never taken this job.

Chapter Twenty-Two

DANNI LOOKED at the water all around them with mounting trepidation. Overnight the camp had become flooded and was now standing in several inches of water. The horses whinnied and neighed repeatedly, and the oxen bellowed in alarm. Austin had left the camp and ridden ahead to see about the road. They were on high ground now; there was no telling how deep the water was in the lower lying areas.

When Austin returned, his expression was grave. He sat on his horse and told them the water was six to eight inches deep in places on the road. The animals could make it now, but if the water continued to rise, all might be lost.

"How far are we from Fort Hays?" asked Kora Blaine.

"Half a day, maybe less," said Austin. "But the rain doesn't show any signs of letting up."

"Are you saying we should stay put and hope for the best, or turn back?" asked Eve.

"I'm saying the choice is yours."

"You're the guide," Quint Corle said gruffly. "What do you think?"

"I think we could make it to Fort Hays if we pushed hard."

"Fort Hays will be just as flooded," observed Arthur Corle.

Austin agreed. "It will. But we'll be that much closer to help if we need it." He glanced at the sky then. "Make the decision now. If we're going, we need to get started."

"We certainly have nothing to lose," sneered Ormond Blaine.

Danni knew he was referring to his stolen cattle. She looked at the faces of the others and saw their uncertainty. She cleared her throat and said, "I say we go on to Fort Hays. Either way we're going to get wet, but we'll be closer to our destination."

Kora looked at Will Drake. "What do you think, Mr. Drake? You've ridden this trail before."

Will lifted both brows. "Never in a flood, ma'am. You'd best listen to Mr. Bourke and do as he says."

Kora's mouth thinned and her husband touched her on the arm. "We'll go," he said.

Quint and Arthur Corle nodded.

Danni felt Austin look at her, but she kept her face averted and stared at the water swirling around their feet.

"Let's move out," he said.

Danni climbed into her wagon and frowned when she saw Jack pulling on his boots. He hadn't been to sleep yet. He had been awake for twenty-four hours.

"You still aren't sleepy?" she asked him, and he looked up with a start, as if surprised to see her watching him. "Not sleepy," he confirmed. "I thought I'd ride the mare today."

"Calliope? Let Eve ride her, Jack. You can sit in the wagon with me."

"Eve can sit with you in the wagon. I want to ride today, even if it is in water."

"If you like," said Danni. Still frowning, she got out of the wagon and quickly found Eve. Eve came and led the horse beside the wagon, so Jack could get on without getting his feet wet. When he was in the saddle he grinned hugely at them, and Danni had to smile at his exuberance.

"It's a good day for me today," he said. "It's a very good day.

I've been thinking about my time in Washington again. I came this close to meeting President Lincoln, Eve, did I tell you?"

Eve smiled and climbed up beside Danni in the wagon. Danni clucked to the oxen and they moved out to catch up with the others. Jack rode happily alongside and began to tell Eve about the people he had met back in Washington; generals and their wives, fancy doctors with manicured nails, and even fancier ladies of society who prided themselves on their care of the poor and the ill.

Danni listened to him but couldn't tear her eyes away from the water on the wagon wheels ahead of them. A sea of water around them, with trees and bushes and the odd pile of stones rising up from the roiling surface. Danni was hypnotized by the sight of the water as it cascaded off the wheels and joined the murky brown river beneath them. In a nearly trancelike state she watched and listened to the sound of Jack's voice droning on and on.

Suddenly she saw her grandmother in her mind, as clear as any day-old memory. She was looking down at Danni, as if Danni were a small child again, and she was humming a song while drumming her fingers on one thigh. Soon she stopped and said, "Help who you can and be a kind person, Danni. Keep your troubles to yourself, but don't hesitate to lend an ear to others."

"I try," murmured Danni.

Jack stopped talking and Eve looked at her. "What did you say, Danni?"

"Nothing. I was just . . . singing to myself."

Jack and Eve went on talking, and Danni returned to her daydream. Her grandmother was frowning now, and she held out her finger as if to scold gently.

"Make sacrifices when you should, but don't make them when you shouldn't."

Danni frowned to herself. She couldn't remember her grandmother ever saying those words to her.

She was surprised at the daydream. She'd never had one so real before. But she had been feeling low lately, and it seemed to help when she thought of the one person in the world who had loved her without fail. Sometimes she was so lonely for the sound of her grandmother's voice she felt she might burst. She thought she'd give anything to have just one more afternoon in the kitchen with her grandmother, listening to her songs and rhymes and laughing and talking with her as they preserved fruits and vegetables from their garden. She had loved her grandmother dearly, and the affection was mutual. All they had needed for a long time was each other. Danni missed being loved that way. She missed the comfort and the warmth. The peace.

"Danni?" said Eve in a low voice. "Are you crying?"

Danni blinked in surprise and felt a sting in her eyes. She forced a smile. "I was thinking of my grandmother. She was very special to me."

"She was all you had, wasn't she?" Eve asked, and Danni looked at her to ask how she knew.

"Jack," Eve explained. "He told me. He said you don't know any of your people. They're all in Oregon."

"When did Jack tell you?"

"The day I gave him breakfast. Don't be upset. He was rambling."

"I'm not upset. And yes, he does ramble." She looked around then. "Where is he?"

"He went ahead. He wanted to ride with Bourke for a while."

Danni swallowed uncomfortably. "I hope he doesn't fall apart up there. Mr. Bourke has enough to worry about right now."

"Mr. Bourke? What happened to Austin?"

"Austin, then."

Eve put an arm across her shoulders. "I saw what happened the night we slept by the railroad camp. I saw him push you away when you tried to comfort him."

Danni's face colored. "You weren't asleep."

"No. Who could sleep with the noise he was making? I was about to get out and shake him awake myself."

"I was only trying to help." Danni looked straight ahead and tightened her hands on the reins. "He told me to stop playing with him. I wasn't . . . playing with him."

"A man might take it that way, Danni. And Mr. Bourke would in particular, since he feels the way he does about you."

Danni looked at her. "What do you mean?"

"I mean he's smitten. You should have seen his face when he found out you took preserves into the railroad camp. He wouldn't have looked that way if it had been me or Kora Blaine. He's angry because he has feelings for you and he can't do anything about it without looking like a complete cad."

The breath came out of Danni slowly. She took her time about taking more in. Finally, she said, "For a time, when we were playing man and wife for the McCandlisses, I sensed something. But once they were gone, he was like a stranger again."

Eve smiled. "I'm sure he felt he had to be. The question in my mind is how do you feel about him."

"I . . . I'm . . . indebted to him. He's wonderful with Jack and he was so good to Kiowa."

Eve's thoughts wandered at the mention of Kiowa's name, but she brought herself abruptly back and turned to lightly pinch Danni in the arm. "That's not what I asked you. Have you fallen for him?"

"No," said Danni automatically. "How could I?"

"You mean because you're married?"

"Yes."

"You're not before a court, Danni. You don't have to say the proper thing. How do you feel about Austin Bourke?"

Danni hesitated before answering. "I think he's the best guide any of us could ever have hoped for. He's caring and considerate, and he says thank you to me for each meal I serve him. He's very courteous."

Eve's look was exasperated. "Danni, are you being thick on purpose?"

Danni looked at her again. "If I did have feelings for him, I wouldn't talk about them with you or anyone else. I'd only make myself miserable if I did."

"Because of Jack?"

"I could never leave him. Never."

"That's what I thought," said Eve with a sigh. "You are a rare person, Danni Coopersand. I've never met anyone like you."

From her tone, Danni wasn't sure if the words were complimentary or not. She didn't want to talk about it anymore. She felt uncomfortable talking about such things with Eve. She would feel uncomfortable talking about them with anyone. She had been brought up to not talk about her feelings. Her grandmother had taught her feelings were private, to be shared with someone you loved. Let the rest of the world see only a benevolent exterior. Privacy had a way of making certain feelings even more special, like love. And it had a way of diminishing those feelings not fit to be aired in public anyway, like jealousy and anger. No one would ever know when Danni was hurt or upset, if she could help it. Her smile was her best face.

"I'm sorry," said Eve suddenly, as if sensing her reticence. "I shouldn't have pushed you."

"You didn't push me. You were curious, and I understand."

"I'm curious about something else," Eve admitted. "When was Jack in Washington?"

"Before his discharge. He was a subject of study for a while, until it was decided nothing could be done for him. He was sent home to me then, with instructions for him to have as much bed rest and as little difficulty as possible in his life."

Danni's mouth was open to go on, but at that moment an unmistakable sound reached her ears; a ripping, tearing sound of earth shifting, branches breaking, and sodden banks crumbling away. There were shrieks and screams up ahead, and Danni had a glimpse of bodies abandoning wagons and heading for the nearest sturdy trees. Her breath caught in her throat then as out of nowhere a monstrous swell of brown water came rushing toward them. The two women stared in horrified shock, unable to move. Then the muddy water was upon them. Danni heard Eve cry out, and her voice was choked off as the wagon bucked and swayed and nearly toppled over.

Her body left the seat, and Danni felt herself being carried backward by the water, into the back of the wagon, where the contents floated up and collided with great force. The wagon bed quickly filled with water and she went under. Panic such as she had never known seized Danni, and she clawed against the muddy brown water to find her way out of the wagon. Boxes and bundles floated into her face to hamper her, and she scrambled wildly to push them away. Lungs bursting, she finally found a slit in the cover and tore at it, hoping it was the way out. She pushed her head through the opening, and then her entire body, and she kicked with her legs to reach the surface and find air.

The current carried her swiftly away from the wagon and try as she might, she could find nothing to hold on to. She fought to swim against the current and soon gave up; it was all she could do to keep her head above the raging water. Her limbs were weakening, but she fought to get to a large cottonwood branch that bobbed in the water in front of her. She gained hold of the branch and pulled herself up, and at that moment the branch slammed into the trunk of another tree. Danni went head first into the tree and knew a second of fierce, jolting pain from the top of her head down to the toes of her feet before the darkness of unconsciousness claimed her.

The branch she hung over was hindered by the trunk for a moment, but soon the water worked it free and sent it rapidly along the current once more, carrying Danni with it.

CHAPTER TWENTY-THREE

EVE CLUNG to the tree for nearly seven hours, until Austin Bourke rode through the water on his horse and found her. The first word he said to her was, "Danni?"

Eve burst into tears, and she could say nothing for several moments. Finally, she mumbled, "The water . . . the water pushed Danni inside the wagon. I didn't see anything else."

A muscle in Austin's cheek worked. He swallowed hard and pulled Eve down out of the tree and onto his horse behind him.

"Where are the others?" asked Eve.

"Kora Blaine was swept away. The others are safe."

Kora. Eve felt a stab of guilt. Then she asked, "Even Jack? Is he all right?"

"He's left us again, but yes, he's all right."

"He doesn't know about Danni?"

"No."

Austin rode through the high water and took her to an abandoned cabin, where the others were waiting on the roof. The Blaines were still weeping, and Eve went immediately to comfort the boys. They allowed her to put her arms around them and hold them. The Corles, like Jack, simply sat and watched, their stares empty. Eve could see a few oxen and some horses tied to the timbers of the cabin, so all the livestock hadn't been lost.

She had seen plenty float by her while sitting in her tree.

After taking some fresh water to drink, Austin rode off again. Eve watched him go and knew he was badly shaken. Kora was gone and he was blaming himself. He would blame himself for Danni as well. His normally erect figure now slumped forward in the saddle; his stubbled chin was low on his chest as he rode away. Eve squeezed her eyes shut and held on to little Joe and John Blaine. Ormond was still sobbing noisily, and Susannah sat by herself near one corner of the roof, crying softly.

After what seemed hours, Will Drake got up and went to sit beside Susannah. He laid a hand on her shoulder and said something low in her ear. She turned and threw her arms around him, and he stroked the back of her head.

Ormond Blaine looked up. He wiped his nose on his sleeve and got shakily to his feet. His reddened eyes filled with loathing as he approached Will and Susannah.

"Mr. Drake, take your hands off my daughter," he commanded.

"Oh, Papa," said Susannah in tearful annoyance. "Will you please sit down and be quiet?"

"I will not. Mr. Drake, I asked you to take your hands off my daughter."

Will's nostrils flared with anger as he turned to look at the older man. "Mr. Blaine, I suggest you sit down. I'm only attempting to comfort your daughter; I'm not going to bed her right here on this roof."

Quint Corle chuckled, and Ormond Blaine's face began to turn colors. Eve could see what was about to happen.

"Ormond," she said in a stern voice. "Don't make things worse than they already are. Please sit down."

"You." He turned his anger on Eve. "You will take your hands off my children this instant. Joseph, John, get over here."

Reluctantly, the two boys left the warmth of Eve's arms and went to their father. Eve released her breath in an angry sigh and saw Quint Corle smiling at her. She turned her head. Ormond sat down heavily on the roof and sneered at Will Drake. "It's amazing what some people will do to intrude on a person's grief. We Blaines need to stick together now and make a plan for our lives now that Mother is gone."

"Plan?" said Susannah suddenly. "I know what your plan is. Your plan is for me to take over as mother . . . and wife, too, probably. I'm not going to do it."

Everyone on the roof stared at her. She went on, her voice raw with pain.

"It's going to stop, Father. All of it. I'm not going on to Utah with you. I'm going back to Leavenworth with Will. The rest of you will have to get by the best you can."

Ormond stood up again, and the anger in him caused him to shake. "You *will* go on with us, my girl. I'm warning you, don't make the mistake of defying me so soon after the loss of your mother. You might join her."

It was Will's turn to stand. His normally jovial expression was grim. He stepped toward Ormond Blaine and said, "I want you to know something. I didn't ask her to come back with me. I haven't spoken to her in days. But if she wants to go back to Leavenworth with me, she's welcome, because you're never going to lay a hand on her again."

"You won't get away with this," Ormond said to him. "I'll see that you don't. There are laws against this sort of thing. She's only fourteen."

"Sit down," Will told him, and he gave the other man such a menacing glare that Ormond was helpless to do anything but what he was told.

The people on the roof then fell into an uncomfortable silence that lasted until Arthur Corle caught sight of Austin Bourke returning to them.

"He's got someone with him," said Arthur, and everyone on the roof squinted in the fading sunlight to see who it might be.

Soon Eve saw who Austin Bourke was bringing back with him: It was Kora . . . dead, white, and slightly swollen.

Susannah started sobbing and the two little boys stared with horrified faces until Eve caught them to her once again. "Don't look," she told them. "It's best if you don't."

Will and Quint got down to help him with the body. They wrapped it in a blanket salvaged from the wagons and put the corpse on the far side of the roof, away from everyone.

"Sure hope the water goes down soon," Eve heard Quint Corle mutter to his father. "That thing's gonna start to stink."

Eve cupped her hands over the ears of the boys and looked at Bourke. "Any sign of the wagon, or . . . ?"

He shook his head. "Getting too dark to see. I'll go out again tomorrow. The water should be down some." He looked at Jack, who had been sitting by the Corles without saying a word. "Any change?"

"No."

"He saved the boys," Susannah said to Eve. "Both of them. When the water came he raced to our wagon and took one boy under each arm. He brought them over to the roof and held them up. I heard the water coming and was already on my way up a tree by that time. So was Father. Mother couldn't . . . make it in time."

Will put his arm around her again, and Susannah leaned against him. Eve looked away from them to Austin Bourke. He took a drink from his canteen and offered it to everyone. Only the two boys were thirsty. Bourke stared at them a long time before getting off his horse and climbing onto the roof. He sat down and put his head on his crossed arms and closed his eyes.

Eve wished she could think of something to say to him. She prayed Danni wasn't dead, but the flood had been so sudden, and the current so strong. It would be a miracle if she had made it out of the wagon.

To lose only two out of twelve was something of a miracle in itself. But they had started out with fifteen, and that meant one third of their number was now gone, with not even two thirds of the journey completed.

Her thoughts came to a halt. Eve blinked as she suddenly realized what the loss of Danni meant. It meant Jack would very likely be sent to a hospital back east, and it meant Eve no longer had anywhere to go. There would be no claim to homestead, no land to work. Her mouth curved in bitter amusement. It seemed she was on her own again after all, with no money, no transportation, and no prospects.

She took the last back as she caught Quint Corle looking at her again. He was certainly no grieving widower. She could throw in with him and his father if she wanted. They would take her. For that matter, she could probably convince Ormond to take her back. With two small boys on his hands and no woman to help him, he would have a rough go of it.

But she knew she wouldn't go with either of them. She'd fare better taking her chances at Fort Hays with the soldiers. Within six months or less she would have enough money to buy her way to California.

Nausea rose in her throat at the thought of returning to such a life, but it would be no different than going with either Quint Corle or Ormond Blaine. She would be earning money to stay alive, the same as during the war.

The depression was slow but sure in coming to her. She was exactly where she'd been the night Robert McCandliss and the Sioux Indians carried her off. Only now there was no Kiowa to come and rescue her. Danni had given her hope for a while. Danni had *been* hope. Now there was nothing but the voice of her memories.

She curled up on the roof with the two little boys and closed her eyes as darkness engulfed them. Will Drake began to sing softly to them, and desperate to escape her own thoughts, she listened to his lilting tenor voice. When sleep came to take her away from her tormented thoughts, it was a blessing.

Chapter Twenty-Four

By the next morning, the water that remained stood in shallow pools in low-lying areas. Everything on the ground was covered with mud and slime, and Austin slid and nearly fell while trying to get on his horse. Butcher picked up his feet and whinnied nervously as his hooves stuck with each step. The black horse shook himself like a dog over and over, keeping Austin on his feet in the stirrups.

Will Drake stirred and lifted his head, and Austin told him to get everyone busy salvaging what they could as soon as they awakened. Will nodded and Austin rode off as the sun creeped over the horizon. He was glad to see the sun that morning and feel its rays on his skin. The warmth would be welcome.

He rode forward, not allowing himself to think about anything but the terrain and the animal beneath him. His eyes scoured every branch and twig for a scrap of fabric or a single sign of Danni, and he paced himself so as not to miss anything on either side of him as he searched.

An hour into his ride he found two of Ormond Blaine's

mules huddled under a tree. He put ropes on both of them and tied them to a branch so they would be there when he came back. Much of the livestock had been drowned, but enough had survived to pull two or three wagons to Fort Hays. Those who had money could buy more oxen at a ranch Austin knew of just beyond the post. The ranch specialized in replacing worn-out animals, so the price would be high. Blaine could afford it, Austin knew. So could the Corles.

As Austin rode he thought of the two Blaine boys, Joseph and John. There was no escaping his guilt in the death of their mother. It had been his decision to go on despite the continuing rain.

He would never forget the looks on their faces when he brought their mother's body to them.

He had found her wedged between two trees, her flame-colored hair floating on the top of the water, her milky eyes staring at him as if in accusation.

Austin didn't know what he was going to do when he found Danni. He didn't think he could bear to look at her when she wasn't alive, when she wasn't shining and smiling at him or even pretending to be unaware of him.

He shook himself like Butcher and fought the thickening in his throat by clearing it loudly. She wasn't dead, he told himself, trying hard to believe it. She was out here somewhere, maybe in a tree, like Eve, and she was waiting for him to come and find her.

When the sun was directly over his head, he stopped his horse by a still-swollen stream and got off to have a drink from his canteen. The water in the stream was surprisingly clear again, made clean by the many rocks and pebbles and grains that lined its bottom. Austin took off his clothes and washed the mud and silt from his skin and hair. Next he worked on his shirt and trousers, which were stiff with mud. He wrung them out as hard as he could and hung them on a low-hanging tree branch to dry while he sat naked on a rock and looked hard at everything around him. Earlier he had seen a strap and buckle from a trunk, and a torn lace shawl he thought he recognized as belonging to Danni. He told himself the water couldn't possibly have carried her this far, but he had known stranger things to happen and he wouldn't give up until he found her.

When he had decided on which direction to take, he pulled his still-damp clothes from the branch and put them on again. He caught up Butcher's reins and mounted him and rode away from the stream at an angle, making a wider sweep of the ground he had already covered and some he hadn't.

Almost immediately he found her wagon. The two rear wheels were half-sunk in the mud, and the cover was a sodden mess. Only one ox lay dead on the ground before the wagon; the others were nowhere to be seen.

His limbs trembling, Austin got off his horse and walked over to the wagon. He stood for several moments before reaching for the cover and yanking it back. His lungs emptied with a huge sigh of relief to find no one inside.

Butcher came and nudged at his back and Austin turned and mounted him before he could start nipping. They moved slower now, Austin being even more careful to note everything around him. Already the sun seemed to be working to repair the damage. Plants covered with mud struggled to receive warming rays, and the grass itself seemed to be trying to stand taller.

Danni was covered with mud, too. So much mud Austin looked at her twice and missed her both times. It was only when he saw the crown of her golden head that he realized what he was looking at. He reined Butcher sharply in and rode up to the grassy knoll where she lay. Her stillness made Austin's heart pound in his chest as he threw himself off his horse and went to kneel over her.

"Danni?" he said in a cracked voice, and he placed his face close to hers to see if she breathed.

He felt nothing.

"Danni," he said more urgently, and he took her face in both of his hands. Her skin looked pale, but it wasn't the pallor of death. Austin laid his head on her chest and closed his eyes when he heard her heart beating faintly.

He spent another minute trying to rouse her, then he picked her up and carried her to his horse. He put her over the saddle in front of him and rode her back to the stream where he had bathed earlier. He found a spot of relatively dry grass and lay down the blanket from his saddle. Then he placed Danni carefully on the blanket. With water from his canteen he washed the worst of the mud from her face and neck. Still she didn't awaken. He began to examine her for injuries, and finding nothing but bruises and scratches he removed her mud-caked clothes and dropped them in a pile. He carried her garments to the stream, and after rinsing out her chemise in the water, he brought it back to wash the mud off her.

Cleansing her body was no simple task, he soon found. The mud was caked, and his fingers quivered as he fought to keep his thoughts on the job at hand. He had never seen anything so perfect. Her breasts were round and full, her waist curved, and her thighs smooth and white. His breathing grew labored as he washed near her private areas and he turned to her legs and feet. He found no serious injuries, and wondered why she remained unconscious. He took the chemise and rinsed it again, then wrung it out and put it on the tree branch.

Finally he decided to look at her head. Using his canteen again, he poured water over her hair until most of the mud was out. Exploring with his fingers, he felt around her skull until he found a large lump just above her forehead. He was relieved to find no accompanying gashes. She probably had a concussion. And maybe she had gone into shock. Austin wasn't a doctor, but he had seen plenty of shock and concussion in the war. Her pulse was stronger for his having moved her, and her breathing was noticeable now. With luck, she would soon begin to stir.

He hung the rest of her clothes out to dry and felt her thin chemise. It was damp yet, but he thought he'd better put something on her in case she awakened. He didn't want her to be frightened at finding herself naked in front of him. He brought the chemise over and drew in a deep, unsteady breath before bending down to dress her.

As he finished pushing the chemise over her hips she began to moan. He held on to her shoulders and propped her head up with his arm. "Danni?" he said, and lightly tapped her cheek. Her lids fluttered and she opened her eyes. First he saw pain and confusion, and then gradual recognition.

"Austin," she croaked.

Unable to stop himself, Austin put his arms around her and gently squeezed. "It's good to see you," he said against her wet hair.

Her arms came up around his neck and she hugged him hard. Austin held on to her, and when she happily placed a kiss on his cheek, he caught her face with one hand and brought her mouth to his. Danni stiffened in shock and put a hand to his chest, but he refused to release her. He kissed her until her hand stopped pushing, and then he kissed her because she was kissing him back and because he couldn't stop. The heat between them was instant, warmer than the sun beating down on their flesh, and suddenly he could think of nothing but touching her with his hands and tasting her skin with his mouth.

What he did next he would not understand or even be able to rationalize to himself. Perhaps it had been the act of cleansing her naked body, or perhaps it was the frustration and helpless panic he had experienced at being unable to find her for so long. He went on kissing her with more and more force until she made a sound of pain and attempted to turn her face away. Austin held her with both hands and forced her to kiss him, the stubble on his face abrading her sensitive cheek. Then he pulled at her chemise and pushed it off her shoulders to reveal her breasts.

Danni looked up at him, her eyes round, and he waited for her to shove him away the way he had rejected her the night beside the railroad camp. A part of him wanted her to, so he would have to stop before things went any further. She only looked at him, her chest heaving and her gaze slightly unfocused.

Austin tugged off the chemise and unbuttoned his trousers, helpless against the tide of sensation rushing through him. The ache in him was too fierce to care if he hurt her. Danni held on to him, pliant and breathless, and when moments later he pushed himself away from her, she shivered. Her eyes were still round as she looked up at him, and her expression was expectant, as if waiting for him to explain himself. Suddenly unable to face her, Austin sat up and fastened his trousers.

Long minutes of silence passed. Soon he felt her move, and then he heard her murmur that her head hurt.

"You've got a lump on it," he told her. He turned to see her wince as she felt around her head. She sat up and drew the chemise to her.

"The others?" she asked.

"Kora Blaine didn't make it. The rest did."

Danni was quiet. Then she asked, "How long have you been looking for me?"

"Yesterday," he answered. "Most of today." He turned all the way around to face her and saw her looking at the ground. Her eyes refused to meet his.

"Thank you," she whispered.

Austin reached for her and drew her against him. After a second of hesitation she timidly placed her arms around him and pressed her lips against his throat.

He buried his face in her damp hair and told her he was sorry for his rough treatment of her.

She lifted her head and kissed his ear.

"Danni . . ." he began, but he could think of nothing to say after her name. He did not know what to say.

He made love to her again before they left the stream to return to the others. He took his time touching her, caressing her silken skin, and he looked into her eyes as he moved over her. For once, the adoration he saw in her gaze didn't unnerve him.

On the way back, Danni rode in front of him in the saddle, occasionally turning her face to him to be kissed. Austin made the ride last as long as he possibly could, stopping to pick up the mules and look for additional livestock as they went, but eventually they drew in sight of the others and he saw Eve look up with a happy cry as she saw them coming. She shouted and cheered and began to clap her hands jubilantly.

Austin was reluctant to let Danni slip out of his arms, but she was laughing at Eve's reception and eager to embrace the other woman.

The two of them ran to each other and did a dance in the slippery mud as they skipped around and around.

"I thought you were dead," cried Eve.

"So did I," said Danni, tears streaming down her face.

They hugged and cried and laughed some more, and Danni finally broke away to see Jack. He sat on the seat of a coverless wagon and looked vacantly at her when she approached. She tried for several minutes before giving up on communicating with him. When she realized everyone had stopped work to watch her, she squared her shoulders and asked what she could do to help.

"Find somewhere to rest," said Austin. "You've had a bad knock and you're not completely sound yet. I want Eve to watch you for a while."

"I feel fine," she told him. "I'd like to help."

"Danni—" he began, and Eve chimed in.

"He's right. There's not much more to be done. We've cleaned up everything we could."

"Danni's wagon is four miles west of here," said Austin. "I'll need to take some animals back with me to pull it out of the mud."

"I'll come," offered Will Drake.

"All right." Austin looked around at all that had been salvaged. More than he had expected when he left that morning. His gaze stopped when several yards behind the cabin he saw a mound of muddy earth with a crude cross sticking out on top. Kora Blaine's grave.

He felt the eyes of Ormond Blaine on him and he turned his head to look at the man.

Ormond said nothing, merely matched his gaze.

Austin frowned and turned his black horse around. "Come on, Will. Mount up."

"My horse is gone. I'll have to take Danni's."

Danni nodded her assent.

Will got on the horse called Calliope—because she sounded like one, Danni told Will—and as they left the cabin area with four oxen behind them, Austin turned for a last glance at

Danni. She caught his look and gave him a swift, sweet smile. He tipped his hat to her.

As they rode away, Will began to chuckle. "And you had me put on report."

Austin looked at him. "Watch yourself, Will."

The tone of his voice was curt enough to make Will raise both brows. "I could've said the same to you. But I didn't and I won't, because I need your help. Susannah wants to return to Leavenworth with me. She doesn't want to be with her father anymore."

"Will, we can't—"

"The hell we can't," Will flared. "We can, and you damn well know it. I don't want that bastard to lay another finger on her."

"She's only fourteen, Will. From a legal standpoint, her father has all the rights."

"What about a moral standpoint? Do we let the sonofabitch continue to do what he's been doing? She wants it to stop."

"She told you that?"

"She told everyone on the roof yesterday."

"What was her father's reaction?"

Will snorted. "What do you think?"

Austin could imagine. "You don't want to be involved anymore, Will. Your record can't take it."

"To hell with my record. This is wrong, Austin, and you know it. I'm counting on you to help."

Austin shook his head. "I told you to stay away from her."

"Damn you, don't you know what it's like to care for someone?"

"Do you care for Susannah?"

"As much as I've ever cared for anyone."

Austin was silent a moment. Finally he said, "Tell her to run away."

Will stared at him. "By herself? Are you crazy? The Cheyenne will get her."

"Not if she goes to Caspar Knowles's place."

"Caspar . . ." Will's voice trailed off. Then he grinned. "The old man who lives on the other side of Fort Hays? The one with the Greek statues in his cabin?"

"She can wait for you there until you come back for her."

Will laughed and reached out to slap Austin on the back. "I knew you'd come up with something. You weren't made a lieutenant for nothing."

Austin shook his head again and rode on. Caspar was a strange old man who read Aristotle by moonlight and played sonatas to the jackrabbits on his piano. The Indians left him alone because they thought he was crazy and Indians were spooked by crazy people. Caspar could spook anyone—until you got to know him. Austin thought he'd be willing to put up the young Susannah until Will could get her to safety.

That is if Caspar was still alive. Austin hadn't seen him for several months, and the man was in his seventies.

"When we stop at the Bullinger ranch outside Fort Hays you stay and help negotiate for new animals," he told Will. "I'll go out to Caspar's place and talk to him."

"Thanks," said Will gratefully. "I mean it."

Austin nodded and rode on in silence. He didn't know if it was the right thing to do—steal a fourteen-year-old girl from her father—but Susannah was no normal fourteen-year-old and Ormond Blaine was no normal father.

When they reached Danni's wagon it appeared to have sunk even deeper into the drying mud. Austin and Will used ropes and heavy branches in a struggle to remove the dead ox in front of the wagon. The animal had become bloated in the sun and the gases emanating from the carcass were enough to make both men retch.

"Thank God I haven't had anything to eat for a day or so," Will said as he wiped his mouth with his handkerchief.

Austin tied his handkerchief over his face and moved in to tie two oxen to the stinking carcass. When the ropes were secured, he yelled and smacked the oxen on their rumps. Nervous and uncomfortable with the smell of their fallen comrade, the oxen leapt forward and dragged the foul carcass out of the mud with a loud sucking sound.

Next came the wagon itself, and all four oxen were necessary to move it from the mud's embrace. Austin picked up all the articles he could find around the wagon and tossed them back inside. Earlier he had found Danni's torn lace shawl again and picked it up. He took that out now and put it with the rest of her things. The wheels, surprisingly, were still in good shape, and the wagon, despite its ripped cover, was all in one piece. Everything was covered with mud, but that could be washed away.

Austin hitched the oxen to the wagon and climbed in the seat after tying Butcher behind. It was dusk when they started back to the others, and just before it grew completely dark they found a milk cow wandering around in the brush. They tied it up and took it with them. Will thought it belonged to the Corles.

They moved quietly through the darkness, Will riding alongside the wagon. Finally Austin heard him clear his throat.

"I don't mean to pry," he said in a low voice, "but what are you going to do?"

"About what?" Austin asked, though instinctively he knew.

"About Danni. And Jack."

"I told you—"

"I know you did, but hell, what can you do, him being the way he is? She can't exactly leave him, and I know you're not the type to stay and farm. So what are you going to do?"

Austin said nothing. Suddenly Will laughed.

"Maybe you've already done all you were going to do, is that it?"

The silence from Austin grew colder.

"Look, I'm sorry, all right?" said Will. "I didn't mean anything."

There was no more conversation between them. Will rode ahead and Austin drove the wagon and stared into the darkness, his thoughts going over what Will had said to him. Will was right. He wasn't a farmer or a homesteader, and there was no way Danni would leave Jack.

Truth be told, Austin didn't know what he was going to do.

Chapter Twenty-Five

In spite of his eagerness to be away, Kiowa found himself fascinated with the life of Brenda, the woman he had inherited. They were not married, had been through no ceremony, but the rest of the Indian camp treated them as a couple and showed neither of them any of the respect accorded to even the lowliest of Indians. Pregnant women would not look upon them, lest their babies be marked, and children were kept away from them. Why they were able to remain in camp was a mystery to Kiowa.

Respect was very important to the Cheyenne, he found. The way Brenda explained it, training began in early childhood. Children were rarely scolded or berated for infractions; instead they were frowned at in disappointment and urged to be more careful of how they were perceived by the rest of the tribe. Soon they learned to see themselves through the eyes of others, and they were always careful to do nothing that might bring shame upon them or their family.

Grown men spent their days hunting, fishing, and occasionally warring and raiding on whites, while women produced children, food, clothing, bridles for the ponies, and took care of the lodges. They dug roots and carried wood and water, tended gardens, and were usually proficient in decorating garments and other items with feathers and quills from birds and porcupine.

Brenda, whose Indian name was something that translated into "woman with fire scar," had not been raised among the Indians. Like Kiowa, she had been given a white person's name and was raised by white people. When traded back to the Indians, she resisted learning their language and way of life and tried to run away. The chief of the tribe thought she would settle down if married, so she was given to a young male in marriage and told to be a good wife to him. Brenda ran away after the ceremony and was brought back kicking and screaming.

Her new husband took her out into the brush and threatened to beat her if she didn't submit. She submitted, but she never went to him willingly and he never took her without a fight. The night Kiowa saw him dance was the night he'd had enough. When Kiowa asked what had made up his mind for him, Brenda smiled and said, "I bedded two of his cousins and told him about it. He wanted to cut my nose off, but the chief told him no. He said to do the dance and be rid of me."

"Why did you bed two of his cousins?"

"Because I knew he would hate me for it and want to kill me."

"You want to die?"

"I would rather die than remain here. By blood I am Cheyenne, but my soul is my own, and I will not give up the God I have come to love for their roots and rituals. I was reared a Christian, and I want to die a Christian."

So it was that Kiowa decided both of them should leave the Cheyenne. In a way he was happy to have been with them and learned what he had of their life. But like Brenda, he had lived with whites, and he knew he would not stay long enough to lose his outsider status and be accepted into the tribe. It was not the future Kiowa saw for himself.

The morning he awakened with no pain, not even a twinge, he told himself it was time to think about planning his departure. Once he left his bed the pain announced itself, but it was diminishing every day, and he had been free of fever for some time. He went outside the temporary, makeshift shelter and found Brenda emptying a rawhide bag of dried meat onto the ground in front of her. The other tribe members were all busy eating and sitting in front of their own hide-constructed shelters.

Most Indian couples lived near the woman's parents, so she always had family close by. Brenda had no one, and since she had proved so contrary, the chief himself told her where to place her lodge, farthest from wood and water and most vulnerable to snakes when the flood came.

The flood did only minor damage to the Indian camp. Many seemed to know it was coming, so everyone was prepared when the waters arrived. A few of Ormond Blaine's cattle were lost, but no human lives were taken by the rushing water. The tribe moved as a whole to the highest ground and prepared to wait it out. When the water withdrew, everyone returned with their bundles and travois used for hauling and set about moving camp.

They had traveled most of the day before, and when Kiowa stumbled in exhaustion the man who had found him came and put him on the back of a pony. It was the Sioux Indian pony. The one Eve had ridden.

Kiowa was not too weak from walking to feel the fear and anger rise in him again. He had asked Brenda a dozen times to inquire about the wagons, and each time she told him not to be foolish. No woman in her position could approach a man in the tribe and ask about a raid. She would be laughed and jeered at should she even try. Kiowa thought of asking the older man who was continually kind to him, but Brenda warned him should he speak he would be taken for a liar, and liars were not tolerated. It was safer for him to remain dumb.

His frustration was building, but since they were moving west he found it easier to keep silent. He kept his eyes open for any sign that the wagons had passed before them, but the Cheyenne didn't travel by the Smoky Hill Road. Instead they traveled some miles to the south, where troops from the forts could be avoided. Kiowa kept imagining he could see Austin Bourke scouting ahead of them, or Will Drake riding a ridge to the north, but the notion was a fantastic one. If the wagons had survived the Indians and the flood, they would be drawing near Fort Hays by now.

He went to join Brenda in front of the shelter and saw her look up with a half-smile for him. Kiowa blinked in surprise and smiled back.

"You look well today," she said. "Healthy. Are you in pain?"

He opened his mouth and she suddenly held up a finger and frowned fiercely at him. He remembered, closed his mouth, and shook his head to her question.

"Good," she said. Then she looked carefully around herself before speaking further. Her eyes were shining with purpose.

"Our departure would go easy during this move," she suggested to him in a low voice.

Kiowa stared. He hadn't said a word to her about leaving.

"Don't pretend with me," she snapped. "You've been thinking of nothing but leaving since you came to us."

She was right, of course, but he hadn't realized it was so obvious.

"Not that anyone will care," she went on, her voice still low. "When we are close to them they can keep an eye on us, like keeping a snake in a basket. But some of the old ones are saying we bring bad luck to the tribe."

Kiowa lifted a skeptical eyebrow.

She looked away from him and her scarred features grew distant. "Many in the tribe are already looking our way because of the flood."

Kiowa's lifted brows met immediately in a frown. They were being blamed for the flood? That was the most ridiculous thing he'd ever—

"Yes, I know," said Brenda, watching him. "Their superstitions seem strange. But no more than our beliefs would seem to them." She paused then. "You are a member of the faith, aren't you?"

Kiowa looked away from her and made no effort to answer.

A snorting sound came from her. She sat back on her buffalo hide and handed him a piece of the dried meat to eat. Kiowa took it with only a glance at her and put it in his mouth to chew.

When he sneaked another look he saw that her gaze was far away again and her eyes had grown moist.

"I had a man, you know," she said suddenly. "Before I was traded. We were a week away from being married when the township decided to give me up. That was in Indianola, north and west of Topeka, where they didn't believe a freed slave ought to be marrying an Indian girl raised white. Too much culture confusion for them. Red, black, white. And the girl they wanted to get back from the Cheyenne was the banker's niece, so there was never any question whether I would go."

Kiowa held up a hand and she stopped talking. He pointed to himself, then to her, and then made a walking motion with his hands. *We'll go.*

Her eyes studied him. "Me, with you?"

He nodded.

"When?"

Kiowa lifted both hands.

"We'll need horses," she said.

He nodded again.

"And food."

Kiowa took the dried meat out of his mouth and handed it back to her to place in the rawhide bag. He noticed others getting up and preparing to move again, and he got to his feet.

Suddenly a shrill scream sounded in the camp, and startled heads everywhere turned to find the source of the noise. Brenda finished tying her rawhide bag and went to see what the commotion was. When she returned, she was frowning. Kiowa took her arm and looked questioningly at her. She shook him off and said, "The wife of the chief's son has chosen this moment to give birth."

Before Kiowa could smile, she continued, "The baby comes much too early. The woman is not more than halfway through her time."

Kiowa blinked and looked around. Many of the Indians sat

down in front of their temporary lodges again and looked at each other with worried eyes. The older ones looked at Kiowa and Brenda.

Kiowa cleared his throat and sat down again, facing away from everyone else.

"They wouldn't kill us, would they?" he asked, trying not to move his lips in case anyone was watching that he couldn't see.

"They might," she answered.

He looked at her to see if she was serious. She was.

"They'll think we're responsible?"

"Yes and no. Some of them will know we're not, but in their grief they'll choose to believe it and want to kill us."

"We should go today then."

"Tonight. We'll need the horses."

"We'll go west to Fort Hays and find out if the wagons made it."

Brenda turned and glared at him. "We'll go east and forget those damned wagons."

Kiowa matched her glare and fought to keep his gravelly voice low. "We'll split up once we're well away from the camp and you can do whatever you like. *I'm* going to find out about the wagons."

"You'll go nowhere if you don't be quiet," Brenda said, and in the next moment Kiowa heard her greet the older man who was his benefactor. Kiowa turned around and looked up at the man whose Indian name translated into Gray Elk. His lined face was worried as he approached them. He spoke briefly with Brenda, then he squeezed Kiowa's arm in affection and said something low to him before turning and walking away.

Brenda's look was thoughtful as Gray Elk departed. To Kiowa, she said, "He warned us to be careful. If the baby is marked, or if either mother or child dies, the news for us will not be good. The old ones are very vocal in this tribe, and they are allowed much respect. They will say our pairing has caused much grief for the tribe, that together we bring white evil into their midst. They are saying we should be gotten rid of."

Kiowa looked in the direction the old man had taken before turning around again. "Why did he come to warn us?"

"He has always treated me well. And I think he is fond of you." Brenda's mouth curved. "Possibly because you resemble Gray Elk. You and he are very much alike. Are you aware of this?"

"Yes," Kiowa said, and his voice was flat.

"You have the same face, the only difference being that of age. How is it possible, I wonder?" she asked.

"It's possible."

"But how? Could he be some relation to you?"

"He could be."

"You don't know?"

He looked at her. "Do you know your father?"

"No," she said. "I don't."

"I don't know mine, either. I don't want to know. I don't care."

She watched him a moment, then said, "You knew your mother, didn't you?"

"Yes. I loved her very much."

Brenda nodded. "Yes, I can see that you did. The mark of a good man is the love he has for his mother. I sometimes wish I had known mine."

"Your Indian mother?"

"Yes. Indian mothers are much more gentle and forgiving than white women." She sighed then. "It's the Indian men I cannot tolerate."

Kiowa pursed his lips and looked down at the ground. He wished there was something he could do for Brenda, but there was no way he was going to take her back east to Indianola. When they left the Cheyenne, he was going to find Danni and Jack and the others.

The rest of the day was passed in waiting, as no one had made even the slightest move to keep traveling west. Kiowa guessed the chief's son and his wife were important members of the tribe to keep everyone in abeyance for so long. When darkness came, fires went on burning, and many gave no indication of sleeping. Kiowa looked frequently at Brenda, but she would only shrug. Occasionally they would hear a hoarse cry from the lodge that had been raised hastily around the pregnant woman, but mostly there was silence in the camp.

Kiowa finally dozed off, and when he awakened it was with a start. Gray Elk was standing over him and motioning for him to get up. Blinking, Kiowa rose and looked around for Brenda. She was sitting astride a pony and waiting for him. Kiowa saw another pony, the one he had ridden before, and he knew his benefactor, not Brenda, was responsible for it. He peered through the darkness at the face of the older man and struggled to see his expression. Gray Elk spoke softly to him, something Brenda couldn't hear to translate, and squeezed Kiowa's shoulder. Without thinking, Kiowa reached forward and put his arms around the man. He hugged him hard, and in a moment of surprise, the man hugged him back. Then he cuffed Kiowa on the head and pushed him away, toward the waiting pony.

With only a glance at Brenda, Kiowa got on the pony and quietly reined it north out of the camp. He didn't look back at Gray Elk, or to see if Brenda was following him; he just rode away.

When he was half a mile from the camp, he kicked the pony into a trot, and using the stars to guide him, he hurried north as fast as the darkness would allow him. Soon he heard hoofbeats behind him, and he knew Brenda was at his heels.

They rode most of the night, and when the first light appeared Kiowa stopped so Brenda could catch up with him. The Smoky Hill Road was visible, and Kiowa pointed it out to her. "Here's where we split up," he said and pointed east. "That way you'll find Fort Harker. Shouldn't be too far, maybe a day or so. Just keep going and the road will take you back to Topeka and Indianola."

She looked doubtful. "What will they do to me?" she asked him.

"Do?" he echoed.

"An Indian woman riding alone. What will happen to me? Will the soldiers know I am a Christian, or will they treat me like an Indian whore? And what if the Sioux find me? What happens then?"

"The same thing that would happen if you were riding with me and they found us," Kiowa told her. "It's a risk both of us have to take."

"Not so much of a risk for you," she pointed out. "You are wearing the clothes of a white. I am not. They may shoot me before asking my business."

Kiowa grew exasperated. "I'm not taking you to Indianola. I'm going west to find out what happened to the wagons I was traveling with. If you'd like to come with me, I won't stop you. But I'm going now."

He kicked his pony again and headed west, riding down to the road. He looked back over his shoulder once and didn't see her, so he assumed she had gone the other direction. He shook his head and rode on. She was the most unlikable woman he had ever met. Hardheaded, mean, and stubborn as an old nanny goat. It was little wonder the tribe had considered her bad luck.

When the sun was directly over his head in the sky Kiowa stopped and found a creek to drink from. He got off and threw the reins down to let his pony rest and graze as he perched on the bank. He kicked himself for not taking any food from Brenda, who had been carrying three rawhide bags full. He got up and looked around and found a few roots to munch on, roots he wouldn't have known were edible if not for his time with the Cheyenne.

As he walked back to catch up his pony again, he saw her. She was standing in the creek about ten yards away and splashing water on herself.

Her head lifted as he approached her, but she said nothing.

"Can you spare some meat?" he asked.

She nodded. "What do they call you?"

"I told you. Kiowa."

"No. I meant your Christian name. The name your mother gave you."

Kiowa turned his back on her to walk away, but something in her proud voice, an unspoken need to be acknowledged, stopped him.

"Nathan," he said. "I was born Nathan McMahon."

"Nathan," she repeated. "It's a fine name. It suits you."

"Evidently not," he said, and he approached her pony to take down one of the rawhide bags.

"What makes you say that?" she called, and she climbed out of the creek.

"No one but my mother has ever called me Nathan." He put some dried meat in his mouth and began to chew. He saw her wring the water out of her clothes and reach for the reins of her pony. He handed the bag back to her, but she motioned for him to keep it. Kiowa thanked her and went back to his own pony. He climbed on again and tied the bag behind him, then together they started for the road. They rode in silence, Kiowa not asking and Brenda not offering to explain her decision to join him.

To the south of them, and east, a tiny Indian boy no bigger than a grown man's hand was born in a hastily erected lodge and just as quickly died. The mother followed her son.

Chapter Twenty-six

At fort Hays six soldiers drowned when the trickling waters of Big Creek grew into a rushing torrent. Elizabeth "Libby" Custer was there, but her husband George had left the fort on the first of June to ride with his troops on a scouting mission to Fort McPherson in Nebraska. Danni received only a glimpse of Mrs. Custer, and the poor woman appeared exhausted. She must have been working hard in the aftermath of the flood, Danni thought.

As everywhere else, much of the fort was covered with dried mud and slime left by the water. For once, the wagons and their occupants were allowed inside the gates of the fort. Everything looked brown and dirty to Danni, the infantry barracks, the stables, and even the officer's quarters. Nothing had been spared.

The inhabitants of the post looked at them with weary, mildly surprised eyes. Many found it hard to believe they had lost only one of their number. Austin asked to speak to the commander, and the rest of them waited in the grass of the courtyard. The

Blaines, the Corles, and Danni had a wagon apiece. The surviving animals had been distributed as evenly as possible among them, to ensure that all the wagons made it to the fort. Now they would visit a ranch beyond the post where replacement animals were sold. It would mean using the remainder of Danni's money, but there was no way to get around it—unless she wanted to homestead here, near Fort Hays.

After looking around herself, she knew she didn't want to. She wanted to see the land Austin had in mind to show her. She glanced back into the wagon to see Jack. He was still in a trance-like state and had barely moved a muscle all day. She had started to spoonfeed him his meal, but stopped when she realized he wasn't chewing anything. She didn't want him to choke.

Jack had never been in one of these states for more than a few hours, and his continued stillness began to worry Danni. The panic that came with the flood had done it to him, she realized; she had been astonished to learn of his heroism in saving the children. She wished he would wake up so she could tell him how proud she was and how wonderful he had been.

Then she would think of the guilt she felt and a part of her hoped he never woke up to see the truth in her eyes. And he would see it, she knew. He would sense her trembling when Austin passed by, and hear the breathlessness in her voice when she spoke to him. Danni's entire body ached with yearning; never before had she experienced such wanting. It was in her mouth and her hands and in every part of her when Austin came near. She wanted to touch him and be touched, and each time he rode by her that day she saw the same yearning in his eyes. He wanted to kiss her and hold her and make love to her again.

It made Danni shiver to think of making love with him. Her body had reacted in ways that made her smile and blush fiercely to herself. She had surrendered both physically and emotionally, and she wanted nothing more than to be with him again. She had to hug her middle a dozen times that day just to keep the pangs at bay, and it was all she could do to keep from beaming at him when he looked at her. She was grateful beyond words for having been allowed to express her feelings physically rather than keeping them hidden in her heart. Danni had never known such sensations were possible.

When he was gone, she would have the most blissful memories. She would think of him every day for the rest of her life.

Beside her in the wagon seat, she felt Eve watching her. Eve had said nothing, but Danni thought she suspected something by the way her mouth curved each time Austin passed the wagon that day. If not for Jack, Danni wouldn't care who knew. But she was, after all, a married woman. And now an adulteress. She didn't care. Her happiness refused to allow it. She would spare Jack if she could, but she couldn't change her feelings. And nothing would change her concern for Jack. He was still hers to worry and fuss over; that wouldn't change because she had fallen in love. Jack would know that.

When Austin finally emerged from the commander's quarters he came and told them it would be all right to camp inside the post that night. He was carrying an envelope that he tucked inside his shirt, Danni noticed. He went to the Blaines and Corles and told them about the ranch where Will Drake would take them in the morning to pick up new animals; then he came to Danni's wagon and raised his arms to beckon her down. She went to him and he lifted her out of the wagon, his fingers squeezing gently as he set her down. "How's Jack?" he asked.

"The same," she answered, and as he helped Eve down she went to the back of the wagon to prepare what supper she could out of the goods that had survived the flood. Austin followed her. "Can you afford more oxen?"

One side of her mouth lifted. "You know I can't. But I'll have to, won't I?"

"How much money do you have left?"

"Enough for one pair of oxen and some seed to replace what I lost. I'll need to buy more staples as well. Most of my supplies were ruined."

Austin stood and watched her. He turned down a biscuit from a tin she offered. Finally he said, "You know I'm not a farmer."

Danni stopped and looked at him. "I know."

"Not a homesteader."

"I know."

"You're still planning to—"

"Yes," she interrupted. "I am." Her face softened then and she smiled at him. "What did you think?"

"I thought you might be thinking of coming with me."

Danni paused. "Where are you going?"

"I don't know."

She smiled again and pulled him by the hand until they were behind the wagon, where none of the others could see them. When they were out of sight she took his face into her hands and pulled him down to kiss her. His mouth covered hers and she made a noise in her throat as a surge of pleasure passed through her body. She felt him tighten his hold on her and moan into her mouth. When the kiss ended, her limbs were shaking.

"Excuse me," said Eve as she came around the corner, and Danni would have bolted, but Austin held on to her.

"I was looking for . . . the biscuits."

Danni pointed to the tin. "There they are."

Eve took the tin and scampered away. Austin looked at Danni's flushed face and touched her cheek with his fingers.

"I have somewhere to go tomorrow, but I'll be back."

"Does it have to do with that envelope in your shirt?" Danni asked.

"No. That's an attack of conscience from my cousin. He sold the stage business and sent me my share. It beat us here by a week."

Danni smiled. "Is it a lot?"

"Five hundred dollars."

"Oh." Danni swallowed. She'd never seen that much money in her life. Austin was watching her.

"Does it change your mind about coming with me?"

She blinked. Then she frowned. "Should it?"

"No," he said, and she saw a muscle begin to work in his jaw. She smoothed it with her fingers.

"I wish I could be with you tonight."

He pulled her hand away and held it. "You want to be with

me, but only until you reach the claim you've come to settle on?"

Danni stared at him. He made it sound as if she was using him.

She said, "I have a lot of responsibility, Austin. People depend on me. Jack, Eve, and Kiowa, too, if he's still out there. If I came with you I'd be letting everyone down."

"If you came with me, it would be because you love me and want to be with me."

Her breath caught in her throat and her stomach contracted. Her words came out a whisper. "Because I'm staying doesn't mean I don't."

He said nothing, only looked at her.

"I do want to be with you," said Danni. "You must know that."

He turned his head. "From the first I've been worried about somehow failing you and not being able to measure up to your ideas of who and what I am. I'll never be anything but what I am right now. And what you're saying is that because I'm not a farmer, I'll never have you."

Danni looked at her feet. "For a while you will, Austin. For a while we'll have each other. And you don't have to measure up for me. All I'll ever want from you is what you are."

His confusion was evident in his eyes. Before she could kiss him again he backed away from her. Danni put a hand out, but he moved out of her reach. "Don't worry about feeding me tonight," he said. "I have no appetite."

He left her standing there, and she shivered again, but with cold this time. What had he expected from her? she asked herself. He knew her circumstances. He knew it would be impossible for her just to walk away. What kind of person would she be if she did? Certainly not someone worthy of his love—or anyone else's, for that matter.

"Hope I didn't interrupt anything," said Eve as she stepped around the wagon. In her hands was the biscuit tin.

Danni's face reddened. "I . . . we . . ."

"Were engaged in a most passionate embrace. I saw you."

"You were spying," Danni accused.

"So shoot me. I was curious."

"About us?"

"Mostly about you. Him, I knew about."

Danni turned away and began rummaging through her stores. She came up with jerky and dried apples.

Eve came and touched her lightly on the back. "I'm sorry for prying, Danni. I really am. I didn't mean anything. I just . . . well, I've read poems about passion all my life, but I don't think I've ever experienced it. I envy you."

"Are there any biscuits left?" Danni asked, and she turned to look at Eve.

"Plenty," said Eve. "And by your expression it's obvious there will be no more personal conversation." Eve handed her the biscuit tin and smiled. "I can take a hint. I'll be quiet. Are we going to try and feed Jack tonight?"

"No. I'm afraid he'll choke. He shouldn't be out much longer. We'll wait."

"Are you going to buy more oxen tomorrow?" Eve asked.

"All I can afford. We'll need to visit the sutler as well and replace what we can."

Eve looked guilty. "I wish I had some money to give you, Danni."

"It would be nice," Danni agreed. "But don't worry. We'll get by the best we can."

Austin Bourke made sure of it. The next morning, Danni discovered he had given Will Drake enough money to buy four oxen and all the staples she needed at the sutler's store. When she protested, Will shook his head and bought the oxen anyway, said Austin was the boss and he was under orders to make the purchases. If she wanted to pick out what she required at the sutler's, that was fine, because if she didn't, then Will was supposed to stock up for her.

Danni waited up half the night to talk to Austin, but he didn't return to the fort. When she asked Will where he had gone, Will grew evasive and told her he wasn't exactly sure but that he wasn't far. Austin would be back, Will assured her.

She knew he would because he had told her so, but it didn't make her any less angry at him for using his money to rescue her every time she ran into trouble. She refused to let him make her feel indebted, and when they reached their destination she was determined to pay him what she could and give the extra food and animals back to him.

When Austin finally returned the next day, he rode his horse right by her and went to confer with Will Drake. She started over to speak to him, but he saw her coming and lifted a hand to halt her. Danni stopped where she was and felt heat creep up her neck. The hurt went deep at the expression on his face. He was exhausted, she saw, and he wanted no part of what she had to say to him. Danni took a deep breath, swallowed the pain, and turned around to walk in the opposite direction.

CHAPTER TWENTY-SEVEN

EVE SAW the pallor of Danni's face when she came back to the wagon. Her gray eyes were on the ground as she walked, and it was a struggle for Eve to keep from asking what had happened. Something to do with Bourke, no doubt, and the way he had ridden past Danni without even looking at her on his return to the fort. Eve mumbled to herself about men and went back to her mending. Half of Jack's shirts and trousers had been lost in the flood, and much of what was left had been torn to shreds. Danni and Eve had been repairing what they could with the needles and thread purchased the day before at the sutler's store. Not everything lost in the flood could be replaced, but with Bourke's money they had managed to obtain most of what they would need.

Eve finished breaking off some thread with her teeth when she heard Jack utter something in the wagon behind her. She got down off the seat and went to him.

"Jack? Jack, did I hear you say something?"

He slowly turned his head and looked at her. His eyes were veined and red. "Kiowa," he murmured.

Eve fixed her gaze on him. "Kiowa?"

Outside the wagon at that moment, Eve heard a joyous shriek fill the air, and she heard Danni shout a name.

Kiowa!

Eve swiveled back to stare at Jack. "How did you know?" she whispered.

His eyes closed and he curled up on his side to fall immediately into a deep sleep. Eve stared a moment longer before scrambling out of the wagon. She saw Danni running out the open gates of the fort, her skirts flapping around her. Beyond Danni she saw Kiowa, looking healthy and strong atop the back of the Indian pony Eve had ridden for so long. He sprang down from the pony and rushed to meet Danni and sweep her up in a hug. Eve held up her skirts and ran toward them. She was amazed at the changes in him since she had seen him last. He looked like a man now. A grown man with a face that needed shaving and hair that needed cutting and—

Eve came to an abrupt halt when she saw the Indian woman on the pony behind Kiowa. A shock went through her system and left her staring dumbly. Kiowa finally released Danni and turned to Eve. His expression as he greeted her was guarded.

"Hello," she said calmly, and she cleared her throat at his coolness. "I . . . are you still angry with me?"

"No," he said. Without another word he turned back to Danni and gestured to the woman on the pony. "This is Brenda. She's with me."

"Hello, Brenda," said Danni with a smile. "It's nice to meet you."

Brenda said nothing, only looked at Danni. Eve stepped forward and asked, "Does she speak English?"

"She does," said Brenda coldly.

"I thought you might," said Eve. "With a name like Brenda."

"Brenda was raised by whites," Kiowa explained. "They traded her to the Cheyenne for a white girl."

Eve eyed the scar on the Indian woman's face. Fire, she thought.

Austin Bourke came to join them then, and a genuine smile lit his face as he shook Kiowa's hand. "It's good to see you again, Kiowa. We've missed your bow skills."

"It's good to be back," said Kiowa with a laugh. "You'll never know how good." He looked around himself then. "Will we be allowed inside the fort?"

"You're traveling with us," said Austin. "I'll go and tell them to put their buffalo rifles away."

As the group moved inside the fort Eve tried to catch Kiowa's eye, but he steadfastly refused to look at her. Not for a minute did she believe he wasn't still angry, but she would bide her time until he decided to talk to her.

If he did decide to talk to her. Now that he had Brenda he might feel differently about Eve.

Brenda was attractive, even with the scar. And there was a quality about her, a stillness, that made a person look and keep looking.

It was when she looked back that Eve had to turn away. Brenda's gaze at Eve was nothing but cold.

Perhaps Kiowa had talked about her to Brenda and she was bitter, Eve thought as she walked along with the group. God knew she was feeling bitter about Brenda, though she didn't want to ask herself just exactly why at the moment. She had never dreamed Kiowa would come back with another woman. A part of her—the part that had believed him when he professed his adoration for her—was still stunned. His feelings for her weren't entirely dead, she knew, because she had seen him looking for her while hugging Danni. And when he caught sight of her there was relief in his face. Then he had become cool.

Fine, Eve told herself. She would play his silly adolescent game if it made him feel better. Still, it was impossible to hide the joy she felt at seeing him again. He was alive and well, had never looked healthier, and Eve found herself attracted to his physical presence.

More than a few heads turned to stare as the two Indians entered the gates of the fort, but nothing was said. It helped that Kiowa was dressed as a white and had lighter skin than most Indians. Brenda was obviously a full-blooded Cheyenne, but the moment they were near the wagons she climbed off her pony and asked for a dress to wear.

Eve and Danni looked at each other.

"A dress," Brenda repeated. Then she pointed at Eve. "Your clothes would fit me. Will you give me a dress?"

"Of course," said Eve, and she climbed into the wagon to find a garment for the woman. She was tempted to give her the least attractive dress she could find, but she overcame the impulse and pulled out a dress in a green shade that would suit Brenda's coloring.

"I can't believe you're really here," Danni was saying to Kiowa as Eve climbed out again. "You were so sick and I was so worried."

Kiowa reached for her to hug her again, then he patted his stomach. "I'm starving for some of your biscuits, Danni. I've thought of nothing else for the last ten miles."

Danni laughed and jumped up to prepare a meal for the hungry travelers. Eve went to Brenda and handed her the dress. "You can change in the back of the wagon. Don't mind the man sleeping inside. He should sleep for some time."

Brenda frowned at her, and Kiowa spoke up. "It's Jack, Brenda. The man I told you about before we reached the fort."

She looked at Kiowa, then climbed into the wagon. Eve took advantage and sat down beside Kiowa. "That pony you were riding—" she began, but he cut her off.

"Came as a result of a raid. Mr. Blaine's cattle were brought to the camp as well."

"So you've been living with the Cheyenne?" Eve asked.

"Yes," he answered.

"Where are they?" Austin Bourke came to stand before them.

"A day from here, maybe more. They weren't moving the last time I saw them, but they have been traveling in the same general direction."

"Did you have any trouble getting away?" Bourke asked.

"Some. A member of the tribe helped us."

Bourke nodded, then he looked directly at Kiowa and said, "The McCandlisses?"

Kiowa matched Bourke's look. "Robert is dead. Luther got away."

"Are you going after him?" Eve asked, and Kiowa shook his head.

"I wouldn't know where to start."

Unspoken in his words was the intimation that Luther too would be dead now if not for Eve's interference.

"We haven't come across any more bodies," Bourke told him, "aside from those left by the flood."

Kiowa looked around himself then. "Was anyone lost? When they brought the cattle and pony in I thought—"

"We were camped beside the railroad gang when the raid happened," Eve told him. "No one was hurt."

"What about the flood?"

"Kora Blaine drowned."

Kiowa looked at the Blaine's wagon, where the two boys sat with their sister, Susannah. Ormond Blaine was nowhere in sight.

He looked further and saw the Corles engaged in a card game. Eve smiled and reached for his hand.

"Not much has changed," she said. "We're all a little older and a lot poorer."

Kiowa removed his hand from her grasp. "You took the dress from Danni's wagon. Was your wagon destroyed in the flood?"

"Yes and no. Yes, the flood took it, but no, it wasn't mine anymore. I've been thrown out of the Blaine family and onto Danni's mercy. She's been very good to me. I'm going to try and be good to her."

Something shifted in Kiowa's eyes, but it was so quick Eve couldn't define it.

"I'm going to try my hand at homesteading with you people," she went on. "I've never plowed a field before, but I'm willing to learn. Danni says she'll teach me."

Austin Bourke excused himself and got up. A second later Danni came and told them their meal was ready. Brenda chose that moment to come down from the wagon, and Eve had to admit she looked very pretty in the green dress. She saw Kiowa smile in appreciation, but he said nothing. Brenda acknowledged his smile and came to thank Eve for the dress.

"It looks lovely on you," Eve guardedly told her.

"Thank you," said Brenda, then she touched Kiowa on the arm and asked if she might be able to post a letter.

Kiowa said he thought so, then he took her by the arm and led her to the food Danni had prepared.

Eve trailed along after them, wondering if her decision had made him angry. Surely an extra pair of hands would be appreciated on any claim. And speaking of hands, the way he had pulled his from her grasp had made her feel utterly stupid, as if she were throwing herself at him to gain his attention and he wanted nothing to do with her. She had actually blushed with embarrassment, something she hadn't done in years.

Unaccustomed to being treated in such a manner, Eve was nearly sick to her stomach by the time everyone sat down to eat. Danni had prepared enough for everyone, so the Blaines and the Corles were invited to come and partake, along with Will Drake and Austin Bourke. Only Bourke refused the invitation. Danni's smile wilted as he walked away from them, and Eve went to put an arm around her shoulders.

Kiowa was watching them, she noticed. Eve squeezed Danni briefly, then released her, not wanting to call attention to the abject disappointment on Danni's expressive face. Kiowa would see the truth soon enough, but everyone else would be better off ignorant.

As they ate, Eve watched Kiowa and Brenda and realized the two of them didn't interact at all. Brenda's stiffness extended itself not just to every white person at the table but to Kiowa as well.

A look at the sleeping arrangements that night would prove what Eve was beginning to suspect, and she prepared herself to wait up and see exactly who slept where. Their bedrolls would be together, certainly, but would *they* be together? Eve would find out.

Well past midnight Eve sat up from her bed on the ground and realized she had dozed off without meaning to fall asleep. She looked around for Danni and didn't see her in her bedroll

. . . but she did see Brenda and Kiowa. Their bedrolls were at least three feet apart. Kiowa's eyes were open and looking at Eve.

"I'm glad you're back," she whispered to him. "I missed you."

He closed his eyes and rolled onto his back.

CHAPTER TWENTY-EIGHT

AUSTIN WAS at Salisbury again, in a crude facsimile of a hospital, and the doctor, a man with a long, greasy moustache, was trying to pour oil of turpentine down his throat to treat his dysentery. Austin whipped his head around in an effort to avoid the medicine, for he knew it wouldn't work. He had seen gallons of it used, and it never worked.

To the left of him was a man who had lost a leg and an arm and now suffered from septicemia. Morphia was given to him frequently. The man to the right of him received daily doses of quinine to control what the doctor thought was malaria. Austin wanted nothing but opium. The opium made the tin tub of human limbs in the corner easier to look at. It made the smell of pus and rot in the air easier to breathe. It made the sight of dying, cadaverous men easier to blink away.

When the morphia and the quinine ran out, the doctor used whiskey. Sometimes he had chloroform for his surgeries; most times he did not. While dreaming, Austin was amazed at all he was seeing. He was seeing things that hadn't existed in reality.

There had been only one bottle each of the morphia and the quinine used by the doctor, stolen from a northern medical transport wagon. The opium was real, though it too had been in severely limited supply.

The doctor in his dream, however, had an entire chest of medicaments at his disposal. Austin could lift his head from his bed and see everything lined up on a shelf above him, all the medicine necessary to treat the wounded and dying around him. Alcohol, ammonia water, creosote, digitalis, ether, hydrochloric acid, morphine sulfate, opium, quinine sulphate, and sulphuric acid. He ticked the names off in his head and tried to think what each of them could do. If the doctor didn't hurry, Austin himself would take the medicines and go out into the camp.

Nearly everyone he had come in with was dead. All but one man, and Austin couldn't seem to remember his name. He was a career soldier, a man who had already fought in the Mexican War and seen much service under the arrogant, wild-eyed Custer. This man too was ill, but his history seemed to be the thing that kept him going. He had seen suffering before and he had seen men starve and die. Never in such great numbers as in this war, but he had seen it just the same. His uncaring attitude kept him rational. He dealt with it all as if it were just another bad day. Or week. Or year. Austin envied him desperately. Not to care would have been a blessing.

In his dream the doctor came to him again and once more offered the oil of turpentine. "It will help you if you believe it will," the man said.

"I don't believe it will," Austin told him. "So it won't."

"So be it," said the doctor, and he turned away. When he came around again he held up a long, gleaming knife. "We'll have to remove them, then."

Austin's eyes rounded. "Remove what?"

"Your bowels," said the doctor. "They're causing all your problems. Don't worry, my good man, I've done this before." He pointed behind himself to the tub in the corner, which was now filled to overflowing with steaming intestines. Austin opened his mouth to scream as the doctor leaned over him.

Nothing came out; his fear was so great his vocal cords had become paralyzed. In panic he thumped on his chest, trying to dislodge the fear. The doctor only chuckled and leaned over Austin's middle to make the incision. Austin did scream then, only it came out as a hoarse, choked whisper, and the doctor immediately clamped a hand over his mouth. Austin struggled to peel the hand away, and as he clawed at the fingers he suddenly realized how small and fragile they were. He crushed them in his hand and awakened to hear Danni's cry of pain.

He opened his eyes and saw her on the ground beside him, under his blanket. He grabbed her hand and held it up to examine her fingers. She flexed the pain away and curled them around his hand. "No harm done," she whispered.

Austin put an arm over his eyes and slowly filled his lungs in an effort to calm his trembling limbs and still racing heart. "I'm sorry," he said in a thick voice. Then he turned his head and looked at her. "What are you doing here?"

"I couldn't sleep," she said. "I wanted to be near you. Are you all right?"

"Yes."

"You were already dreaming when I found you. I tried to wake you, but you didn't respond. Was it bad?"

Austin said nothing.

She rose up to look into his face. "Don't be angry with me. Do you want me to go?"

He hesitated before answering. Finally he said, "You know I don't."

She released the breath she was holding and leaned forward to place her lips against his chin.

Austin sighed and put his arm around her, amazed at how easily she chased the tortured images from his mind, as if her unique brightness somehow forced the darkness away. He cupped her face and kissed her lips in mute thanks. She opened her mouth to him and he closed his eyes as a shivering spasm of pleasure passed through him.

He soon rolled over with her, and she took his hand to guide it beneath her nightgown, where his fingers met her warm, bare flesh. Her hands moved to unbutton his trousers.

Austin didn't think about where they were or whether some guard might be watching them; he thought only of her warmth and softness and how beautifully smooth her skin felt to his calloused hands. He thought only of pushing himself inside her and of hearing her small cry in his ear, and of losing himself in her mouth and in her body at the same time for as long as he could stand it. And after he had reached his quaking, shuddering finish, he thought only of holding her as close to him as he could so she would still be a part of him somehow.

Making love to Danni was in its own way as unreal to him as his dreams. He had never felt for anyone what he felt for her, nor had he ever been more helpless and unsure. She had to love him. He knew she did. It was in her eyes, her hands, her mouth, everything about her. But apparently it wasn't going to change any of her plans.

He didn't know what he was supposed to do. He loved this woman and he had always believed that would be enough. If it were any other woman, Austin thought it would be. Danni was different, independent, married to a trauma case, and intent on homesteading. Austin had never farmed, had never wanted to. With the money in his pocket he could offer her a home far away from Kansas doing almost anything else. But she wouldn't go. She was rejecting him because she believed people depended on her for a way of life, a means to survive, and she couldn't let them down.

Austin understood that. But he wanted to know where *he* fit in.

The truth, he guessed, was that he didn't. And that was why Danni clung to him with such fierceness now. Because soon they would reach their destination and he would have to go on to Wallace and leave her. He wouldn't return to plow fields and plant corn just because he loved her. Doing so would make him feel worthless as a man. He would hate his life and soon he would grow to hate her for making him live it. He knew himself well enough to know there would be no sacrifices made on his part.

He breathed in deeply and exhaled, and the breath coming

out of him caused Danni's hair to flutter. She responded by tightening her arms around him.

"Stop thinking," she whispered. "I can almost hear you."

He wished it were that easy. If it were, he would turn off his nightmares just as easily and get some sleep at night.

She rose on one elbow to look at him and after gazing at her face for a long moment he pulled her down to kiss her. Within seconds the urgency arose in him again, and with the aid of her lips and warm, inviting body he managed to cease thinking for a while.

At first light it was she who awakened him. She kissed his cheek and his mouth, and then she crawled from his blanket and slipped away. Austin felt a chill where her body had been, and once again he had to wonder at how well he slept, how deeply, when he knew she was beside him.

He rolled out of his blanket and sat up to pull on his boots. Today they would leave the devastated Fort Hays, and that night Susannah Blaine would run away. Austin had made all the arrangements. Caspar Knowles, the wild old man who lived on the prairie and played piano, would be expecting her.

Austin had inquired about the rumored cholera epidemic and had been told only a few isolated cases existed around Fort Wallace. It would be perfectly safe for them to go on. Austin didn't trust government information, but he intended to stop short of Wallace anyway and show Danni and the Corles the land he had promised. He would have to escort the Blaines all the way to Fort Wallace, where Austin would collect the rest of his money and officially complete the job he had begun.

He was still surprised at having received his share of the business from his cousin. He supposed there had been a change of heart on someone's part—either his cousin or his cousin's wife. He wasn't going to question his good fortune.

He strapped on his guns, rolled up his blankets, and thought of everything he could do with the money. He could buy himself a ranch and raise horses like his father, or he could travel farther west and see California and the Pacific. He thought he might like to visit San Francisco some day. A few papers and magazines he had seen made it sound like a wonderful, bustling place, where something exciting was always happening.

He walked over to Butcher and ducked his head as the black horse swung his long neck around for a nip. Austin smacked him on the nose and strapped on his bedroll. He'd told Will to look for another horse at the replacement ranch, but only mules and oxen were available. For the time being, he was stuck with Butcher.

Near the wagons he saw Danni making a fire to start breakfast. He walked toward her, drawn by the shy smile on her face, and saw Jack clamber down from the wagon behind her. He looked slightly dazed, and Austin went to give him a hand.

When Austin touched his arm, Jack looked at him and said, "I can't find my rifle, Captain. Have you seen it?"

"No," Austin told him. "You're off duty today, Corporal. You don't need it."

"I am? Oh, you're right. Sorry, I forgot myself there for a minute. Am I late for breakfast?"

"No, you're right on time." Austin sat him down beside an oilcloth Danni had spread over the ground. "We'll have bacon and biscuits in a minute."

"That's good," said Jack. "I could eat my way through a quartermaster's storehouse about now."

"In that case I'd better put on more bacon," Danni said, and she leaned over her frying pan.

"That's right nice of you, Miss . . . ?"

Danni turned to look at him. "I'm Danni, Jack."

"So you are. That's awful nice of you, Miss Danni. Everything smells delicious."

Danni opened her mouth to say something, then she changed her mind.

Austin put on his hat and walked away to find somewhere to relieve himself.

As he finished, he heard a commotion from the Blaine's wagon. He walked back to see Ormond Blaine shouting at his two sons. The boys cowered against one another in the face of their father's fury.

"I asked you where she went," Ormond yelled. "I know she

told you, and I want you to tell me right now or by Heaven I shall whip both of you till you bleed."

Susannah. Susannah was already gone.

"Dammit," Austin muttered. He had told Will to make her wait until they were away from the fort. Now Blaine was going to have the entire post up in arms about his missing daughter.

Will rolled out of his bed then. He got up, listened to what Ormond Blaine was saying, then he walked over to the man in his stockinged feet. "What did you do to her?" he said through his teeth. "Did you try to touch her again last night? What the hell did you do to her?"

"What I did or did not do to her is none of your business, Mr. Drake. If you know anything about her disappearance I demand to be told this minute."

"Even if I did know, I wouldn't tell you."

"Oh, you will," Blaine promised. "You will, because I'm going right to the commander of this fort and tell him about your doings with my fourteen-year-old girl."

Will laughed in his face. "You do and I'll tell the commander what *you've* been doing to that fourteen-year-old girl. I'm a cavalryman, Mr. Blaine. You're nothing but a failed Mormon."

"Failed?" Blaine echoed incredulously. His reddened eyes found Eve, who was just folding up her blanket. "You've been listening to her. All of you. You've been listening to that filthy, lying, hellbound harlot. You have actually taken the word of a whore over the word of a man of God. Well, let me tell you people, I won't falter. I will persevere. Through death, sorrow, and loss, I will go on, and no mortal man can stop my quest. If I arrive at Salt Lake with only my two boys beside me, then it must be the will of God."

The two boys didn't look so happy, Austin noticed. They were obviously frightened of their father and already missing their sister. When their father stormed off to his wagon, they gazed at each other and seemed ready to cry. Eve's heart was ready to break for them, but she knew their troubles would only be made worse if she dared to comfort them. Danni stepped up and beckoned the boys over for breakfast. She gave them each a plate and sat them down on the oilcloth beside Jack. They looked grateful.

As soon as Austin could, he motioned Will over to where the horses were tied and asked about Susannah.

"You know as much as I do," Will told him. "When I talked to her she said she'd wait until I gave her the go-ahead. I guess I shouldn't have given her the directions so soon." He wiped angrily at his face. "That bastard must have tried something last night."

"You'd better hope he doesn't try to see the commander today."

Will smirked. "The commander's too busy with the cleanup. And Libby Custer. Did you see her walking around giving orders yesterday? Danni and Eve were staring like a pair of schoolgirls. And when she actually said hello I thought they were going to bust."

Austin nodded. He had seen. He looked at Will then. "I thought of something last night. What are your orders after we reach Fort Wallace?"

"I won't know till we get there. Why?"

"Susannah thinks you're going back to Leavenworth. What if you don't?"

Austin could see Will hadn't thought of it.

"I don't know. I always assumed I would."

"Captain Bloom didn't give you specific orders?"

"He said my new orders would be waiting for me at Fort Wallace, when and if we arrived." Will frowned and touched his forehead. "Damn it, why didn't I think of that? What am I going to do if I get transferred? And what the hell is Susannah going to do?"

Austin shook his head and Will grabbed him by the arm.

"If I get transferred and have to stay at Wallace, will you go get her?"

"And do what?"

"Bring her to me."

"What are you going to do with her?"

"I don't know. I'll think of something." Will's face hardened then. "It was your idea for her to run away. You owe it to me to go get her if I can't."

Austin knocked Will's hand away and walked over to get some breakfast. *San Francisco,* he told himself, and he patted the envelope in his shirt.

CHAPTER TWENTY-NINE

KIOWA FOUND himself just short of amazed at the changes that had occurred while he was away. The mumbling, soft-spoken Ormond Blaine was now a raging, religious madman; Danni and Eve had become the best of friends, with Eve making the decision to throw in with Danni; and most surprising of all, Danni was sneaking around with Austin Bourke. Kiowa hadn't said anything to her about it, but he had seen her leave her wagon the night before and disappear in the direction of Bourke's bedroll.

A part of him had been shocked, and Kiowa lay there utterly speechless, unable to believe the Danni he had known would behave so. Then Eve had sat up from her own bed and looked at him. It caught Kiowa off guard when she whispered to him, and he had to turn away.

When he was finished wondering what had come over Danni, he allowed himself to think about the black-haired Eve. He knew she was curious about his relationship with Brenda, and he wasn't doing much of anything to set her straight. Kiowa was still wondering at the changes in her, and in the way she looked at him.

No longer was she the tragic, beaten victim raped by Robert McCandliss and the two outcast Indians. Her bruises were all gone, her face mostly healed, and she smiled more than he had ever seen her smile before.

The names Ormond Blaine called her hadn't affected her in the least. Minutes later she was smiling at Danni and taking hot biscuits from the deep pan Danni used to bake them in over the fire.

Brenda watched everything with a faintly amused expression. After breakfast she told Kiowa that Ormond Blaine reminded her of the man who had traded her to the Cheyenne. He, too, had called himself a man of God.

"The pig," muttered Brenda.

Kiowa turned to her. "Did you write your letter?"

"I have nothing to write on. Nothing to write with."

"Danni has writing things. You can ask her."

"You ask her."

He paused. "Why don't you want to?"

"I see the pity she has for me. It makes me sick to my stomach."

"No," said Kiowa and shook his head. "Danni looks at me the same way. It's not pity, it's caring. She's one of the kindest women I've ever known."

A snorting sound came from Brenda. "Oh, yes. I saw her kindness to a man other than her husband last night."

"You want the paper," said Kiowa tightly, "you ask her yourself."

Brenda smiled. "I also felt the stab it gave you to see her. The martyr fallen down. But she's not the one who makes Kiowa hard, is she?"

Sudden anger flared in Kiowa as he looked at her scarred face. He wanted to hit her. His fists clenched at his sides and his jaw turned to rock.

"It's the other one," she continued. "The whore. She's the one who makes your loins shiver." Brenda gave an abrupt laugh. "Whites are so much more interesting than the Cheyenne, don't you think? Everything is open with the Cheyenne, even relations between men and women. They have nothing to hide, nothing to be ashamed of but bad behavior and loss of respect. To the whites, relations between men and women *is* bad behavior unless sanctioned by a church."

"We're not so different," said Kiowa stiffly. "Your husband grew angry when you slept with two of his cousins."

"Of course he did," replied Brenda. "But he grew angry because it was *my* decision, not his. He gave me to others on occasion and told me to be good to them. It was a courtesy on his part. When I took it upon myself to choose my own bedmates I became like your Eve, a whore."

"She's not a whore."

"Oh, but she is. She's a whore to everyone in this camp. Everyone but Danni, and to Danni she's just another poor stray to take in. My eyes have been open and they've seen much in my short time here. I won't be taken in by the pretty blonde with the open legs and the heart of gold. She can do nothing for me."

"You disgust me," Kiowa said to her.

"Go on," Brenda told him in a voice full of disdain. "Go find Eve and be that big, gangly puppy that drools all over her faded gowns."

Kiowa got up and walked away from her. He had to. He had never struck a woman in anger, but Brenda was about to make him lose control.

Danni lifted her head and smiled when she saw him coming. "Kiowa. Did you and Brenda get enough to eat?"

"Yes."

"Are you ready to leave?"

"Yes. I have to talk to you, Danni. I have to know if things have changed.

Surprise rounded Danni's eyes. "Changed?"

Kiowa cleared his throat. "You and Austin Bourke."

Her gaze dropped and she was silent for several moments. Finally, she said, "You saw me go to him?"

"Yes. What's going on, Danni? What about Jack and the claim?"

"Nothing has changed," Danni told him quietly. "Everything we planned before will still happen. It's just that I . . ." She fell silent again, and Kiowa had to prompt her.

"You what?"

"I . . . I can't seem to stay away from him. I know it all must seem terribly . . . wrong . . . to you."

The halting words took their time in coming and her face glowed pink when she finished.

Kiowa exhaled through his nose. Her frank admission confused him. "Does he feel the same?"

She smiled and nodded. "Yes."

"What about Jack?" Kiowa had to ask.

"Nothing will change for Jack. He's still in my heart and in my care. I'll never let anything I do hurt him, and you should know that."

"I do," said Kiowa. "I do know that. So you're still going to homestead?"

"Yes."

"What's *he* going to do?"

"Austin?"

"Yes."

"He's not a farmer," said Danni. "He has no interest in homesteading."

Kiowa was more confused than ever. "Then what's going to happen? What will you do?"

Danni lifted both shoulders. "Say goodbye."

"Say goodbye," Kiowa echoed. "He must care for you an awful lot to leave you on the Kansas prairie with a feeble husband and a woman who's never even seen a farm."

"And you, Kiowa," Danni reminded him.

"You didn't know I was still alive. What kind of man is he to—"

"He's a very good man, Kiowa. He shared the cost of fixing my wheel, and he gave me money to replace the animals and supplies I lost in the flood."

"And look what he's getting in return," Kiowa said darkly.

"What a surprise," said a hard voice behind him, and he

turned to see Eve move past him to climb in the wagon. "T find out you're just like all the rest, Kiowa."

"I didn't mean—" he began, but the expression of hurt o Danni's features stopped him.

"Austin is ready to move out now," she said, looking pas Kiowa to the gate of the fort. Kiowa turned and saw Bourk astride his large black horse and signaling everyone to get read to move. Reluctantly, Kiowa left the women and went to hi pony.

He looked around for Brenda and felt his jaw drop as he sa her on the wooden porch of the officer's quarters talking to th woman Danni had pointed out to him yesterday as Elizabet Custer, George Custer's wife. Kiowa stared as Libby Custe placed her arm around Brenda's shoulders and turned to lea her inside the small dwelling.

"Brenda!" he yelled, and when she turned to look at him h gave her a beckoning wave. "We're leaving now."

Smiling brightly and with incredible sweetness at Mrs Custer, Brenda gave him a facetious wave goodbye.

Kiowa dug his heels into his pony's sides and rode after th wagons. A user. That's what Brenda was. She had used him t get away from the Cheyenne, and she was now going to us Libby Custer to get back to her lover. Kiowa hoped the ma was married by now. With children. It would serve Brend right for being so callous. Not to mention crude. He stil couldn't believe the things she had said to him.

The truth was Kiowa didn't know what he felt anymore. H was confused and unsettled. Before, his sole purpose had bee to find his stepbrothers and kill them. He had done that, wit the exception of the lecherous Luther, and there was no tellin where he might be. Kiowa had figured to kill them and the help Danni get her farm started, but so many things ha changed.

He was tempted to turn his pony and just ride away in th opposite direction. But he couldn't. He couldn't leave Danni t go it by herself, no matter what she had done. And Eve. He stil cared for her, but he couldn't forget how easily she had be trayed him. Jack hadn't even recognized him, the poor man

He appeared not to recognize anyone, except for Bourke, whom he kept calling "Captain."

Kiowa's chin sank to his chest as he rode along. He wasn't a farmer himself, but he knew how to turn the ground and plant seeds, mostly from watching the slaves on his stepfather's farm. At one time Kiowa had thought of becoming a teacher. His abduction by his stepbrothers put an end to that aim. It was probably a good thing, Kiowa told himself. Being a teacher had been his mother's idea, not his.

He supposed he could start a search for Luther, and that would give him something to do for a while after he left Danni and Jack.

And Eve.

Though Kiowa doubted Eve would be there for very long. Not a woman like her. She would get tired of the callouses and the cramped muscles, the backaches and the brain-frying heat. She would shriek at the grasshoppers and cower during heavy storms and twisters. She wasn't the pioneer type.

He rode closer to the wagon and looked at her. Her face and hands were more tanned than he remembered. Her black hair hung loose. Her green eyes were cool as she turned her head to look at him. Kiowa matched her gaze, then kicked his pony and rode on ahead. He couldn't look at her for too long. She would see everything.

He found Austin Bourke riding a half mile ahead of the wagons. Kiowa rode up beside him and Austin turned to speak. "Where is Brenda?"

Kiowa told him, and Austin frowned. "I suppose she knows what she's doing."

"Do you?" asked Kiowa.

Austin shot him a glance. "Concerning what?"

"Danni."

They rode together in silence, Austin looking straight ahead. Then he said, "It's between her and me. Leave it that way."

"The same way you're going to leave her?"

"It's what she wants."

"I don't believe that."

"Then you don't know Danni. She's got it in her head everything's going to end the day she stakes her claim. She's not interested in making a life with me."

Kiowa looked at the stiffness of Austin's shoulders and thought he detected a note of regret in his voice.

"Farming is the only life Danni's ever known," he said in explanation. "She's never known anything else."

Austin only looked at him.

They rode together the rest of the morning, and when the sun indicated it was past noon, Austin finally pulled up and waited for the wagons. He had picked a semi-shady spot to stop and rest and take some lunch. Kiowa rode his pony to Danni's wagon and hopped off to help her and Eve down from the wagon. Jack was up and looking around with curious eyes. "Where are we?" he asked. "Does anybody know for certain?"

"We're about ten miles west of Fort Hays," Kiowa told him. "We're doing good, moving a lot faster without the cattle. Should get ten more in today before we quit."

Jack smiled at him. "You been with this regiment long?"

"This isn't—" Kiowa stopped and started over. "No, I haven't. Why don't you come and have some lunch with the rest of us?"

"That's mighty nice of you, son. Say, have you seen my rifle today? I had it here with me just a minute ago, but I seem to have lost it."

"I haven't seen it, no. Can you get out all right?"

"Oh, sure." Jack lumbered out of the wagon and walked with Kiowa over to where the oilcloth was spread on the ground. Austin Bourke talked briefly with Will Drake, who intended to use the lunch stop to catch up on his sleep. When he finished, Austin came to place a hand on Jack's shoulder. "How are you today?"

"Fine, Captain. Just fine. Did that artillery keep anyone else awake last night? Damn noise is enough to drive a man insane. Must be giving 'em hell over in Fredericksburg."

Kiowa looked at Austin, and Austin was nodding. "I'd say so, yes."

Jack glanced up then as Danni came and began to dish out the bread and beans she had prepared earlier. He accepted a plate from her and thanked her, all the while watching her. He took a forkful of beans and elbowed Kiowa.

"She looks an awful lot like my late wife. It's almost spooky."

Austin paused with his bread halfway to his mouth. "Late?" he said.

"Lost her in a flood. Just swept her away one day while we were traveling west in some wagons just like these."

Danni stopped what she was doing and stared at her husband. "Jack, it's me. I wasn't swept away. I survived the flood and I'm here with you right now."

Jack shook his head. "No, honey. I lost my wife the day of the flood. She's gone to me now."

Danni's face was stricken. The look she gave Austin held so much guilt Kiowa thought she was going to burst out with a sob.

Austin started to speak, but Danni held up her hands and backed away from the cooksite. She turned and ran to her wagon. Austin put down his plate and went after her.

Kiowa glanced at Eve. She lifted a shoulder, then turned to help the Blaine boys. Their father was eating lunch with the Corles. When Ormond Blaine turned to see his sons being fed by Eve, he stamped angrily over to her.

"Just what do you think you're doing?"

Eve barely glanced at him over her shoulder. "I'm giving Joe and John some of Danni's beans."

"I gave them dried beef back at the wagon."

"They were still hungry."

Ormond Blaine glared at his sons. "Is that right?"

Neither boy said a word, and Blaine looked at Eve again. "You lured them over here, didn't you? You coaxed them to you."

"I did no such thing," Eve said angrily.

Jack abruptly rose and let his plate clatter to the ground. Kiowa didn't look to see where he was going; he was too busy watching Ormond Blaine, whose face had gone from white to red.

"I should have known it was you who convinced Susannah to run away," Blaine said in a low, trembling voice.

"I didn't," Eve responded. "But I'm certainly glad she did. Better than spending her life chained to a degenerate like you. It won't be long before the boys have the same impulse."

"You leave my sons alone," warned Blaine. "You're not going to take them from me with your filthy lies."

Eve's nostrils flared. "Someone needs to take them, but it won't be me. It will probably be some court in Utah, once you're finally declared a raving, mentally diseased lunatic."

Blaine's eyes went dark. Suddenly he drew a small blade from his coat pocket and lunged at Eve. Kiowa leapt from the ground and jumped on his back, grabbing him from behind and throwing an arm around his throat in a headlock. The blade slit down the front of Eve's dress and cut her above her navel, but Kiowa managed to spin him away before any further damage could be done. He reached for the arm with the knife and had it in his grasp when a deafening shot assaulted his ears. He felt Ormond Blaine go stiff beneath him, and the man began to stagger. Suddenly Blaine's legs gave out, and Kiowa toppled with him to the ground. Kiowa looked up in alarm and saw Jack standing a few yards away, his chest heaving, his face white as he gripped the rifle he had taken from Austin Bourke's saddle. He was still staring at Blaine's prone form.

"It's finished, Sergeant," he said in a quavering voice. "It's over."

"Jack, put down the rifle." Austin Bourke had left Danni's wagon and was walking slowly toward him.

"No. Don't come any closer, Captain. I had to do it. I couldn't let him hurt anybody else."

"I know that, Jack. You did what you had to do. Now, point the rifle into the air or put it down."

"I can't. Don't come any closer, Captain. Please. I know what's going to happen to me. I know I'm going to face court martial, and then I'll be shot. I know all that, so just stay away. I don't want to hurt anyone else."

"Jack, if you don't put down the rifle, I'm going to have to shoot you. I won't have any choice. Do you understand?"

"No," said a white-faced Danni as she emerged from her wagon. "Please, Austin, don't hurt him."

"I'm sorry, Captain." In a single motion, Jack aimed the rifle and fired. The bullet knocked Austin to the ground, and Danni screamed as he fell. Before Jack could fire again, Quint Corle grabbed him from behind and wrestled him to the ground. Arthur Corle took the rifle away and hit Jack over the head, rendering him unconscious.

Kiowa scrambled away from the dead Ormond Blaine and moved over to where Austin lay gritting his teeth. Danni was busy ripping his shirt off and barely looked up when Kiowa spoke to her.

"How bad is it?" Kiowa repeated, and still she ignored him. Finally he saw an oozing hole just under the left shoulder.

Danni's lips were purple in her bloodless face. "I'm going to have to take the slug out. Kiowa, get my bag and some clean linens from the wagon. Bring my herbs."

Kiowa moved to do as he was told, and once everything around Austin was as clean as she could make it, Danni was ready to perform surgery. She was good at it, Kiowa knew. He was walking proof. Her face was the picture of concentration as she leaned over Bourke and went to work. He didn't pass out, Kiowa noted. His pain-filled eyes stared at the sky.

With only a minimum of digging, Danni removed the slug. Then she fixed up a poultice and applied it. After she bandaged the shoulder she called for Kiowa and the Corles to move the patient into her wagon.

Quint nodded and came over, and Kiowa looked to where Arthur Corle had been standing guard over Jack. Only there was no Jack. Kiowa looked all around the camp before saying, "Jack's gone."

Chapter Thirty

"We'll find him later," Danni said shortly and turned to concentrate on Austin once more. "I can make some tea to help you rest and maybe sleep."

He only looked at her.

Kiowa and the Corles prepared to move him. Not much attention was given to the two little boys who stood with fearful eyes while staring at the body of their father.

A half hour later, Will Drake stumbled sleepily into camp and gazed in shock at the dead Mormon. He walked over to Danni's wagon and looked inside. When he saw Bourke he asked what the hell had happened, but he received no answer from Danni. Bourke lay pale and silent, his brow pinched with pain. Will walked over to the two little boys and put his hands on their backs. "Can you tell me what happened here, boys? Where is everyone?"

"Kiowa and the Corles are digging a grave for my father," answered Joe. "Mr. Coopersand shot him. Father was going to stab Eve."

"Who shot Bourke?" Will asked.

"Mr. Coopersand."

"I'll be damned," said Will softly. Then he brightened suddenly. "How would you boys like to see your sister again?"

Joe and John both looked at him. "You know where she is?" asked Joe.

"I think I can find her. You need your sis now, don't you?"

Both boys nodded, and John began to sob. "We don't have anybody left. You have to find Zannah."

"Zannah?"

"It's what he calls Susannah," explained Joe, and his eyes too began to fill. "Would you go and find her for us, please?"

"May take me a day or more," Will told him. "Think you can keep a secret that long?"

"What's the secret?"

"That I'm going to find Susannah."

Will knew Bourke would be expecting him to take over and guide the wagons until he recovered, but these little boys needed their sister, and at this point they were only twenty-five to thirty miles away from Caspar Knowles's place. If he waited, Will might not get a chance to bring her back. Bourke would know what Will was doing, and it might be a day or more before he could even be moved.

In a split second Will made his decision. He walked to Blaine's wagon and gathered some food before jumping on his horse. As he rode by the two boys he placed his finger over his lips to remind them, and both boys nodded.

When he was gone, John looked at Joe. "Is she really coming back?"

"I don't know," said Joe.

"Are you going to cry, Joe?"

"I don't think so."

John sighed and wiped his face. "Me either."

The two boys walked away from their father and went in search of Eve, who was just coming out of Danni's wagon. She looked at them, they looked at her, and then she climbed down and gathered the boys into her arms.

Inside the wagon, Danni finished making a fresh batch of tea and poured some into a cup for Austin. The wound in his shoulder was serious, and it had to hurt, but he made not a sound. His eyes were still open, but he stared at nothing in particular. His breathing was steady and even. On his bare torso she found several other scars, one from a bullet, the others made by either bayonets or blades of some kind.

It struck Danni that while she had made love with him several times, she had never seen his body.

After holding the tea to his lips, she impulsively leaned over and kissed the scar that angled across his right breast. His gaze shifted and focused on her, and Danni leaned back to look at him.

"Speak to me," she asked. "Please, Austin. What are you thinking?"

"How much it hurts."

"I'm sorry. The poultice burns, but it will draw out any infection."

"I wasn't talking about the poultice." He turned his head. "Did I hear Kiowa say Jack was gone?"

"Yes. He's wandered off somewhere. We'll find him, don't worry."

"I'm not worried. I was going to kill him."

Danni drew in breath and froze. Austin looked at her. "I wanted to," he said. "I wanted to kill him."

Danni was stunned. "Why?"

"Because he's crazy and miserable, and because he's married to you."

Hot tears began to roll down Danni's cheeks. "Oh, Lord," she murmured, "what have I done?"

Austin was silent.

"Please don't kill Jack. I know he's miserable and crazy, but he can't help it. He doesn't deserve to die for being married to me." Danni's gray eyes were red-rimmed. "I can't change anything that's happened, Austin. I can only say I don't regret what we've done. I love you so much I thought my heart would burst from fright when I saw Jack fire that rifle. He might have killed you."

Austin finally looked at her. "It would have been quicker

than the way you're doing it. I'm as close to insane right now as I ever want to be, and I'd appreciate it if you leave me alone."

"Austin . . . don't."

He ignored the pleading in her eyes. "I have to get away, Danni. The sooner I get away from you, the better off I'll be."

With supreme effort he lifted himself from the bed of the wagon. His face turned white as he searched around himself for his shirt.

"Austin, please don't get up. I'll leave. You need to rest or the bleeding will start again."

He shoved her away from him as she attempted to grasp his arms. "I'll be in the Blaines' wagon. Send Kiowa to see me later."

Danni felt as if part of her very existence was leaving the wagon with Austin. She wanted to cling to him, throw herself at his feet and beg him not to go. But the coldness in his eyes stopped her.

Helplessly she watched him swing down from the seat and stagger over to the only empty wagon available. She could almost feel his pain as he climbed inside. The desolation she felt was overwhelming. Never in her life had she known such utter despair. The sobs that came up from her chest and out through her throat sounded alien and animallike in their intensity. She cried until she grew nauseated and lost the contents of her stomach; then she cried some more.

Finally Eve came. She climbed into the wagon and took Danni in her arms. Danni held onto her and cried all the harder until she grew exhausted by her tears and could only hiccough softly.

She fell asleep in Eve's arms, and when she awakened she was surprised to find it was dusk outside. She was alone in the wagon. Immediately she rose and went outside to see about Austin. Eve, the Corles, and the Blaine boys were gathered around a fire and eating supper. Kiowa stopped Danni when she approached the Blaines' wagon. She looked at his hand on her arm and Kiowa said, "He doesn't want to see you. He asked me to keep you away from him."

Danni's eyes threatened to well up again. "But what about his wound?"

"I can see to it if you'll give me the things for the poultice and the bandages."

All Danni could do was nod. "Has Jack come back?"

"No. While you were asleep I went looking for him. I tracked him on foot for some time—he was heading west—but it grew dark and I couldn't see."

"Is he armed?"

"No."

When Danni said nothing, Kiowa rubbed the back of his neck and went on, "Austin wants to get moving tomorrow. He says he knows where Will Drake has gone. We're moving in the same direction as Jack, so unless you have any objections, I'm going to ride scout and the elder Mr. Corle is going to drive Blaine's wagon."

"I have no objections," Danni said, her voice dull. "Tell him I have no objections at all."

Chapter Thirty-one

Two weeks after Jack Coopersand shot Austin Bourke, Eve awakened inside a tent on the prairie and found herself listening to the stillness. There was no rush to get a meal and get everyone fed, no hustling and bustling about to make tracks. No creaking of wagon wheels or bellowing of oxen. There was no sound but the wind and a faraway meadowlark. Eve lifted herself on her elbows and looked for Danni. The blonde lay on her side facing away from Eve. Eve put a hand on her shoulder. "Danni, it's light already. Time to rise."

"I'm awake," said Danni.

Eve withdrew her hand and inwardly sighed as she pushed away the blankets and got up to get dressed. When she left the tent she saw Kiowa emerge from his own shelter. They smiled tentatively at one another. Since the day Austin Bourke showed them the claim, Eve and Kiowa had reached a truce of sorts, and in the past two weeks they had done well together, working as a team to cut up the sod they would need to build a home.

There was no timber for a cabin. The few trees in the area

bordered the stream nearly a quarter of a mile away. Until a well could be dug, daily walks to the stream would provide them with water. Eve didn't complain. She had heard of people who walked four miles or more every day for water. The benefit of such treeless, rockless land was that there was nothing to clear when it came time to plow and plant crops. Danni intended to put in wheat, corn, and oats as well as a large vegetable garden.

The Corles, who after drawing straws had won the claim closest to the water, planned to put in tobacco and hemp as well as wheat and corn. Rainfall had been plentiful, and the land appeared green and fertile. The placement of their claims would keep them away from any flood waters, and the other settlers in the area assured them all had gone well in their time as farmers. Austin Bourke had made a good choice for them.

And then he had left, his arm in a sling, taking Will Drake, Susannah, Joseph, and John Blaine with him on to Fort Wallace. Before his departure he assured Danni every effort would be made to locate her husband. Kiowa had followed Jack's trail for some time, only to lose it in a stream bed. He was of the mind that Jack had doubled back and gone north, and when he had time Kiowa occasionally rode off on his pony to search.

Eve believed Jack didn't want to be found. If one took into consideration his state of mind, it only made sense that he believed himself a deserter who was to be shot on sight. Jack would hide from anyone he thought was looking for him, including his own wife, whom he no longer recognized.

"Is Danni awake yet?" Kiowa asked.

"Yes," said Eve, and she hastily made a fire to put on some coffee.

"Look at your hands," Kiowa said after a moment, and Eve opened her hands and looked at them. The blisters on her palms had hardened into rough callouses.

"Look at yours," Eve returned, and Kiowa grinned lopsidedly at her as he held up his own calloused palms.

"I suppose this means we're becoming farmers," observed Eve.

"That, or we should have brought gloves," said Kiowa.

They smiled at each other until both grew uncomfortable, then they turned away to attend to daily chores, Eve thinking how pleasant Kiowa could be first thing in the morning. He was the same every day, always quick with a witty observation or clever, humorous comment. And while they worked he was always encouraging, never demanding or critical. He helped with all aspects of work around the homesite, lending himself to cooking, washing dishes, whatever needed to be done.

When Eve saw him sitting with a sewing needle and a torn shirt in front of his shelter, she went over to inspect his work. He saw her looking and held it up to show her. "I need a new shirt. This one has so many repairs it's impossible to see the original seams."

The repairs were well done, Eve noted. "You could wear one of Jack's shirts," she suggested, and Kiowa slowly nodded. "I could, yes."

He rubbed his face then and smiled at her. "Which do you want today? The sod cutter or the spade?"

Before Eve could reply, Danni emerged from her tent and said, "I'll get behind the sod cutter today."

Her face looked pale to Eve. Her eyes had lost their shine and her golden hair had lost its luster. She rarely smiled anymore, and when she did it was a brief, fragile curving of the lips that was swiftly gone. Danni refused to discuss her problems, so it was difficult for Eve to know which affected her the most, Jack's continued absence or the coldly abrupt departure of Austin Bourke. Danni would give away nothing.

Kiowa, too, was worried about her. "Are you sure you're up to the sod cutter today?" he asked. "You don't look well, Danni."

"I'm up to it," she replied. "If you'll harness the oxen for me, we'll get to it right after breakfast."

And so they did. Danni drove the oxen with the sod cutter, cutting out four-inch-deep strips of earth that Kiowa came along and chopped into two-foot-long slabs that measured a foot wide. Eve drove the wagon and together she and Kiowa loaded the large, fifty-pound blocks of earth into the back. In the afternoon they took the blocks back to the homesite they had selected and stacked them, grass side down, into layers that made up the walls of their sod home. In all, they stripped almost two acres of land to build their "soddy," since Danni felt it was important to have a bedroom separate from the main room. When the home was completed ten days later, when the cracks were all sealed with mud and the roof was covered with willow branches and cottonwood poles and extra blocks of sod, they allowed themselves to sleep late the next day in celebration.

Eve awakened first and left the tiny bedroom to go to the sole window and push away the sewn-together rabbit skins that served as a cover. The sky was clear and so blue it took her breath away. Eve had lived many places in her life, but never had she seen anything like the blue of a Kansas sky. Just looking at it created an ache within her.

She let the skin fall and looked around the inside of the soddy. Only a few of Danni's belongings had survived the flood, mainly the larger items, like the bed, a dresser, and other pieces of furniture, along with most of her cooking utensils, which had been tied onto the back. The cracked and broken clock on Danni's worn trunk read ten minutes to eight. A noise to her right caught Eve's attention and she turned to see Kiowa shift in his sleep. He slept with his blanket by the cold ashes of last night's fire. Eve eyed his broad, naked chest and exhaled softly.

Beside him was a piece of paper with some writing on it. Eve slipped over and noiselessly picked it up. Her name was written at the top, and below it were the carefully penned lines of a poem.

I am restless to touch her,
Helpless to tell her,
Frightened to hear what
Her lips might say.
I have loved her so long,
Even hated her once,
But never have I loved her
More than today.

Eve smiled and closed her eyes as she held the poem to her breast. When she opened them she saw Kiowa awake and looking at her. Slowly, she folded the poem and placed it inside her dress, next to her heart.

Kiowa blinked and started to sit up. Eve placed a hand on his chest and pushed him back down. She knelt and lowered her head to kiss his mouth. She felt the jolt in him when their lips touched and she smiled as she kissed him. Then she lifted her head again and whispered, "I was afraid you no longer cared for me."

He touched her black hair with his hand and said, "I tried not to. I told myself you wouldn't last out here. You'd start whining and complaining and want to leave. I kept expecting to wake up some morning and find you gone on one of the horses."

"I'm glad I surprised you," said Eve, and her chest swelled suddenly with pride and emotion. *She* had been afraid of the same things. Eve, the pale-skinned professor's daughter, the woman with a past, had fully expected herself to cave in and give up long before a month had passed. She was glad she hadn't. The hard work had felt good to her, right somehow, and she had stayed and made Kiowa proud of her. It mattered to her that he was proud.

It mattered very much.

"Kiowa, I—"

He sat up, and before Eve could finish what she was going to say, he put his arms around her and guided her mouth to his for a gentle kiss. When he leaned away, he took her chin in his hand and made her look at him. He said, "It's already mid-July. My birthday is the fifteenth of August. If you're still here then, I want you to marry me."

It was Eve's turn to blink. "Marry you?"

"Me," Kiowa confirmed. "In August. We'll invite all the neighbors. Arthur Corle said he heard a store is going to open a few miles from here. We'll buy you a pretty white wedding dress and have a dance to celebrate."

Eve was shaking her head in astonishment. "But . . . I'm seven years older than you, Kiowa. Everyone knows I am."

"And no one cares. You'd better say yes, because Arthur told me his son Quint intends to come courting as soon as he gets around to it. They need a woman on the place, he says."

"He can look elsewhere. I've had dealings with Quint before, and he's no—"

Kiowa's brows met. "When?"

"It doesn't matter. They don't want a woman, they want a slave. Someone to clean and cook and do all their chores."

"If you were my wife, he'd have no business coming here."

Eve looked worriedly at him. "Can I give you an answer in August?"

Kiowa's eyes narrowed as he studied her. "Give me back the poem."

"What?"

"The poem. Give it back to me."

"Kiowa, I want to keep it. It's the loveliest thing I've ever seen. You know how I love—"

"All I know is the fear I see in your eyes, Eve. Are you so afraid of what people will say?"

She said nothing for a long time. Finally she took the poem from her dress and handed it to him.

Kiowa was crushed; she could see it in his face. He took the poem from her, swallowed heavily, and crumpled the paper in his hand.

Unable to bear his heartbreak, Eve threw her arms around his neck and clung to him.

"I'm sorry," she cried. "I'm so sorry, Kiowa. Yes, I'll marry you. Just promise you'll be patient with me. I don't want to be afraid of anything, I want to be with you."

Kiowa pulled back and looked at her. His hoarse voice was uncertain. "Are you sure?"

"I'm sure," she said, and buried her face against his neck.

"I'm confused, Eve," Kiowa admitted. "I don't know what to make of you."

"I'm the one who's confused," she told him. "I don't know what I'm saying or doing. All I know is I love you. I love everything about you. I've never known anyone so wonderful."

Kiowa tightened his arms around her, and when she lifted

her lips to his he kissed her with so much passion Eve was left panting for breath. Her cheeks were flushed as she stared into his dark eyes. With one look she knew what kind of lover he would be.

He read the thoughts behind her gaze and drew in a deep breath. "I can't wait to be alone with you. I've thought of nothing else for days."

"Have you ever . . ." Eve began, but she couldn't finish.

Kiowa grinned at her. "We start early in the south."

"You do?"

"Yes, ma'am," he said, affecting a southern drawl.

Eve grinned back at him, and they both turned as Danni emerged from the other room. When she saw them entwined in each other's arms, she smiled genuinely for the first time in weeks and said, "You two look happy."

"We're going to be married in August," Kiowa announced.

"If I'm still here," Eve said, and Kiowa pinched her hard on the rump.

"You'll be here." Danni moved to the window to pull back the skins and Eve glimpsed color in her cheeks and lips. She was wearing a blue ribbon in her hair. Eve left Kiowa and got up to speak to Danni. "You look very pretty this morning. Your face, your hair . . ."

Danni smiled at her again, and it was the stunning smile of the old Danni. She put her arms around Eve and gave her a hug. "And you look radiant. I'm so happy for you. Will you invite the neighbors to the wedding?"

"All of them," said Kiowa. Then his dark eyes softened. "And don't worry, Danni. We're not going to desert you."

"Nonsense," said Danni. "You need to register another claim right beside me. We can share the well, when we get it dug, and farm together."

Eve looked at Kiowa and he shrugged. "We can try." The Indian half of his ancestry might prove an obstacle.

He lifted himself from the floor and excused himself to go outside. While he was gone, Eve turned to Danni again. "I'm worried," she admitted. "People will talk. Will I make a fool of myself by marrying him?"

Danni shook her head. "You'll make yourself happier than you've ever been. I've seen the battle going on inside you these past weeks."

"It's terrifying," Eve confided. "Nothing in my life has managed to stay good. I want this one thing to be good, but I can't stop the questions in my mind, most of them beginning with the words 'What if.' "

Danni's tone was gentle. "You and I have wasted too much of ourselves on 'What if.' It's time for us to start living, wouldn't you say?"

"Yes," said Eve, and when Kiowa reentered the soddy and smiled at her, she repeated herself with heartfelt force.

"Yes."

Chapter Thirty-Two

Austin shoveled the last pile of earth onto John Blaine's grave and stood back. Joseph's grave had already settled in the six days since his death. The row of graves beyond were sunken, filled with the victims that had died since the beginning of the cholera outbreak. Susannah and Will were sick, both of them vomiting until they blacked out and then waking up to vomit again. Austin himself had been spared. He had touched none of the water, eaten none of the fort's food. He lived on boiled water—a survival skill learned at Salisbury—and the victuals forced on him by Danni before his departure. And he took care of those afflicted.

Susannah was going to die next, he knew. Her body was dehydrated by the constant vomiting and diarrhea, and she was close to complete collapse. Grief over the loss of her brothers and the rest of her family hadn't helped her condition. Austin could only stand and shake his head as he stood over the young boy's grave. An entire family wiped out on one short journey, and he alone was responsible. For his insistence in pushing on in spite of the dangers of the flood; for not realizing the potential for violence in Jack Coopersand; and for believing the government reports about the cholera outbreak at Fort Wallace. In each instance, he should have known better. The Blaines—even little John—had put their trust in him, and he had failed them.

"I didn't want to," he said aloud to the fresh earth of John's grave. "I didn't mean for this to happen. If I had known everyone was sick, I would never have come here."

There was no money for him to collect. The fort had spent every available cent on medicines to fight the cholera.

Not that the medicines would do any good. No more than any of the Confederate medicines had done for the sick at Salisbury. The sickness was too great; it was a huge, horned monster that spewed its fetid breath on all who came within reach. Only a few were spared, and they were left as witness to the monster's insatiable appetite for the young, the weak, and the old.

Austin knew he should go while he was still uninfected. There was a loose quarantine, but it would be easy to break. It wasn't that he felt he had to stay with Will Drake. Will's orders had indeed transferred him to Wallace, and it was here he would stay, live or die. It was Susannah that Austin was reluctant to leave. If he were to leave now she would believe it was because she was dying, and Austin couldn't do that to her. Not after everything else he had done.

He carried his shovel back into the fort and went to check on her in the crowded hospital. Susannah was awake, her sunken eyes staring at the ceiling. Austin knelt down beside the cot she rested on and looked into her face. Her gaze drifted down to him. "Did you bury John?"

"Yes."

"Right beside Joe?"

"Yes."

"How is Will?"

"I haven't checked on him yet. He was sleeping the last time I saw him."

Susannah swallowed painfully and asked for some water. Austin fetched her some of his own and gave it to her in small sips. Finally he took it away from her. "You'll heave it up again if you take more."

She leaned back, her eyes still on him. After a while she said, "This isn't your fault, Mr. Bourke. I can see you think it is, but it isn't. This is my punishment for allowing my father to do what he did."

"No," said Austin. "You're not being punished. If that were so, then tell me what John and Joseph did to deserve to die?"

"They were Blaines."

"That makes no sense, Susannah. They were innocent children, no matter what name they carried. They died because I was foolish enough to bring them here."

"You didn't know."

"There were rumors. That should have been enough, but I ignored everything in my push to get here."

"You were upset with Mrs. Coopersand," said Susannah, and Austin looked at her wan face. She passed a thin and trembling hand over her mouth. "Will and I talked of it . . . you and her. Danni was so pretty. And good at heart, always wanting to help."

Austin said nothing. Soon he felt Susannah's hand touch his. "Talk about it if you like," she suggested.

"You're tired," said Austin. "You need to rest."

"I'm tired of resting," she responded. "Today I couldn't get up. My legs are too weak. I wet myself in the bed here, and cried myself to sleep. I'm not going anywhere, Mr. Bourke, and I know it. Whatever you tell me, I'll take to the grave."

"There's nothing to tell, Susannah." He looked down at her bedclothes then. "Would you like me to find some fresh linens?"

She nodded. "And a clean nightgown, if you can find one."

It took Austin time to find everything, and as he looked through her wagon he thought about her request. He thought of making up something to tell her, something a romantic fourteen-year-old would enjoy, but he knew he wouldn't. When he had fresh linens and a clean nightdress he went back inside the dreary hospital and found her vomiting up the tiny amount of water he had given her. She heaved and heaved, and Austin did his best to hold her over the pan that was kept under her cot.

When she could heave no more she passed out in his arms, and Austin lifted her gently back on to her cot. When he picked up her wrist from the floor and laid it across her chest, her lids opened. She gazed at him a moment, and then she stopped breathing.

Austin's mouth hung open. He picked up her wrist again to feel for a pulse, then he laid his head on her chest. Nothing. There was nothing.

With a sharp intake of breath he tore himself away from her and walked to the opposite side of the room, to tell the doctor in charge. The doctor saw him coming and began to shake his head. "I'm sorry. We did everything we could."

"Yes, I know," said Austin. "I—"

"He went quietly."

Austin looked at him. "He?"

"Your friend, Will Drake. He died half an hour ago."

Feeling as if the breath had been knocked out of him, Austin looked over his shoulder. "Susannah's gone, too."

"We'll all go, I'm afraid," said the doctor. Then he put a hand on Austin's arm. "Take a rest, Mr. Bourke. Then I'll ask you to dig more graves. You and three others are the only able men I have left."

Austin could only nod. He left the hospital on feet that felt as numb as the rest of him. He felt like heaving himself. He wanted to vomit up the stench of disease and death he was sure had come to live in his soul.

He rested, but he did not sleep, and when he arose he dug the graves all alone in an effort to exhaust himself. Later, when he went to cover Will Drake in the linen sheet he had slept in, Austin thought to himself that Will looked nothing like the man he had been. There was no buoyant grin, no jokes or laughing or scheming. Nothing but death in the shape of Will.

He buried Susannah beside John and Joseph and put Will on the other side of her. Then he got on Butcher and rode away from the fort in the cover of dusk. No one stopped him. No one even noticed his departure.

For a week he lived on the prairie, eating off the land and resting on the earth at night. He slept little. The dreams were back at him again, the Salisbury doctor and his knife interspersed with images from the tiny hospital at Fort Wallace. At times he found himself sitting and staring at objects while his mind whirled away from him. He would try to rein it in and drag it back to the present, to the here and now, but he would find himself helpless to move, powerless to gain control of his own thoughts. This loss of control frightened him like nothing ever had. Not the enemy, not the doctor, not even the threatened loss of limb had frightened him so much.

Instinctively he found his way back to the place he had felt the sanest, the point where he had left Danni and the others behind. He needed to see them again, he told himself. He needed to know he hadn't killed everyone, that some had survived and were now doing well.

He rode into the first homestead he saw and spent an afternoon in the company of the man who intended to open a store a few yards away from his soddy. He was temporarily without funds, so the opening would be a bit delayed, but the lumber had already been shipped and paid for, and all he needed was the manpower to build the store. He'd go about stocking it when the money from his crops came in.

Austin asked about Danni, Kiowa, and Eve and learned there would soon be a wedding. The half-breed Indian was going to marry the black-haired Eve come August. The man had ordered a wedding dress for her especially, so she wouldn't be disappointed about the store not opening. The Corles were doing well. They had already built two shelters alongside the soddy they shared. They were determined men, and it appeared that both were courting separate widows on different claims. They had applied for all the extensions they were entitled to and were looking to increase their own claim, was the way Walter McCurty saw it.

Austin thanked Walter McCurty and took his leave of him, riding east and south. Just before dusk he reached Danni's claim, and he saw Kiowa and Eve out front, sitting on stools in front of the soddy. They were peeling potatoes and laughing.

He got off Butcher and sat in the cover of the tall grass, out of their line of sight. Soon Danni came out and tossed scraps to some chickens near the soddy. She stopped to listen and then laugh with the others, and Austin's exhalation was long at seeing her. She was pretty as ever, full of smiles, and shining bright as the sun. A part of him ached to know she was so near, the part that slept so soundly beside her because she chased away his nightmares. He could sleep right where he was on the hard ground just knowing she was within reach.

While he was looking, he saw her head turn his way and she frowned into the growing dimness, as if sensing something. Austin grew very still, and when it was completely dark, he got on Butcher again and rode away. He had seen what he came to see. Everyone was healthy and full of life. The three of them had never looked happier. He hadn't seen Jack, but it didn't mean he wasn't around. He might have been asleep in the soddy. Or he might not have been found yet. Danni hadn't appeared disturbed. She had what she wanted. Austin was curious to know which category she would file under when she got around to registering her claim. She wasn't exactly a widow.

He rode past the Corles' place and saw a light burning in their soddy. He didn't stop. He rode on through the night and most of the next day, pausing only to water Butcher and to drink from his canteen.

When he reached Caspar Knowles's place it was close to midnight. He smiled to himself to see a light burning inside the wood cabin.

The smile died when Caspar met him at the door with a shotgun in his hand. "Bourke?" the old man barked in his high, crackling voice. "Is that you?"

"Expecting trouble?" Austin inquired as he reached for the hand the old man extended.

"Could be, yessir. What the hell you doing out here this time of night?"

"Looking for a bed and a hot cup of coffee," Austin told him.

"I got both. Come in."

Austin went in and inhaled deeply of the smells of Caspar's cabin. Spices and oils and the remnants of a stew in a pot over the coals of a dying fire. Then there was the piano, soft gleaming wood and ivory keys.

"Been playing much?"

"You bet. Keeps my fingers nimble." Caspar bustled about, fixing a cup of coffee and a bowl of stew before he gestured for Austin to sit down. Caspar sat across from him. "Tell me, whatever became of young Susannah and wicked Will?"

Austin stopped with his spoon poised above the bowl. "They're both dead of cholera."

"Cholera?"

"Around Fort Wallace."

"You didn't get sick?"

"No." Austin placed a spoonful of stew to his lips. It tasted good.

"Where you headed now?" Caspar asked.

"I don't know. Nowhere."

"Job's all done."

"That's right." Austin paused. "Who did you think I was when I came to the door?"

Caspar waved an impatient hand. "I had this fella come to me, a man not right in the head, and I put him up for a while because I could see he needed some looking after."

"What was his name?" Austin interrupted.

"I'm not sure he ever told me. In fact, I don't believe he did. I just called him 'fella.' Anyway, he stayed here with me for a couple weeks, until this other young fella showed up and seemed to recognize him. He carried on like they were old buddies or such, and the poor silly boy had to go along with it, because how would he know?"

"What about the second man?" Austin asked. "Did he give a name?"

Caspar put a finger to his temple to help himself think. "This one did, but damned if I can remember what it was. Lucius, or Luther."

"Luther?" Austin repeated, and thought immediately of Luther McCandliss.

"That's it," Caspar confirmed. "He called himself Luther. Didn't give no last name. Anyhow, he looked pretty skinny and worn out himself, so I fed him up real good for a couple days, and then I got to noticing the way he was looking at my things here around the cabin, like maybe he was wondering what he'd be able to sell 'em for somewhere. I told him I thought it was time he got a move on, and damned if he didn't hit me over the head with a gun and take off with half the food in my larder. He stole a horse and took off with the poor silly boy, too. I ain't seen either one of 'em since." He stopped then. "From the way you're looking at me, I'd say you know one or both of these boys."

Austin nodded. "I do." It had to be Jack Coopersand and Luther McCandliss.

"Are they dangerous?"

"One of them is, one of them can be. Any idea which way they went, Caspar?"

"Tracks headed west. I didn't exactly go out looking for 'em."

"How long ago was this?"

"A couple weeks. Out robbing folks and roaming the countryside, I'd say."

Austin thought of Danni and the others. Luther had had plenty of time to find them. But only if he was looking. If Kiowa saw him first, Luther would be dead.

Then there was Jack. Crazy Jack wandering the prairie with a murderer.

Before Austin finished his stew he knew he would have to go back. He found himself oddly relieved.

Chapter Thirty-Three

When Kiowa heard of an Indian attack on some settlers just seven miles away, he grew worried. An entire family had been killed—husband, wife, and four children. The youngest, a child of only two, had been picked up by the heels and smashed against the side of a two-foot-thick soddy. It wasn't known whether the attacking Indians had been Cheyenne or Sioux, but Kiowa had his suspicions. Gray Elk's band had been traveling in the same direction as the wagons. He imagined they were camped somewhere near the Smoky Hill River.

It was hard to imagine the Indians he had known perpetrating such savagery, but he had seen only one side of their lives. Several of the younger men, Brenda's former husband in particular, were doubtlessly capable of marshaling their anger in such heinous form. Kiowa had no idea what would happen if the Cheyenne saw him again. He imagined he would be slaughtered on the spot, unless perhaps Gray Elk was there to intervene, and Kiowa could not be certain even of him.

One thing about a soddy, Kiowa told himself as he worked on

the house he and Eve would share: you couldn't burn one. And he had taken the precaution of digging a hidden root cellar just off the back of the soddy; it would be somewhere to hide in case of attack. He told himself he would go over and dig one for Danni when his soddy was finished. He and Eve didn't like the idea of leaving her alone for so long while they worked on their home, but it couldn't be helped.

And he needed time alone with Eve.

They talked and laughed and worked and sometimes dropped everything to make love right in the middle of a field. The first time Kiowa made love to her was at dusk, on the site where they planned to build their soddy. He was clumsy and passionate and anxious to please her. She made him feel as if he could do nothing wrong.

The stories of slaughter and the threat of marauding Indians put an end to those carefree days. Kiowa kept his head up and his eyes constantly on the distant horizon, searching for any sign that someone was watching. Danni and he had agreed to fire their rifles into the air in successive shots if trouble was coming, and if that method somehow failed, he had shown her how to smack her shovel against her plow to make a loud clanging noise that would reach Kiowa should she need him. So far she had needed him only once, when coyotes came and spooked her horse, Calliope, into breaking her lead. Kiowa found the horse unharmed at the stream the next day.

Bill Ottleway, the old trapper back in Illinois, had taught him horses were as good as guard dogs when it came to sensing trouble, and Kiowa watched his pony constantly to see if its ears stayed pricked at attention for too long.

That was how he knew someone was coming later that afternoon. The pony's head lifted and his nostrils flared repeatedly as he stared south. Kiowa dropped the sod cutter and scanned the southern horizon. First he saw feathers on a lance, then he saw an Indian. Two more came behind the first, riding in single file.

"Eve," Kiowa called, low and harsh. "Get in the cellar."

She dropped the spade in her hands and didn't ask questions. She went immediately to the cellar. Kiowa's impulse was to follow her, but something kept his feet rooted to the ground. He waited and watched while the Indians approached. They weren't painted. They rode naked on their ponies, carrying only the lance and the bows slung over their backs. When they saw him they stopped.

They were too far away for Kiowa to recognize any of them, but he thought he knew one of the horses, the big chestnut mare in front.

Soon the trio started forward again, and Kiowa stepped closer to his rifle, propped against one of the four walls of the foundation he and Eve had completed.

They aren't going to attack, he told himself. These are hunters, out looking for prey.

There were few buffalo or antelope near. Kiowa and Eve had picked up plenty of chips to store and burn when winter came, but they had seen little game in the area other than rabbits and birds.

The Indians stopped fifty yards away and Kiowa squinted at their faces. He knew them, and from the recognition in their features, they knew him. One of them started talking and gesturing angrily. It was the man who had been married to the volatile Brenda.

Kiowa moved closer to his rifle, keeping his gaze on their hands. One of the other men seemed to be arguing with the angry man, attempting to reason with him. The third man said three words to the others and wheeled his horse around to ride away. The second man soon followed, and finally the angry agitator spat on the ground and left. Kiowa breathed a deep sigh of relief and picked up his rifle.

"Who were they?" Eve asked as she crept from the cellar.

"Three men from the Cheyenne tribe. One wanted to kill me but the others talked him out of it. They've probably gone to consult their holy man."

Eve's eyes were round. "They'll be back then, and we shouldn't be here. We have to leave, Kiowa. We need to go away." Her eyes grew even rounder then. "What about Danni? We have to make sure she's all right. They could have killed her and then come here."

"No," Kiowa told her. "They rode in from the south, so they missed Danni's place."

"Are you sure?"

"Reasonably. When I traveled with them we rode south of the Smoky Hill Road, and we're seven miles from that, so they must be even farther south."

Eve pulled at his arm. "We need to leave, Kiowa."

He looked at her, then he shook his head. "No, Eve, I can't. Where would I go? There's a man among them, the man I told you about who helped me escape. He's called Gray Elk. He may be able to talk them out of their intentions. He's a respected man in the tribe."

"And what if he can't? Are we going to stay here and be murdered?"

"You're not," Kiowa told her. "You're going over to Danni's, and then I want the both of you to go to the Corles. They have plenty of guns and ammunition, and they'll be able to protect you in a raid."

"I don't want to leave you," Eve said to him.

"I don't want you to stay," he told her, his tone firm.

"What will you be doing while we're sitting around waiting for this raid?"

"Working on the soddy."

Her face creased with worry. "I'll take the pony to Danni's and you hide in the cellar when they come. They'll think you've gone and they'll ride on."

Kiowa put a hand out and brought her close to him to kiss away her frown. "I want you to go now, while you've got plenty of daylight left."

"You think they'll be coming back today?"

He nodded.

Eve threw her arms around his neck and hugged him tightly. "Promise me you'll be all right. I want a wedding and I want a groom."

"I'll be there," he promised, though an uneasy sensation in his gut made him wonder if in fact he would be. "Go on, now," he told her, and he kissed her hard before releasing her. "Get Danni and ride over to the Corles."

Eve released him and went to catch up to the pony. A sudden fear gripped Kiowa as he watched her ride away, and he was tempted to yell at her to gallop hard, but he managed to restrain the urge. He forced himself to get behind the sod cutter again and pick up his switch to flick at the backs of Danni's oxen. Eve and Danni would be all right. The Corles had much more ammunition than either Kiowa or Danni possessed, and they were both good riflemen. Until Kiowa was certain the danger had passed, the women would be all right with Quint and Arthur.

He had plowed nearly a quarter of an acre when the hair on the back of his neck lifted and he sensed they were coming again. More than three this time. At least a dozen men on horses rode into view, and Kiowa dropped his traces as quickly as he could and unhitched the oxen. He switched them on their backs to make them run, then he grabbed his rifle, that Henry Austin had given him, and scrambled into the cellar, sliding down the earth and filling his clothes up with dirt as he went.

It seemed hours before he heard them approach the sod foundation he and Eve had laid. There was the stamping of hooves and the snorting of horses, and a low murmur of voices, their tone indistinct. Suddenly Kiowa heard an ox bellow in pain, and he knew one of the men had shot the beast with an arrow. The poor dumb animal hadn't run fast enough or far enough.

There were lifted voices from the men, some laughing and cheering, and then another voice quieted them. Kiowa knew this voice. It was Gray Elk. He spoke for several moments, and while Kiowa understood nothing that was said, he thought it sounded as if the old man was urging them to take the meat of the ox and ride on. There was disagreement from several, and Kiowa put his head on his arms as he lay and listened to an angry discourse from the man he was sure was Brenda's former husband.

He was glad of the coolness of his hiding place, for the sun outside had been miserably hot. A bug or a worm would do to satisfy his thirst until it was safe to leave his camouflaged hole. It appeared the Cheyenne would be staying for a while.

When he heard a sudden cheer arise again, his curiosity forced him up to peek out through the sparse cover of his cellar. What he saw made the anger rise hot and fierce in him. They were destroying the sod foundation, using their horses to pull the blocks out and drag them across the ground in every direction. All the hard, grueling work he and Eve had done was being obliterated to satisfy the sheer destructiveness of these men. Kiowa's fingers gripped his rifle until they were white and bloodless.

His angry mind worked, calculating how many he could take with his repeater in the first moments of surprise. As the destruction went on, his rage built, until it became too much for him. With a bloodcurdling yell, he burst forth from his hiding place and began to fire. One, two, three Indians fell right away, and the others turned in stunned surprise to see him. Kiowa shot one more before he himself was hit by an arrow in the left thigh. An Indian came at him with a lance, and Kiowa went down to one knee and shot him in the gut.

Out of the corner of his eye, he noticed one Indian still sitting on his horse, making no motion toward his bow. It was Gray Elk.

As he looked at the older man, Kiowa was hit by an arrow in his right side, and another that went through the meat of his left arm. He got off a shot and hit Brenda's former husband in the jaw, creating a red trench along the bottom of his face. Kiowa dragged himself behind the remaining blocks of his foundation and had resigned himself to death when he saw two Indians fall face forward off their horses. Surprised faces turned, and the pain in Kiowa seemed to dissipate in a surge of triumph when he saw Austin Bourke ride up with a revolver in each hand. Bourke turned Butcher with his knees as he shot and fired, and one by one the Cheyenne fell. The arrows they shot at Bourke tore his clothes and sliced his skin but none found flesh to sink into.

Kiowa had just managed to lift his rifle when he saw Gray Elk draw his bow to shoot Bourke. Kiowa shouted, and Austin turned, but Gray Elk did not. His face was filled with purpose as he drew back his bow. Kiowa leveled his rifle and fired at the same moment Gray Elk released his arrow. The arrow went through the meat of Butcher's neck, causing him to go to his knees and spill Austin onto the grass. After a breathless moment, Gray Elk fell forward on his horse. He bowed over the horse's neck, then he rolled slowly off the animal's back and hit the ground.

The angry husband of Brenda was the only Indian who stayed when the others rode away. He whirled on his horse and screamed in rage at Kiowa as he rode hard for the foundation behind which Kiowa hid. The word he screamed was one of the few words Kiowa recognized from his time with the Cheyenne. The man was screaming, "Father!"

Gray Elk had been the man's father. Brenda's father-in-law.

Perhaps my brother? Kiowa's mind asked, a second before the enraged man landed on him with a knife and attempted to cut his throat in the manner that Kiowa's stepbrother had done before him.

My brothers are always trying to kill me, Kiowa thought abstractedly as the sharp blade bit into his skin. He held the arm off as long as he could, but he was rapidly weakening and losing ground. Austin Bourke threw himself over the short wall and grabbed the man from behind, jerking the hand with the knife up and then shoving it down again, burying the blade in the Indian's own abdomen. A ragged cry came from the man's mouth, and he staggered back and fell into a sitting position against the wall. He died that way.

Kiowa let his head loll while he panted out his gratitude to Bourke. Austin came to kneel over him, and his own breathing was labored as he surveyed the damage done to Kiowa. "What happened to the women?" he asked as he removed his bandanna.

Kiowa had to blink to stay in focus. He wondered if he was going to die. "I sent them to the Corles. What are you doing here?"

"I was at Danni's claim when I heard the shots."

"I'm glad you came," said Kiowa.

Austin nodded and grabbed hold of the arrow sticking through Kiowa's arm. "We'll take this one first," he said. He broke off the end of the arrow, and Kiowa cried out in agony. His vision darkened, but he managed to hold on to consciousness.

He smiled to himself in weak triumph. He was doing it. Just like Bourke had when he was shot. Kiowa was handling it.

Then it was time for the arrow to come out.

When Kiowa tasted that pain, he willingly, gratefully gave himself up to darkness.

Chapter Thirty-Four

Danni was tending to the chickens she had purchased from a neighbor to the east when Eve rode up on her pony and breathlessly relayed her news. Upon hearing the word *raid,* Danni wasted no time in enclosing her chickens in a rickety pen she had fashioned from cottonwood poles. She grabbed her rifle from the cabin and as much ammunition as she could carry and handed them to Eve to hold while she hurriedly saddled Calliope. Together they rode for the Corles, with Danni taking only one glance over her shoulder at the small farm. There was no great fear of leaving her home, for it had become lonely beyond measure for Danni to live there. Her reasons for starting the place had all seemed to disappear with Jack. And though they promised to farm with her, the departure of Eve and Kiowa would leave Danni on her own. For a time, anyway. The child she carried would be born in the spring, if she managed to carry the pregnancy to term. She prayed she would.

From the moment she realized she was pregnant, Danni became determined to shake herself free of the gray, cheerless gloom that had settled over her since Austin's departure. The pregnancy itself was one reason to smile, for she would have precious evidence of the love she had known. It was also reason to worry, because of her two previous miscarriages. Danni had been as careful as possible to get plenty of rest and not exhaust herself. She ate well, kept the worrying to a minimum, and so far this pregnancy had outlasted her others. She was beginning to believe this child would be born. Yesterday for the first time she felt the tiny stirrings of life inside her womb. Danni had hugged herself and wept.

As they rode for the Corles, the worry crept in, and she found herself wondering how she could possibly protect herself once the baby was born. What if the Sioux or Cheyenne surprised her at the soddy? Danni didn't think any Indians lived out here on the prairie; she had never seen any. According to Austin, many of them moved about, taking their entire village from place to place. If they lived in such a way, then why attack the white settlers who chose to farm and live a more permanent life?

Danni already knew the answer. Because more and more whites were settling, leaving less and less land for the Indian to hunt and survive. The whites were taking and the Indians didn't care for what they were giving in return. How could they? They were like tigers and birds sharing a vast jungle: the tigers staked off territory and ate all the meat they could catch, even swiping at the birds when the opportunity presented itself; the birds nested where they could and ate what the land offered, shunning the remains left by the tiger and occasionally diving at his head in anger. There was no question of which was mightier.

Something similar was happening in Kansas, Danni knew. The whites were the insatiable tigers and the Indians were the scattered birds, both living in the only fashion they knew.

But it was the savagery that affected Danni. The two-year-old child smashed against the side of the soddy. The brutal rape and torture of women.

The skinned corpses of Quint and Arthur Corle lying side by side in the brown grass outside their soddy.

Eve gasped and nearly fell off her pony in a faint. Danni caught her and held her up until she gave a nod she was all right. Danni slowly dismounted her horse and walked over to look at the bodies. Her stomach threatened to heave and she backed away again, sickened by the grisly sight.

Eve whispered something to her and she looked up at her on the pony. "What?"

"I said we should be careful. They might still be—"

The buffalo skin covering the door of the soddy was pushed abruptly aside and a man came out carrying a rifle.

Luther McCandliss.

His eyes narrowed at sight of the two women. Then he recognized Danni and grinned in delight.

"I'll be damned. If it isn't Mrs. Bourke."

Danni and Eve traded a glance, but Luther interpreted it and pointed the rifle at Eve.

"You get down off that pony now. You ain't goin' nowhere. You don't want to get caught by Indians like these two poor fellas, do you?"

"Is that what happened to the Corles?" Danni asked, her voice cold.

"Sure looks like it, don't it?" said Luther, and he grinned again. "We was camped just over the rise there last night and we came upon 'em this morning."

"We?" Danni echoed.

"Why, me and your brother-in-law, Mrs. Bourke. Good old Jack and me hooked up a couple weeks back and we been together ever since."

Danni dropped her reins and walked past him to go inside the soddy. It took a moment for her eyes to adjust, but she soon saw Jack asleep on a bed in the corner of the room. He was thin, and his face was covered with a grayish beard, but he looked all right. She went to him and touched his cheek. "Jack?"

He didn't respond to her. He was in one of his deep, almost comatose sleeps.

"Has he slept long?" she asked when she heard Luther enter the soddy behind her.

"All damn day," Luther answered, and from the stertorous quality of his reply, she looked to see what he was doing.

He was using a thin piece of rope to tie Eve's hands behind her back.

Danni straightened. "What do you think you're doing, Mr. McCandliss?"

"I'm tying up the little whore so she can't run away while I'm talking to you."

"Mr. Bourke will be here shortly," Danni lied. "He told us to come here and wait for him."

Luther patted the revolver strapped around his waist. "I can handle Bourke. Sonofabitch left George in the middle of the road. He'll pay for that. Him and Nathan, for killin' Bob the way he did."

Danni frowned. "Nathan?"

Luther yanked at the rope on Eve's hands and then pushed her away from him. "Kiowa. The one who ambushed us in the brush. Daddy always knew he'd revert to his savage ways."

"Like the Indians who murdered the Corles," Danni said.

"That's right. Like them." He laughed then at the look Danni was giving him. "Aw, come on now, you don't think I could've done something like that, do you?"

"They had bullet holes in their heads," said Danni. "Mr. Bourke says the Indians don't have many guns, and they certainly don't waste their ammunition on people; they save it for buffalo and other game."

Luther chuckled suddenly and approached Danni. "Okay, I give. I sneaked up here after Jack bedded down last night. He's kinda funny about them things, so I skinned 'em like that to make it look like Indians done it. He wanted to bury 'em, but I told him we should eat first, to get our strength up. We came in and got breakfast and poor old Jack went to sleep right in the middle of his plate."

Danni's mouth was dry. "Why? Why did you kill the Corles?"

Luther lifted his shoulder in a shrug. "They had food and shelter, something me and Jack needed. And they knew where you and the others were."

"What did they tell you?" Danni asked almost breathlessly.

Luther grinned again. "I woke up the old man and said I'd spare his son if he told me what I wanted to know. He told me, and damned if I didn't kill 'em both anyway."

"What did he tell you?" Danni repeated.

"He said the little whore there and Kiowa were buildin' a place of their own, gonna get married. And he said Mr. Bourke went on to Fort Wallace. I was comin' to look for you today, because he also told me you and Bourke ain't truly married, never were, and that your real husband is none other than my good buddy Jack. Is all that true, Miss Danni?"

Danni turned away from him and looked at Eve, who was white with fear. It was obvious Luther intended to kill them. He wouldn't be talking so much if he didn't. But he wouldn't kill them before he got what he wanted, and his eyes gave away his intentions.

Danni's legs weakened and she backed up against the bed to give her support. Luther moved toward her again.

"What do you say we shove old Jack over and have us some fun, Miss Danni? You know the kind of fun I mean."

Danni glanced helplessly at Eve. Perspiration rolled down Eve's cheek; her mouth was trembling.

"Send her away," said Danni in a cracked voice.

"Why? We won't do nothin' she ain't seen before. I can guarantee it."

"I won't fight you if you send her outside," Danni told him.

Luther gave her a crooked smile. "I'll tie her to the post out there. Be back in a minute."

He took Eve outside, and while he was gone Danni turned to Jack and shook him violently.

"Jack," she whispered fiercely. "Jack, please, wake up."

His lids fluttered and promised to open, but before she could shake him again, Luther returned. He walked toward Danni with his hands open, and she gripped the bed behind her and kicked up with both feet at the same time, catching him square in the gut. The force of her kick propelled him backward and Danni screamed at the top of her lungs and grabbed an iron pot near the cook pit. Before he could recover his breath, she hit him hard over the head with the iron pot. A large purple dent was the result, and the dent seemed to fill with blood under the skin as she watched.

As he lay stunned, Danni dropped the pot and grabbed a knife from the table to run outside and cut Eve loose. She had time to cut the bonds and free Eve's hands before Luther staggered out of the soddy. He howled in rage and drew his revolver. Eve instinctively hopped on the back of her pony. Danni ran to Calliope, but the horse shied away from her and took off with the pony. Eve started back, but Danni shouted for her to go on and get help. Luther aimed his revolver and started firing. Eve bent her head low over her pony's neck and kicked the animal hard.

Still holding the knife, Danni ran at Luther and stabbed at the hand holding the revolver. He wheeled and knocked her to the ground with one blow from his fist. Enraged, he drew back his foot and kicked her viciously in the ribs. She cried out in pain and he lifted his leg to kick her again. Before he could complete the motion, a voice from the door of the Corles' soddy roared at him to stop. It was Jack. In his trembling hands was a rifle aimed at Luther. His face was ashen.

"Don't touch that woman again, traitor. You'll die if you do."

"Jack," Danni gasped in relief.

Luther lifted his hands and tried to laugh. "Jack, I keep tellin' ya I ain't no traitor. *You're* the traitor. I was trying to help this poor woman. She's hysterical."

Jack looked confused. He opened his mouth to speak and Luther cocked his revolver and shot him in the heart. Jack's rifle went off as he fell. Danni shrieked and looked at his face, just yards away from her own. For a moment, in the split second before he died, there was a glint of recognition in his eyes.

A booted foot stepped on her arm then, dragging her attention painfully back to Luther. She dropped the knife she held and he kicked it away from her. Then he hauled her up from the ground and dragged her over Jack's body and into the soddy again. He threw her on the bed and held the revolver to her face as he began to tear at her dress.

"You gonna fight me now?" he said. "I don't think so. You

don't know what's good for you. Hell, I might keep you with me for a while, Miss Danni."

Danni said nothing to him, knowing that anything from her mouth would make him angrier still. He might hit her again and possibly knock her unconscious, and while a part of her wished for unconsciousness in the face of what was about to happen, the rest of her knew she needed to be ready for any available moment of escape.

Impatient with tearing at her dress, he shoved her down on the bed and pushed up her skirts. Then he lifted himself onto the bed and forced the barrel of the revolver into her mouth with one hand while unfastening his trousers with the other.

Looking at his grinning face, tasting the oil and grease of the metal in her mouth, Danni knew she had never in her life felt as much hatred for a human being as the hatred she experienced in that moment for Luther McCandliss. She had never in her life wished anyone dead the way she wished for the death of the filthy, slobbering pig above her.

As she was about to squeeze her eyes shut, she saw a shadowy form momentarily block the light coming in the cabin door. In the dimness behind Luther, like an apparition formed by her will, she saw Austin Bourke appear, and in the second before he descended upon her attacker, she saw what a splendid soldier he must have been. His jaw was set with fierce purpose, his mouth was hard and determined, and his eyes burned with flickering fury. He snatched Luther McCandliss from the bed, disarmed him, and then lifted him bodily from the floor and flung him out the door of the soddy. His eyes raked over Danni, then he went out after Luther.

Danni could only mouth Austin's name. She wanted to shout, but her throat was too full. She stumbled off the bed and went to the door to find him. Austin had Luther by the hair, and his fists were bloody as he smashed Luther's face again and again. Danni opened her mouth to tell him to stop, but she closed it again without uttering a sound. She closed it for Quint and Arthur Corle, and she closed it for Jack. Luther McCandliss deserved to die.

CHAPTER THIRTY-FIVE

AUSTIN DIDN'T kill Luther. He threw his unconscious form over his horse, turned the animal in the direction the Cheyenne had ridden and gave him a hard slap on the rump. Luther would be shown as much mercy as he deserved.

Next came the burial of the Corles, and Austin put both into one grave. Danni requested that they take Jack back to her claim, so Austin fashioned a travois behind Butcher and put Jack on it. He lifted Danni into the saddle, and they started back to her soddy, with Austin tiredly leading his horse.

He patted Butcher's head and praised the animal for being so stalwart. The wound in his neck wasn't life-threatening, but it had made the large black horse surprisingly docile.

Halfway to the soddy, Danni asked Austin how he had come to be at the Corles'.

"Eve came while I was with Kiowa at your place," he answered. "Kiowa was injured when the Cheyenne attacked."

"How badly?" asked Danni.

"He'll need plenty of your poultices," Austin told her, and he wished he could tell her not to worry, but he was concerned himself.

"What of the Blaines?" she asked. "Did they make a change of plans and start back to Leavenworth?"

Austin shook his head. "They died of cholera at Fort Wallace. Will Drake joined them."

Danni sucked in her breath. Her already reddened eyes grew moist again. "It must have been awful for you. What made you . . . why did you come back here?"

Austin saw her soddy ahead. A light burned inside. "I came to warn you about Luther McCandliss."

Danni lowered her gaze. "And arrived in time for another heroic rescue."

He curled his aching hands. "Danni, I'm no hero."

"Tell that to Kiowa. I'm sure you saved his life today. His real name is Nathan."

"Who?"

"Kiowa."

Austin helped her down when they reached the soddy. She started to go inside, but he stopped her. "Where do you want me to dig?" he asked.

She looked at the travois and then pointed to a spot west of the house. "Over there, on that small ridge." She paused then. "You don't have to do it this evening. You can sleep and then—"

"I'll do it now," he said, and he asked her for a shovel. Wordlessly she fetched it for him and then went inside the soddy to see about Kiowa.

Austin walked up the ridge and set about digging, his muscles aching in protest. His hands were so calloused from digging graves he might have been taken for a farmer.

When he was ready to put Jack in the grave, Danni and Eve came out to help him. Danni had cleaned up and put on another dress, and she placed some flowers over Jack's body. Eve said the Lord's Prayer, and Austin began to fill up the grave. Danni stayed until he was finished, then she took the shovel from him and led him inside the soddy. After showing him where to clean up, she fixed some coffee.

Eve was hovering worriedly over her now-conscious patient. Kiowa nodded painfully at Austin. "Good to see you again."

"Good to see you, Nathan."

Kiowa frowned at him. "Where did you hear that?"

"It's not important," Austin told him. "I suggest you use Nathan rather than Kiowa in Kansas. Particularly when you file your claim."

"You might have a point."

Danni handed Austin a cup of coffee and brought him a chair. He thanked her and took one sip before his head began to nod. He shook himself and looked up to see Danni watching him. She took the cup from him and pulled him from the chair to lead him to her bedroom. She pushed him down on the bed and pulled off his boots, then she leaned over him to unbutton his shirt. Austin didn't know what else she did, because he fell immediately into a deep sleep.

She must have slept beside him, he told himself when he awakened, because he experienced no nightmares. Nothing but dreamless, refreshing sleep.

He looked around and saw his boots on the floor beside the bed. He didn't know where his shirt and trousers were. He pulled the quilt from the bed around him and walked into the other room. Kiowa lay dozing, while Eve sewed on a shirt in her lap. She looked up and smiled when she saw Austin. "I think he's going to recover. He asked for something to eat."

"Good," said Austin. "My clothes?"

"Drying outside. Danni washed them."

Austin's mouth twisted. They probably smelled. He hadn't had a chance to bathe for some time. He went back to the bedroom and looked for a basin to wash in. He saw a small brass tub instead, half-filled with water. Beside the tub was a cloth and some soap. A moment after he seated himself in the cool water of the tub, Danni appeared with his clothes. She smiled when she saw him squeezed into the tiny tub. "Not very comfortable, is it?"

"No."

"Call if you need anything."

"I will."

She backed from the room, her eyes lingering on his naked torso. When she was gone, Austin reached for the cloth and the soap.

Something was different about her, he decided. He couldn't say what exactly; it was something he sensed more than saw. Almost as if she had a secret no one else knew.

When he finished bathing he dressed in his clean shirt and trousers and pulled on his boots. Danni had a warm meal ready for him and put a plate on the table as soon as he came out. He thanked her and sat down in the same chair he had used the night before.

"I'll go see to my chickens," Danni said, and she left him alone in the soddy with Kiowa and Eve. Kiowa was awake and finishing off a second plate of breakfast. As he ate, Austin glanced at Kiowa and Eve and found both looking at him. He lifted a brow inquiringly.

Kiowa said, "Danni was miserable after you left here."

"She was devastated," said Eve. "We didn't know if she was ever going to pull out of it."

Austin shifted uncomfortably in his chair.

"Eve and I are going to be married," Kiowa told him. "Danni will be alone here."

"Congratulations," said Austin.

Eve looked at him in exasperation, as if he were missing the point.

"Is it pride or stupidity?" she said harshly, and Kiowa shushed her.

"What it is, is none of your business," Austin told them, and he put down his empty plate and walked outside.

He saw Danni clucking to her chickens and he watched her a moment, enjoying the sight of her on a summer day. She saw him looking and walked over to join him. "Did you get enough to eat?"

"Plenty."

"Are you . . . have you made any plans?"

"For today? No." He looked up on the ridge and saw a coyote

sniffing around Jack's grave. He went for his gun, but it wasn't on his hip. Danni touched his arm.

"I covered the grave with all the rocks I could find this morning. They won't get to him." She sighed then and turned her face toward the wind. "I'm surprised they could find it, with this breeze."

Austin nodded and walked over to look after Butcher. The black horse actually nuzzled him when he approached, and Austin stopped to pat his muzzle. "How's the neck this morning?" he asked. "Sore?"

Butcher tossed his head a bit and once more Austin had to marvel at the change in him.

Danni came over and Austin told her he was going to the stream. "My horse needs some water."

"I need some as well," said Danni, and she went to the house to get the buckets she hauled water in.

As they walked along, Austin looked at the expression on her face and asked if she was thinking of Jack.

"Yes," she admitted. "I can't stop thinking about the way he looked just before he died."

Austin was silent.

"And then I think about you, and the way you looked when you came into that soddy for Luther McCandliss. You were like a knight going into battle."

He looked at her in annoyance. "Don't do that, Danni. I'm not a hero or a knight. I'm just a man, and there are days when I'm not sure of that. I question my sanity daily and I dread the coming of darkness. I'm the worst kind of coward. I'm afraid of myself."

Danni moved in front of him and turned around to walk backwards. "Nothing you say will change the way I feel about you. You are what you are, and I knew what you were the first moment I saw you. You're the best kind of hero, Austin. You're a hero who doesn't know he's a hero."

Austin swallowed and walked on, quickening his steps so she was forced to turn around and hurry to keep up. When they reached the stream he turned Butcher loose and reached for the buckets to help Danni fill them. Butcher drank long and deeply of the crystal-clear water, and Austin sat down on the grassy bank to watch him. Danni left her buckets and came to sit beside him. When several minutes had passed, she looked at him and said, "I've missed you more than I could ever tell you."

His eyes met hers. He said nothing.

Her voice wavered as she went on. "I have no more obligations, Austin. There's no one left who needs or depends on me." She paused and touched her throat, as if to help herself find the words.

When she fell into frustrated silence, Austin held out his hand. She glanced at him and clasped his palm gratefully.

"I need you," he said.

The fingers around his raw-knuckled hand stopped squeezing. She stared at him. "You do?"

"Yes," he said, and he knew it was true.

Danni gazed at their entwined fingers and whispered, "Austin, would you marry me? We don't have to stay here on the claim. We can go anywhere you like."

Austin went still. After a thoughtful silence, he said. "I want to visit San Francisco. Then maybe I'll buy into McCurty's store. I told you I'm not a farmer."

Danni took his hand and guided it to her abdomen. Her gray eyes were dark as she looked at him.

"Will you marry me?" she repeated softly.

Austin stared at her as his fingers encountered a slight roundness. He searched her eyes for meaning and saw the truth.

"When?" was all he could manage.

"Late February."

His fingers went on exploring, while his mind went to Danni. She was going to have a baby. His.

Austin remained silent, awed by the world that had opened up for him with two words from her mouth. She was waiting, watching him breathlessly, and he knew he had to come up with an answer for her. He said, "Do you know a preacher?"

"He's coming next week to marry Eve and Kiowa."

Austin nodded.

"Does that mean you want to?" asked Danni.

"I have to."

Her expression was hurt. "No, you don't have to," she said in a low voice. "You don't have to at all. I thought you might want to."

She didn't understand. Austin was trying to tell her he had no choice but to be with her if he wanted to lead a rational, productive life. Danni and the baby she carried were his protection against the nightmares. His feelings for her were all that gave him hope and reassured him of his own humanity. She made him feel like a capable, worthy man again. She made him feel sane.

He looked at her and said, "I would have come back to you, Luther or no Luther. I can't let you go. If we're married, I won't have to."

Danni threw herself at him and hurled them both to the ground as she covered his face with kisses.

Austin held her and squeezed her as tightly as he dared, letting the joy settle over him as Danni settled on his chest. He told her he loved her and heard her tell him the same a dozen times over as she kissed him.

Soon their lips began to linger, and her fingers moved to unfasten the buttons of his shirt.

He caught her hand and looked questioningly at her. She ignored him and began to kiss him again. She opened his shirt to slide her hands down his chest to his trousers. Austin jumped at the coolness of her palms and put his hands on her wrists to keep them still.

"Jack once told me you'd had trouble with pregnancy. Will it hurt anything?"

"It will hurt worse if we don't," she told him, and the logic of that statement coaxed a smile from him.

"I missed you so much,." she whispered against his mouth. "I thought I would die when you went away."

"Kiowa told me."

"He did?"

"And Eve."

Danni frowned and tried to lift herself, but Austin held on to her and undid the buttons on her dress. She drew in her breath and closed her eyes at the warmth of his touch. Austin spanned her belly with his hands and reached around her hips to draw her close to him. He could never get close enough to her. Never.

EPILOGUE

"THERE'S NO one, Danni." Austin's voice was strained as he loaded his wheelbarrow with heavy bags of flour. Danni stood and watched, one hand on her round belly. Her face was disappointed. "No one at all? Not even a cousin?"

"My father was an only child. My mother's sister was struck by lightning at fourteen and her brothers died in a fire. They had no children. I've told you all of this before."

"I know," she said. "I was hoping there was someone you had forgotten. I'd love to have some family to write. Someone to tell about the baby."

Austin stopped what he was doing and went to put his arm around her waist. "I don't have anyone. I grew up by myself, with only my parents to talk to. I know how much you want to share this with others, but you'll have to settle for me and the McMahons."

Danni smiled and lifted herself to kiss his dusty cheek. "You three will do just fine. I'll leave you to your work now. I'll be in the house."

Austin squeezed her and returned to his flour.

The store was his responsibility, and he took pleasure in running it. Upon their return from a leisurely visit to San Francisco, Austin and Danni had worked out a partnership deal with the affable Walter McCurty. It was agreed that the Bourkes would manage the store, leaving Walter McCurty free to work his land and farm. Austin had helped with the actual building of the store, along with the cabin he and Danni shared. The lumber had been brought all the way from Pennsylvania, as well as real glass for the windows. It was the finest house either of them had ever lived in.

Danni was in her eighth month of pregnancy and ready for the baby to arrive. One room of their home was filled with things made by Kiowa, Eve, Danni, and even Austin, in preparation for the birth. Austin made a cradle much like the cradle his father had made for him. It was his one contribution, and it was the item Danni loved the most. She would rock the cradle and sing songs and talk to the baby in her womb as if it were already born and able to hear her. Austin enjoyed watching her.

He went to the door and saw her knitting by a window in the house. He was turning away when he saw a wagon arrive. The oxen pulling the wagon came to a snorting halt in front of the store. Austin knocked the flour dust from his clothes and went out to greet his customers. He saw a man and a woman climb down from the wagon seat. From the back came another woman and a teenage boy. Ordinarily, Danni would have come over to chat, but Austin could see her attention was on her rows.

These folks looked road-weary, Austin thought. The Smoky Hill Road had brought him many tired travelers in the short time the store had been open. Disgruntled people leaving the west to go back east, or hopefuls coming to Kansas dreaming of settling on five acres of land, all of them foolishly braving the risk of Indian attack, and many losing their lives along the way.

Kiowa had mended well, save for a numbness that often plagued his left arm, and a limp that came on when he walked too much. He and Eve worked hard on their claim and had gotten along well on the land.

There were continuing problems with the Cheyenne. In fact the tension seemed to be escalating all the time, leading Austin and Kiowa to construct a hidden storeroom beneath the store to hide money, valuables, and people, should the need arise. They had been lucky thus far.

Austin shook hands with the man from the wagon, who smiled wearily and handed him a list. As he filled the list he made small talk with them. A woman dressed in black—a widow, Austin assumed—was the most talkative, and she told him they had left California for New York, where her brother hoped to practice medicine and find a decent school for his son. On the way, they thought to stop and look up some kin in Illinois.

Austin told them his wife was from Mattoon, and the woman said that was exactly where they were headed. She told him the name of the relative and Austin looked out the window to see if Danni was still in the house. He thought she might know the woman, having come from the same town. At that point the man asked him about dangers on the trail ahead, and Austin told them all he knew, sparing none of the facts. The family listened attentively, and their faces were grim as they turned to leave the store.

Once they were gone, Austin returned to his bags of flour. He lifted first one, then another, and then he paused to think. The name the woman had given him. Louise Ogden. Louise Ogden from Mattoon.

Austin straightened and stared at the door, his brows furrowing as the realization hit him.

Danni's real name was Louise Danielle, and her maiden name was Ogden.

Louise Ogden was Danni.

Austin dropped the bag of flour he held and ran for the stable where Butcher was kept. He forced a bit through Butcher's teeth and threw a saddle on his back and raced out of the stable at a dead run. Out of the corner of his eye he saw

Danni come out of the house and raise her eyebrows in surprise at his hasty departure.

Stay there, he silently told her. *Stay right there, Danni. You wanted family and I'm going to bring you some.*

He kicked Butcher and urged him to go faster, and within seconds they drew in sight of the wagon. Butcher galloped hard to catch up, and the man and woman on the seat frowned when they saw him. The man slowed the oxen and Austin rode up alongside them.

"Did you say you were looking for Louise Ogden from Mattoon, Illinois?"

"Yes," the woman said cautiously.

"You don't have to go to Illinois," Austin told them. "She lives right here. My wife's name is Louise Danielle Ogden. Everyone calls her Danni."

The woman in black looked at her brother in shock. "Could it be?" she asked, her voice breathless.

Austin looked closely at her, searching for some resemblance. He didn't see any until she turned back to look at him again. Her eyes were the same gray as Danni's.

"Will you come back?" he asked.

"Of course," said the man, and he began to turn the oxen. Austin rode alongside them, and the woman asked him how Danni had come to leave Illinois. Austin told her, and then he asked how she and her brother had come to leave Oregon.

"When my father died, six of us decided to go south," she answered. "We settled in California. After my husband died last year, Willie asked me to come to New York with him."

"Six of you?" Austin repeated. "How many are there?"

"Twelve, counting Louise."

Austin sat back in his saddle and drew a long breath. Danni had said she wanted someone to write.

When they arrived at the cabin, Danni came outside, followed by Kiowa and Eve. Austin greeted them warmly and Danni smiled briefly at the people in the wagon before looking curiously at Austin. "Is everything all right?"

He nodded and got off his horse. "Everything's fine, Danni. I'd like you to meet Willie, Clarissa, and Peter Ogden. And this is Minerva Ogden Jordan."

Danni automatically extended her hand and began to walk forward when she stopped suddenly and stared at the family.

"Ogden?" she said. "My name was . . ." She paused and turned to look at Austin. He nodded.

"My lord," whispered Minerva. "You look just like our sister Loraine when she was pregnant. Doesn't she look like Loraine, Willie?"

"She does," Willie agreed. He held out his hand. "Hello, baby sister. It's good to finally meet you."

Danni ignored his hand and threw her pregnant bulk into his arms to hug him. After leaving him breathless, she turned to her sister and doled out the same treatment. When all three were misty-eyed, Danni turned proudly to introduce her companions. "This is Nathan McMahon and his wife, Eve. They are my very dear friends. You've already met my husband, Austin Bourke."

The Ogdens grew busy shaking hands with the McMahons, and Danni turned to Austin. The surprise and happiness and wonder she felt were evident in her eyes.

"Thank you so much," she whispered.

Austin smiled at her. For the first time in his life, he felt like a hero.